H. L. Sidney Lear

Henri Dominique Lacordaire

A biographical sketch

H. L. Sidney Lear

Henri Dominique Lacordaire
A biographical sketch

ISBN/EAN: 9783337011642

Printed in Europe, USA, Canada, Australia, Japan

Cover: Foto ©Raphael Reischuk / pixelio.de

More available books at **www.hansebooks.com**

RI DOMINIQUE LACORDAIRE

A Biographical Sketch

BY

H? L. (SIDNEY) LEAR

"In la sua Voluntade è nostra pace"

NEW IMPRESSION

LONGMANS, GREEN, AND CO.
39 PATERNOSTER ROW, LONDON
NEW YORK AND BOMBAY
1905

PREFACE.

THIS sketch of a great man and his career has been framed entirely upon his own writings—his Conferences and others—the contemporary literature, and the two Memoirs of him published by his dearest friend the Comte de Montalembert, and by his disciple and companion Dominican, Père Chocarne. I have aimed only at producing as true and as vivid a portrait of Lacordaire as lay in my power, believing that at all times, and specially such times as the present, such a study must tend to strengthen the cause of Right, the cause of true Liberty, above all, of Religious Liberty.

H. L. SIDNEY LEAR.

May 1882.

CONTENTS.

I.

SECULAR LIFE.

"*ABION un rey, l'aben perdut !*" Such was the heartfelt cry of a poor woman from the mountains, one among the crowd of all ranks and ages gathered at Sorèze, November 28, 1861, to render the last tokens of love and respect to the mortal remains of one of the greatest men France has given to Christianity, although they be not few. A king in the world of thought, of patriotism, of influence over the hearts of men ; and verily these are royalties dearer to the noble soul, made after the image and likeness of God, than all that this world's pomp and power can give. A great part of Lacordaire's life may simply be described as a reign over the hearts and spirits of his fellow-creatures. But my aim is not to write his panegyric, and facts will suffice to set forth in true yet glowing colours the strangely blended beauty and harmonies of his career.

They were wild, fierce times in which Lacordaire entered into this world. His father, Nicolas Lacordaire, was a doctor in the little country town of Recey-sur-

Ource, not far from Chatillon-sur-Seine in Burgundy —a man of strong Liberal opinions, but seemingly of the same large, generous heart which in his son was so marked a feature.

It was in the year 1793 that the Curé of the town, a certain Abbé Magné, having refused to accept the Civil Constitution which was then being pressed on the French clergy, and being resolved to render to Cæsar only the things that be Cæsar's, reserving to God those that be His; when, surrounded by a tumultuous mob, which pursued him to the very steps of the altar, where he daily renewed his pledge, this venerable man, while sabres and guns were pointed at him on all sides, steadily made reply, " Cut me down an you will ; but as to a sacrilegious oath, never will I take it ! " Their good angels saved them from the cowardly crime of shedding the brave priest's blood, but they drove him forth from the village with savage execrations and threats of vengeance should he ever return, and then forgot their personal spite in the excitement of pillaging his poor presbytery. For a while the brave priest wandered in the forest, then journeyed to Rome; but eventually, yearning after his own country and his own people, he made his way back to Recey, staff in hand, knapsack on shoulder ; and while fully realising the danger of his position, he felt such confidence in Dr. Lacordaire and his true generosity of heart, that it was at his door that the Abbé sought refuge, and found it. He was kindly harboured and carefully concealed, and there an altar was secretly raised, where the faithful found access to the Sacraments and to the Word of God. Here, on May 12, 1802, the future great Dominican was born, and baptized by the true-hearted confessor of the Faith to whom his father had thus shown no little kindness. Four years later that father died of consumption, not at Recey, but at Bussières; and the mother (Anne Marie Dugied, daughter of a Burgundian *avocat*) was left with four young sons, of whom Henri was the second.

Dr. Lacordaire had been married before, and had a son born 1789 by his first marriage. In a letter to Madame Swetchine, August 20, 1835, Lacordaire describes the last hours of this eldest brother, who had lived the quiet life of a chronic invalid: "His mind was cultivated, and he had such perfect taste in Art matters that in the family he was habitually called 'the artist.' Horticulture was his favourite pursuit; no other garden produced such marvellous fruits and vegetables, or was kept with such exquisite neatness and order. This was a tradition from my father, whom he resembled personally more than any of us, he alone possessing blue eyes, which were penetrating in spite of their sweetness. His other passion was '*la chasse.*' He had bought some land on the slope of a hill (at Aisey le Duc), and had built a pretty house. He had been in possession barely two months—his life's dream fulfilled—for twenty-nine years he had held his hand because he thought his life too uncertain to build. At last he had gained confidence, and scarcely had he laid down and risen up twenty times in his house, when he laid down to rise up no more."

Madame Lacordaire was one of those strong-hearted, morally powerful women who are so often moulded by times of danger and disaster when the weak and purposeless are winnowed out by the storm. Lacordaire described her himself in three words: "Christian, courageous, strong."[1]

She was naturally undemonstrative, dignified, and perhaps somewhat severe, intensely anxious to bring up her sons to a high level both of faith and education. The picture we gather of her in her widowhood, surrounded by her four boys, is a noble one; reading aloud with them the classics of their language, specially Racine and Corneille; talking to them of the sovereign greatness of the Faith, of honour, uprightness, and an unsullied name; of the necessity of a clear, strong will for what is good; lessons stamped upon the lads by their mother's own firm, decided, truthful character. The father had been a man of considerable intellectual power and cultivation; his varied acquirements and a singularly happy

[1] "Chrétienne, courageuse, et forte."

manner of expression, added to a very attractive manner, gave him much of that gift of fascination which was so marked a characteristic of his son through life. It was a great inheritance to begin with; and though Lacordaire barely recollected his father, he always held his memory in most loving remembrance. An old friend of the family tells how, going to see the Dominican Father at the height of his career, their whole conversation was concerning details familiar to the elder man; and how, when he rose to take leave, Lacordaire, holding both his hands, exclaimed, "Tell me more about my father!" Not long before the close of his life he revisited the old house at Recey, and seemed to recall the scenes of fifty years past. Nothing was changed in the house; and when Lacordaire expressed his surprise at finding all so unaltered, the owner answered without hesitation that all was so precious to him because of the memories and name it cherished, that in his lifetime at least no rude hand should touch a detail. His own warm clinging to these early links finds vent in many of his utterances; *e.g.* in a Conference of 1845 at Notre Dame he exclaims, "O the hearth and home of Christian men! that father's home, where from our first hour we drank in with the air and light of day pure love of all things holy; verily we may grow old, but we must ever return to you with a youthful heart; and were it not that the Eternal calls us forth, we could scarce comfort ourselves that we must perforce depart and not watch the shadows deepening and the sun going down on your beloved walls !" [1]

After her husband's death Madame Lacordaire settled near her own family at Dijon, devoting herself to her sons, of whom Henri himself says that he was the favourite, giving as the cause that the gentleness of his character suited hers. "What hand is delicate enough, discriminating, tender enough," he says in his Conference on Family Life, "to manipulate the wild beast just born midway between good and evil, who may turn out a scoundrel or a saint? No need to seek far. His training has begun at the breast which bore him. Every thought, every prayer, every sigh of his mother has been a holy nourishment flowing into his soul, a very baptism of honour and saintliness. . . . And when our heart first wakens to affection, and our mind to truth, it is beneath the hand, the word, the force of a mother's love that this marvel is achieved. And as childhood passes away, and youth asserts its instinctive liberty; as education becomes more perilous, though not less necessary; when all authority is felt as a yoke, but one refuge remains, if not intact, at least respected. We can still listen to truth from the mother who holds fast to God; her glance has not lost all authority; her reproof has not lost its power to awake remorse; and

[1] Conferences, xxxiv.

when she has no other weapon left, her tears are a
last utterance which we cannot dare to resist.
Unknown to us, she works out hidden channels to
the very most hidden depths of our heart, and we are
amazed to find her there where we supposed ourselves
most entirely alone." [1]

We all recoil from marvellous childhood in the
story of great men; and it will suffice to say that those
who remember Lacordaire as a child describe him as
very beautiful, a medley of gentleness and petulance,
of docility and vehemence, such as many another has
been. His old nurse, Colette Marquet, loved to tell
how he used to play at being a priest, and preach to
any who would listen, though it must be owned the
much-enduring nurse seems to have been for the most
part the sole congregation. "Sit down, Colette, for
to-day's sermon will be long," he too often predicted.
And when the little boy's vehement oratory frightened
poor Colette into beseeching him to be quiet, she was
met with the characteristic reply, "No indeed; there
is too much sin going on! I don't mind being tired;
I *must* go on preaching!" And sometimes he would
take up his station in the open window as a pulpit
and read Bourdaloue's sermons aloud, with many
copied gestures and much declamation, to the astonished passers by.

Henri Perreyve published a few autobiographical

[1] Conferences, xxxiv.

fragments of his friend, which must be quoted here in reference to Lacordaire's earliest days :—

"My personal recollections begin to take shape from about seven years old. Two facts have stamped this period on my memory. It was then that my mother put me to a little school for elementary classical education, and that she took me to the parish priest to make my first confession. I crossed the sanctuary, and found myself alone, in a large stately sacristy, with a venerable old man, altogether kindly and gentle. It was the first time I had come into personal contact with a priest; so far I had only seen such at the altar in an atmosphere of incense and ceremony. The Abbé Deschamps (that was his name) sat down on a bench, and placed me, kneeling, beside him. I forget what I said and what he said; but the memory of this first intercourse between my soul and God's minister left an impression on me at once pure and profound. Never since have I entered the sacristy of Saint Michel de Dijon, or breathed its atmosphere, without renewing the vision of my first confession, together with that fine old man and my own childish simplicity. For that matter, the whole church of Saint Michel has retained a share in my reverent remembrance, and I have never revisited it without a certain emotion which no other church has ever since awakened. My mother, Saint Michel, and my new-born religion form a sort of structure in my heart, the earliest, the most pathetic, and most enduring that I know.

"When I was ten my mother got me a scholarship in the Lycée at Dijon, and I went there three months before the end of the scholastic year. Then, for the first time, I made acquaintance with suffering, and therein I was led to God with a vivid, warm, practical impulse. From the first day my companions turned upon me as their sport or victim; I could not stir without the reach of their brutal fun. For several weeks I was forcibly deprived of all my food except bread and soup. To escape from this ill-usage I used, whenever I could, to take refuge during recreation time in the schoolroom, and hide myself under a bench, from masters and schoolfellows alike; and there alone, without protection, altogether forsaken, I used to pour out my devout tears before God, offering my childish miseries as a sacrifice, and striving to unite myself fervently to the cross of His dear Son.[1]

[1] In a letter of December 10, 1850, Lacordaire refers to this time, saying: "I have never brought up anybody, and I can hardly say I was ever brought up myself, although I had the best and most perfect of mothers. But she was obliged to send me to school when I was only ten; and God knows if there was one single shadow of education to be had at that school beyond military discipline and the reciprocal blows of the scholars shut up within four walls. Religion, morals, civilisation, disappeared one after the other, and whatever good we retained must have been from the impressions of our early childhood. For all my

" Brought up by a mother at once so Christian, so courageous, and so strong, religion had flowed from her breast into mine as a pure milk; now pain changed that into blood, which made it my very own, and child as I was, a sort of martyr. My miseries came to an end with the holidays; and when term began again, either my persecutors were tired of the game, or possibly my own loss of innocence and simplicity achieved the exemption. Just at this time there came to the Lycée a young man of twenty-four or twenty-five, fresh from the École Normale, whence he was transferred to the mastership of an elementary class. Although I was not one of his pupils, he came across me and took a fancy to me. He occupied two rooms in an isolated corner of the building, and I was allowed to go there and work under his care during part of my schooltime. There for three years he lavished the most careful literary teaching upon me. Although merely a scholar in the sixth form, he made me read and learn by heart whole tragedies of Racine and Voltaire, and even had patience to hear me repeat them. Devoted to literature, he sought to give me his own tastes; a thoroughly upright, honourable man, he sought to make me kindly, pure, sincere, and generous, and to subdue the impulsiveness of a naturally indocile nature. He was a masters save M. Delahaye I entertained the most profound indifference, enlivened by a tolerably perpetual rebellion."

stranger to religion ; he never alluded to the subject to me, and I maintained a like reserve towards him. Had he not been deficient in this precious possession he would have been the good angel of my soul as well as of my intellect ; but God, Who sent him to me as a second father and true guide, was pleased in His good Providence to suffer me to go down into the depths of unbelief, so that I might one day more wholly realise the full brightness of revealed light. And so my dear master, M. Delahaye, left me to be carried away, like my fellow-pupils, farther and farther from all religious belief; while he kept me on the highest elevations of literature and honour, where he had himself taken up his post. The events of 1815 deprived me prematurely of his care : he entered upon office, but I have ever associated the thought of him with all that has been for good in my life.

"I made my first Communion in the year 1814, when I was twelve years old ; that was my last happiness in religion, and the last ray of mutual sunshine between my mother's soul and mine. The shadows soon closed in upon me ; the chill of darkness took possession of me ; and my conscience ceased to be stirred by any sign of God within me.

"I was but an indifferent pupil, and no success marked my early studies ; my intelligence deteriorated

as well as my morals; and I was going on in that path
of deterioration which is the retribution of unbelief
and the inevitable side of mere rationalism.   But all
of a sudden the literary seeds sown by M. Delahaye
sprang up, and I made a great success in rhetoric,
and before the year was out sundry prizes came to
kindle my pride rather than to reward any worthy
work.

"A meagre course of philosophy, without breadth
or depth, completed my classical course, and I left
school at seventeen, my religion effaced, and my
moral life imperilled; but nevertheless honest, frank,
impetuous, alive to honour, keen for literature and
all that is beautiful, and putting before me as my guid-
ing star an ideal of earthly fame.   It was perfectly
natural.   There had been nothing to sustain our
faith in an education where the Word of God was
faintly heard, without force or sequence, while our
everyday life was moulded upon the examples of
heroic antiquity.   We had been kindled by the virtues
of the heathen world set before us in its sublimity;
while the new world of Christianity was still unknown
to us.   We were entirely unconscious of its great men,
its saints, its civilisation, its moral and civil superiority,
and of the progress of mankind under the standard
of the Cross.   We knew but little even of the history
of our own country, which had not touched us, and
we were French by birth without any patriotic life in

our souls. Not that I mean to throw myself into the war waged of late against classical education. We owe our taste for the beautiful, our elevated feeling for intellectual pursuits, many precious natural virtues, many grand memories, many noble links to great times and characters, to the classic authors ; but they did not lead us high enough to reach the threshold of that building which is Jesus Christ Himself, and the friezes of the Parthenon concealed the dome of S. Peter's from us."

At this time Lacordaire is described by those who remember him as beginning very decidedly to exercise the power and influence over those around which became one of the most marked features of his after-life. His tall, well-made figure, his handsome face, with those large flashing eyes, that broad, strong forehead, and that mobile, ever-changing, sensitive play of expression, won the admiration even of the lads around him ; and his marked success during the latter part of his school-days made him a sort of hero, the ideal student of his fellows. One of these re-members how the *externes* used to climb the railings before their hour for opening, and cry out as Henri Lacordaire was seen passing within, "See ! see ! there he is !"

Leaving the Lycée, to go on in his own words, " I entered the École de Droit, and returned to my mother's little home, with its blessed homeliness, so loving and simple. There was no superfluity in that house, rather a strict economy and a severe simplicity, the aroma of a day that is past, where somewhat sacred attached to the virtues of a widow, the mother of four children, already growing up around her, in whom she fondly hoped to leave a generation of honest men at least—possibly of distinguished men. Only a heavy cloud lowered upon that devoted mother's heart when she realised that not one of her children was really a Christian, not one of them ever accompanied her to God's House or shared the sacred mysteries of the Faith with her.

" Happily for me, among the two hundred students who frequented the Law Schools there were some dozen whose intellect had gone beyond the Civil Code, who sought something higher than mere law, and to whom their country, eloquence, fame, civic virtue, had a more lively meaning and attraction than the mere vulgarities of successful money-making. They were drawn instinctively together by means of that mysterious sympathy which, if it fuses vice with vice, and mediocrity with mediocrity, no less welds together souls of higher bent and aim. Nearly all these young men owed their natural superiority to their Christian faith; and although I was devoid of that, they recognised me as one of their set, and it was not long before our long walks and our friendly gatherings brought us face to face with the greatest problems of philosophy, politics, and religion. As might have been expected, I neglected the study of mere law, attracted as I was by the impulses of a higher intelligence, and I was but as sorry a law student as I had been a sorry schoolboy."

Such may have been his own impression; but his fellow-students, and especially M. Lorain,[1] speak enthusiastically of Lacordaire's share in the eager discussions which were for ever arising concerning all things in heaven and earth, his bursts of eloquence, his exquisite power of appealing to the higher feelings of his audience, his speaking looks; of the firstfruits, in short, of all that made the future preacher of Notre Dame the noblest orator of his times.

"Lacordaire took his full part in all," M. Lorain writes in the *Correspondant*,[2] "and was at once *facile princeps*. I can yet fancy I hear his dazzling improvisations, his ingenious arguments, his unexpected sallies, his plastic power of resource; I can see his bright flashing eyes, so fixed and so piercing, as though his glance went down into the depths of thought; I can hear his clear, vibrating voice, quivering, breathless, lost to all else in the force of his conviction, giving itself up without reserve to the unchecked flow of his rich mind. O happy years, so quickly fled! O precious, magnificent *jeux de l'esprit*,

[1] Doyen de la Faculté de droit de Dijon.
[2] Tome xvii. p. 821.

surely ye gave the promise of a matchless athlete in God's cause ! "

M. Lorain goes on to speak of the papers Lacordaire read at this period (1821-22) before the Société d'Études Dijonnaise; such subjects as the Siege of Jerusalem, Liberty, etc., being the most remembered. "Were I permitted to describe by antithesis," he goes on to say, "I should describe Henri Lacordaire as one series of remarkable contrasts. That impulsive nature was capable of long, persistent, stedfast work; that energetic nature was patient, it united eagerness and gentleness. That lively, impatient imagination was capable of grappling with deliberate design; his quick perception was combined with the most sustained thought, the most continued calculation. Side by side with his luxuriant youthfulness you had the serious anticipation of maturity; wild fun and almost childish merriment together with thoughtful meditation. Combined with his ardent, passionate temperament, there was a natural taste for order and method, for neatness in trifles, the most refined simplicity, the most studied precision and nicety. He could always stop at will in the midst of his phrase, whether verse or prose. The friend who ventured to intrude upon his study was safe to find all in the most symmetrical order; no confusion among his books, his paper, pens, inkstand, penknife, all arranged most correctly on his little black table, and carefully eschewing all uncouth angles. There was the same regularity and neatness in his manuscripts, in his writing, in everything he did or touched; in short, there was a kind of material symbolism in all of that wisdom of the serpent and simplicity of the dove of which he speaks in one of his Conferences, where he says that, like S. Francis de Sales, he would gladly give twenty serpents for one dove!"[1] This love of order clung to Lacordaire through life. In his latter days we find him writing of his "reparations" at Sorèze: "I cannot endure any spot out of order in the house I inhabit, were it a hundred feet underground."

The scepticism which at this time enthralled Lacordaire, and so grieved his mother's Christian heart, was almost the inevitable condition of his training and circumstances. As he himself exclaimed in Notre Dame, "The social condition to which we have been born is a wondrous chaos. Raging storms have rocked our cradle; we have striven through a thousand contradictory theories!"[2] But it was not the active danger so much as the passive which had overthrown the boy's early faith. There was nothing to uphold it[3] in the training offered by public schools

---

[1] Conferences, xxviii. 1844.   [2] Conferences, viii. 1836.

[3] "Rien n'avait soutenu nôtre foi, dans une education où la parole divine ne rendait parmi nous qu'un son obscur, sans suite et sans éloquence, tandis que nous vivions tous les jours avec les chefs-d'œuvre et les exemples d'héroisme de l'antiquité."

in France, a memorable warning in these days when precisely this is the danger which threatens us all. But in Lacordaire's case the early training, though for a time stifled and starved, was not eradicated. He was no "impious tribune or democratic atheist," asserts the friend already quoted. "The Deistic student dabbled somewhat with Voltairian sarcasm, or more correctly, with a tinge of Rousseau, who suited the conscientious seriousness of his mind better. . There is no denying this, France was passing through that stage; but my Dijon schoolfellow never went further."

His law course ended, "my mother, in spite of her very straitened means, resolved to send me to the Bar at Paris. She was stimulated by her maternal anticipations of my success; but God had otherwise ordered things, and she, not knowing it, sent me to the gate of Eternity."

In a letter written shortly afterwards (1824) he speaks of himself as floating between truth and error, equally friendly to both, confusing them unknowingly. The soil was ready for God's seed. "Paris did not dazzle me," he writes. "Accustomed to a laborious, strict, and honest life, I went on living as I had done at Dijon, with this painful difference, that I had no longer any fellow-students or friends, nothing but a vast solitude, where no one cared for me, and where my soul preyed upon itself, without finding either God or Creed therein, nothing save the lively pride of hoped-for fame."

M. Riambourg, President of the Cour Royale de Dijon, had promoted Lacordaire's legal start in Paris by an introduction to M. Guillemin, Avocat au Conseil; and in this lawyer's office he worked on, as he says, with "patient fervour," following the Bar, poor and lonely, leading a dull life for a man of twenty, without any external amusements or agreeable connections, devoid of taste for the outer world, unattracted by the theatrical excitements which were so powerful for most of his contemporaries, without any great eagerness, as he himself said, for anything in the surrounding sphere unless a vague, not powerful, longing after fame. Some seasons of success in the Cours d'Assises slightly moved him, but not to any great extent. M. Guillemin, himself a Royalist and a Catholic, introduced his Liberal, sceptical pupil to a Society called des Bonnes Études, composed of young men who were both Catholic and Royalist, hoping thereby to influence him; but alike from both points of view he felt strange among these companions.

"An unbeliever from my school-days, I had become a Liberal while at the École de Droit, although my mother was devoted to the Bourbons, and had given me the name of Henri in honour of Henri IV., the cherished idol of her political faith. But all the rest of my family were Liberals, and I was so myself instinctively; so that scarcely the faintest echoes of public affairs reached me before I followed

my generation in the love of liberty, as, unhappily, I
had already followed it in ignorance of God and of
the Gospel."

M. Guillemin's hopes of converting the talented,
solitary youth were not fulfilled; he made no friends,
and received no light from his connection with the
Society.   There he remained in his little room at the
top of a house in the Rue Mont Thabor, oppressed,
lonely, controlling by strength of character and habit
of self-domination the restlessness of his unsatisfied
longings; not indeed realising why he was unsatisfied,
and striving to throw himself into the monotonous
work, which he already felt was not his true vocation.

"This vivid imagination and this enthusiasm which
consume me," he wrote, "were not given me to be stifled
by the frost of law, to be crushed under all its realism.
But I am kept in my present position by force of
reason, which tells me that trying all things and chang-
ing condition is not to change one's nature. . . . I
am continually distraught by the struggle within me
of two opposite principles; cold, hard reason reacting
upon an ardent imagination, and causing more disen-
chantment than the latter had caused illusion."[1]

With reference to this crucial period of Lacordaire's
life, his friend Père Chocarne remarks forcibly : "One
needs to remember what that epoch was in order to
understand how it told upon Henri Lacordaire.   We

[1] Lorain, *Correspondant.*

had not then, as now, a France come to her pre-cocious maturity through paths strewn with dispersed illusions and cruel experiences, or turning aside through weariness. All was youthful then, full of enthusiasm and vigour; keen for the present age, its poetry, its liberty. The heart of France had been crushed beneath a weight of bloody memories and humbled pride—thanks to the ruin and defeat brought by the first part of the century—and her long-repressed energies were bursting forth before the first bright rays of liberty and life, rays which assuredly gave birth more to blossom than to mature fruit; but all the same, there were fair flowers and a noble life. A man such as Henri Lacordaire could not be indifferent to the season of universal outburst in which he first came to Paris; not in vain could he hear the triumphant harmonies which celebrated the awakening of a nation, or behold the grand spectacle of social reconstruction into which enthusiasm, hatreds, aspirations, regrets, the wildest, most generous dreams were cast wholesale. Those whose tendencies led them to foster the more hidden, interior, mental revolutions were met by in-toxicating visions from the prairies of America, such as flew to the brain of our youth and made them well-nigh delirious. Henri tasted of this cup like the rest, but he was able to stop himself short of folly; and while his imagination wandered amid the enchanted solitudes of the New World, his patient pen persisted

in its daily toil of copying papers and drawing up con-
sultations." [1]   One of his Conferences in 1848, treating of man as a social being, draws freely upon
Lacordaire's own early mental experiences.   " We have
been told," he says, "that society is a purely human
institution, the source of all our woes, and that our
decadence began together with our civilisation.
Which of us in early days has not imagined himself
wandering at will amid the solitudes of the New World,
with no roof save the sky, no drink save the waters
of unknown rivers, no food save the unsown fruits of
the earth or the wild game that he himself had shot ;
no law save his own will, no delights save the consciousness of his independence and the excitements of a
boundless life on a soil which owned no master ?
Those were our dreams. . . . Our soul burst forth
from its oppression into such ideal regions, and came
back painfully to the monotonous burden of reality.
Was this true ?   Was this effort to rush forth from
society an aspiration towards the primitive condition
of creation, or was it merely a rebellion against the
established order of God's Providence ?   Sirs, it was
a rebellion, a burst of egoism impatient of the limits
fixed for us by universal communion with our fellow-
men, a striving to wrest the universe to the purposes of
our own individuality !" [2]   Yet though he described
himself as the " child of an age which scarce knows

 [1] Vie Intime, vol. i. p. 36. [2] Conferences, li.

how to obey, born and bred in independence," he had self-command enough to plunge into no heroics ; and while crying out, " Where shall I find a heart that can enter into mine, and that will not stare because the very name of Great Greece makes me shiver and weep ! The mind of these men is not made to understand mine ; it is sowing on polished marble ! " he was nevertheless calm, self-reliant, and doubtless far more than he knew shielded by the influences of his early religious education.

Always a passionate friend by instinct, and destined to form friendships of the noblest, deepest character, it was the want of any friend that should satisfy his ideal that tried him most at this period. " I was very young ; God had perished in my soul. . . . I beheld this capital, where curiosity, imagination, and thirst for knowledge led me to suppose that I should read all the secrets of the world. But its weight crushed me." [1]   Paris was at that time, he said, a vast desert to him ; he craved to people it with friendships. There is a most characteristic letter written at this period to a young friend, which gives us a very living portrait of the writer.

" PARIS, *November* 10, 1823.

" MY DEAR CONFRÈRE,—When I saw you this morning I felt more than ever how far off we are from each other, and I saw sorrowfully that our

[1] Speech before the Cours d'Assises, January 31, 1831.

meetings would be passing, and would fail gradually to take that intimate form which long habit and mutual sympathy in heart and mind establish between men. Yet I must own one of my favourite notions, one which had been most attractive to me in looking forward to my life in Paris, was the hope of attaching myself closely to you. I was disposed to comfort myself for the loss of friends who would be afar, by the thought that I had found some one who would replace their everyday friendship by the welcome kindliness which every one needs both to give and to receive. I told myself gladly that you, like them, held those religious principles which I value without having as yet accepted them; that you too held sound political principles without the addition of that bitterness and littleness which sometimes dishonour truth; that you too are pure in taste and morals. I loved the living likeness of my friends in you, and I augured happily for my future life that I seemed thus destined always to come across people worth more than I am. So the prospect of your friendship peopled this vast desert of Paris to me, and I looked to you as the complement of my life. But we are so far apart, that if we do not take care our souls will travel on in parallel lines without ever touching; and of a truth there are so many lovable but unknown people in the world that it is a great mistake to let go such as actually come in our way. Moreover, the time during which we can hope to win friends will soon be past; in riper years men are more easily drawn together by interest than by affection; the spring of one's heart slackens as youth departs. As we are both young, and you can understand me, as you know me well enough to appreciate both the good and the bad in me, I offer you a friendship which will be lasting, begging you to give me yours in return. Well, then, I have a mind to describe myself to you, so as to give you a firstfruit of confidence —the handsel of affection.[1]

" Two rival principles are for ever struggling within me, and sometimes make me very wretched : a chill reason meeting a fiery imagination, the one disenchanting more than the other had enchanted me. No one could be guilty of more follies than I on one side of my being, unless I were withheld by a mental process which makes me see things from all sides. I have watched the working of this world's material interests, and without having ever drunk deeply of its

---

[1] The whole of Lacordaire's life was in keeping with this early view of friendship—a full revelation of self, its faults and weakness. "On veut bien se mettre à nu devant une âme qu'on aime," he writes to Henri Perreyve, February 2, 1854. "Si vous m'aimiez bien, vous entendriez ma réponse à travers l'espace;" and, "Il est si doux de s'humilier devant ce qu'on aime ! Et si l'orgueil nous retient, si nous voulons être un theâtre même devant notre ami, l'aimons nous? Il est certain que la confiance est le premier élément de l'amitié," etc. October 11, 1859.

pleasures or intoxications, I am convinced that everything under the sun is vanity, the result of this same imagination which knows no limit save the infinite, and this reason which analyses whatever it comes in contact with.

"I have a very religious soul, and a very sceptical mind; but as it is in the nature of the mind to yield to the soul, probably some day I shall be a Christian. I am calculated alike to live in solitude and to plunge into the whirlpool of human events; liking quietness when I think of it, liking excitement when I am in the midst of it. Sometimes making a castle in the air of a country parish; saying good-bye to such a thing directly I reach the Pont Neuf; kept where I am by the belief that to change my position would not be to change my nature, and that there are some needs which this world can never satisfy. I possess great activity, and so ready a power of conception that I often misuse it. I have loved men, but never yet women, and I shall never love them in the ordinary way. I believe that my epitaph might be, 'He had faults, but he was worth as much as many another.'"

"Here, dear ——, is a sketch of myself. See if it suits you, and believe that I shall love you all my life with a frankness and sincerity which may bring some grains of happiness into your life. That is always worth something!"

 ¹ "Il eut des defauts, mais il en valait bien un autre."

It is remarkable that this hopeful friendship came to nothing, and he says of himself that he lived on alone, without any cheering sympathy. To a certain extent this may have been owing to the extreme reserve, and sometimes almost chilling silence, which, paradoxical as it may seem, formed part of Lacordaire's external side. His most cherished friend, Montalembert, alludes to this in later years, speaking of the passionate taste for order and neatness already mentioned : "It was stamped upon his most trifling habits of life, as will be witnessed by all admitted to the cell where he used to receive friends, disciples, above all, young men, with such effusion ; but where, nevertheless, some had no resource than to gaze hopelessly around when he received them with that freezing silence, which no one knew how to put forward more boldly than himself in respect of indiscreet or inquisitive visitors." [1] Later on he himself said, "When any one puts a quarter of a mile between himself and me, I put ten thousand, and think no more of him." [2]

But this was not said in any spirit of resentment or pride. Quite the contrary ; it was applied to those who calumniated or injured him. With regard to such men, as Montalembert says, he "raised alike against the pettinesses of jealousy a more formidable

[1] "Ce silence glacial dont personne n'a poussé l'audace aussi loin que lui " (Montal. p. 181). [2] *Correspondant.*

opposition, a strong rampart of silence." There was no real coldness or hardness in his character; in fact, nothing strikes one through his after-life so much as its warm, impulsive love and tenderness; but in earlier days, especially while he would have given up almost everything to win affection, he was too undemonstrative to let it appear. "It is a strange thing," he wrote, "people think me hard! At the moment I am most touched I am taken to be cold! They do not discriminate between the real and the fictitious man in me; what I am and what I appear. I cannot, like Sterne, weep before the public; I am ashamed of tears."[1]

We must then, especially in these early years, keep the real and fictitious man in mind while looking at Lacordaire's life; nor can one doubt that this moral solitude was the mould in which the future apostle of Christianity was being formed. Disappointed in his yearnings for friendship and sympathy, he worked on at his, not wholly uncongenial, profession. Speaking was a natural gift, and he enjoyed exercising it. "I was amused by my pleading this morning," he writes. "The cause was detestable, but I wanted to feel sure that I could speak before the Bench without any nervousness, and that my voice would be strong enough; and this trial has convinced me that the Senate of Rome would not alarm me, though I don't know how I contrived to say anything!" He was

[1] *Correspondant.*

then under the authorised age for a barrister, but that mattered little. "If I were to be summoned before the Conseil de Discipline," he said, "it would be a fine opportunity for making a great speech, and that's all! A young barrister who was condemned by the Council, after having argued successfully, might boast of his condemnation!"

That Lacordaire was successful is undoubted. Berryer declared that if he was watchful over his exceeding facility of speech he would become a leading advocate, and the Premier Président Séguier exclaimed that he was another Bossuet. Nevertheless, he was not satisfied or happy in his legal career. God had better things in store for him, and he could find no rest for his longings in these secular achievements. "I am growing old in mind," he wrote, "and I am conscious of mental wrinkles beneath the flowers I strew. I care little for existence; my imagination has exhausted it. I am satiated with everything without having really known anything! If you only knew how melancholy I am! I like melancholy; we are familiar friends. Men talk of the fame of authors, of public positions; I have had such fancies. But honestly I despise fame, and can hardly imagine how people take so much trouble in pursuing the silly little goddess. To live quietly by one's own fireside, without pretension and without notice, is surely better than to sacrifice one's peace to fame, to receive in return a few gilded straws! I shall never be content until I possess three chesnut trees, a field of potatoes, another of corn, and a cabin in some Swiss valley."

Lacordaire gives an eloquent description of this mental condition from his own experience in a Conference of the year 1850 :—

" Eighteen years have barely passed over us before we begin to experience longings whose object is neither the flesh, nor love, nor ambition; nothing, in short, that can take shape or name.   Wandering, whether in lonely solitudes or amid the splendid streets of great cities, the youth is weighed down by objectless aspirations; he turns from the realities of life as from a prison which stifles his heart, and he seeks from all that is vaguest, most uncertain—from the evening clouds, the autumn winds, the fallen leaves—sensations which feed while they wound him.   But all in vain! the clouds disperse, the winds lull, the leaves decay without teaching him wherefore he suffers, without satisfying his soul more than his mother's tears or his sister's love had satisfied it.   O my soul, why art thou so cast down?   Hope in God.   Yes, it is God, it is the Infinite stirring in our twenty-year-old hearts which Christ has touched, but which have carelessly strayed from Him, and in which His precious grace, failing to produce its supernatural influence, now stirs the storm which it alone can lull." [1]

[1] Conferences, lx.

The oppression became daily greater. "People prophesy a brilliant future for me, and yet I am often weary of life. I have no pleasure in anything; society has little attraction for me; the theatre bores me; I am becoming a negation in the order of material things. No enjoyment save self-love remains, and I am wearying even of that. Every day I feel more and more that all is vanity! I would not lose my heart in this puddle!"

His friends, for he had friends, although they were not yet such as could touch the penetralia of his heart, noticed his depression, but they could not understand the cause. They saw less and less of him; he became preoccupied and absent. Now and then some one caught sight of him in some church, kneeling behind a pillar, motionless, wrapt in meditation. They could not make him out. One young fellow (the same to whom his friendship had been so fervently professed) came to see Lacordaire in his lodgings; and finding him alone, sitting at his writing-table with his face between his hands, no book, no occupation in hand, he entreated to be told the cause of his trouble, offering a hearty sympathy. Lacordaire thanked him, but kept his secret, promising that when he saw daylight as to his perplexity this man should be one of the first to know. It was not long after that he returned the visit, and utterly overwhelmed his friend by the announcement, "I have made up my mind. I am going to the Séminaire."

His own account of this joyful loosening of the bonds which held him must supersede any other :—

" It was in my weary state of isolation and mental sadness that God came to seek me.   No book, no man, was the instrument between Him and me.   M. Riambourg had introduced me to the Abbé Gerbet, but in vain.   It was also in vain that I had been taken once to a dark room in the Bureau de la Grande Aumônerie to see M. de la Mennais.   I felt only curiosity at seeing and talking with him, neither had any Christian oratory won my attention.   M. Frayssinous had become Minister of Ecclesiastical Affairs, and no celebrated preacher had taken his place in the pulpits of Paris.   At the end of eighteen months I was as much alone as the first day—a stranger to all sides, carried on by no stream, unenlightened by any influence, upheld by no friendship, cheered by no home delights.   Such an entire and severe isolation was a trial unquestionably, but it was part of God's dealing with me.   I crossed this desert of my early life in weary toil, unknowing that there were its Sinai, its lightnings, and its flowing waters in store.

" It is impossible for me to tell the day, the hour, or the manner in which the faith I had lost for ten years reappeared in my heart as a flame not wholly extinct. Theology teaches us that there is another light besides that of reason, another impulse besides that of nature, and that this light and impulse, proceeding from God, work while we know not whence they come or whither they go. 'The Spirit bloweth where it listeth, and thou hearest the sound thereof, but canst not tell whence it cometh, or whither it goeth' (S. John iii. 8). An unbeliever yesterday, a Christian to-day; certain with an invincible certainty: it was no sudden surrender of my reasoning faculty to an incomprehensible authority; on the contrary, it was the extension of my sight, a glimpse of all things beneath a wider horizon and a clearer light. Neither was it the instantaneous submission of temperament under a strict cold rule, but the development of its energy by a motive-power beyond nature. Neither was it the renunciation of heart-gladness, but its fulness and exaltation. All that was the man himself remained, only to that was added in him the God who made him.

"He who has never known such a moment has not fully realised life; a glimpse thereof has entered his veins by inheritance, but the full stream has not swelled into keen energy. It is the actual fulfilment of our Lord's words, 'If a man love Me, he will keep My words : and My Father will love him, and We will come unto him, and make Our abode with him' (S. John xiv. 23). The two greatest gifts of our nature, truth and beatitude, at once flow to the very centre of being, begetting one another, sustaining one another, creating a mysterious rainbow which tinges all our thoughts, feelings, virtues, and actions, till the last—death—is touched by the light of eternity. Every Christian knows something of this condition, but it is never more clear and vivid than at the hour of conversion, and for that reason one is tempted to say of unbelief when once conquered, what has been said of original sin, *Felix culpa.*

"Once a real Christian, the world did not vanish before my eyes ; it rather assumed nobler proportions as I myself did. Instead of a mere empty fleeting theatre of ambition, alike petty whether deluded or achieved, I began to see therein a noble sufferer needing help ; a mighty misfortune resulting from all sorrows of ages past and to come, and I could imagine nothing comparable to the happiness of ministering to it, under the Eye of God, with the help of the Cross and the Gospel of Christ."[1]

"A great heart in a little dwelling-place is what has always most deeply moved me," Lacordaire wrote many years later (1846), and of a truth it was no bad characterising of himself. A very great heart his was, that could do nothing feebly or by halves. Directly that his mind was clearly made up, and his unbelief gone, he went straight at the highest point, and without hesitation offered himself as a student at Saint Sulpice. Hesitation or looking back were

[1] Mémoires H. Perreyve, p. 464.

utterly foreign to his nature. His own simple announcement of the fact cannot be surpassed :—

"PARIS, *May* 11, 1824.

"MY DEAR FRIEND,—Few words are needed to say what I have to say, and yet my heart longs to expand. I am giving up the Bar; we shall never meet there any more; our last five years' dream will not be fulfilled. To-morrow morning I enter the Seminary of Saint Sulpice. Yesterday the world's visions were still in possession of my soul (although Religion was asserting her presence), and the aim of my future was fame. To-day I have a higher hope, and on earth I ask but obscurity and peace. I am greatly changed, and honestly I cannot tell you how it has come to pass. When I examine my line of thought during the past five years, my starting-point, the steps of my intellectual process, the definitive result of this slow, hard-beset progress, I am amazed, and can only lift up my heart to God. Dear friend, it can only be felt by one who has passed from error to truth, who realises all his former fancies, who can grasp their connection, their incongruous combinations, their gradual course, and so compare them at the divers stages of his conviction. It is a sublime moment when the final ray of light pierces the soul, and gathers all stray and scattered truths round their common centre. There is always so mighty a gulf between the moment which follows and that which precedes this same ; between what one was before, and shall be after, that the word *grace* was perforce invented to express the marvel, the lightning-flash. I seem to see a man blindfold, moving on at haphazard ; the veil is loosened, he is conscious of daylight, and then the moment his bandage drops he finds himself face to face with the sun ! " [1]

In the first moment of surprise and disappointment, for unquestionably Lacordaire's decision was the sacrifice of a great legal success, his friends and family were inclined to question the reality, the motive of his action. He had told no one but his mother of his intention ("I was certain to meet with nothing but blame," he said, "and I preferred not asking counsel to flying in the face of it when given "), and while asking her consent and blessing, he knew that even to her there would be an element of pain mingled with her thankfulness. "To know that I was a Christian would be unmixed comfort to her, but that I should be a *Séminariste* would be all the greater blow to her, that I was her favourite child, on whom she had always reckoned as the stay of her declining years. She wrote me six letters, in which her joy and her sorrow struggled touchingly ; but seeing that I was immovable, she consented to my giving up the world."

The Vicar-General, M. Borderier, presented Lacor-

[1] Lettres aux Jeunes Gens, i.

daire to the Archbishop, Mgr. de Quélen, who received him with fatherly kindness. "You have been pleading perishable causes before the world's bar hitherto," he said to the young lawyer; "henceforth you will defend a just cause, which is eternal. You will find it very variously judged by men, but Above there is a final appeal, where we are certain to win."

And so it was that Lacordaire closed for ever the chapter of his secular life. At twenty-two he had thoroughly grasped De Chateaubriand's assertion, " In Christian thought lies the world's future," and with him to believe was to act. As he wrote fifteen years later from his Novitiate at La Quercia, "When we become monks, it is with the intention of being monks to the uttermost."[1] So now he entered Saint Sulpice, going to the branch house, called La Solitude, at Issy, May 12, 1824 (the anniversary of his baptism), re-solved to be a student for the priesthood "*jusqu'au cou,*" and he kept his resolution.

[1] " Quand nous nous faisons moines, c'est avec l'intention de l'être jusqu'au cou " (Lettres aux Jeunes Gens, p. 131).

II.

ISSY AND ORDINATION.

O N entering La Solitude at Issy, according to custom, a senior student (since then an archbishop) was told off to befriend Lacordaire, and initiate him into the ways of the house; and he has recorded the frank and simple happiness of his companion's first days as a seminarist, his delight in the bursting leafage, and the spring flowers, and the May sunshine. A young barrister, one of Lacordaire's friends, had gone with him to Issy, and when his former master, M. Guillemin, presented the two, asking the seminarist to guess which was his future comrade, he at once pronounced upon the graver, less cheerful man, a mistake which delighted Henri Lacordaire. An early letter to one of the friends left behind puts forth his mental position:

"SÉMINAIRE D'ISSY, *June* 1824.

"Though you may not recognise my handwriting, you were never indifferent to me personally, and I have so lately received proofs of your interest and recollection, that I am glad to think your friendship is not estranged at a season which must leave so marked a stamp on my life alike in its cause and its results. You have seen me floating between falsehood and truth, alike friendly to both, because I involuntarily confused them; the hour has come when it pleased God to give me light, and to make me realise the helplessness of reason and the necessity of faith. And being thus brought near to you by religious belief, I rejoice to find in you a brother that I fain would have discovered earlier. It is true that I am leaving you, by forsaking the career which you have already made your own; but if your triumphs cease to be an object of emulation to me, if I dream no more of Miltiades' trophies with a view to being Themistocles, believe me that I shall always rejoice in them, and take pleasure in your success." [1]

In after days Lacordaire always spoke of the calm stillness and the serene content of those among whom he found himself at Issy as having made a most lively impression on him. Coming as he did from the noise and clatter of the outer world, his imagination was profoundly touched by the silence, the regularity, and the simplicity of his new home. " I shall never have to say ' *linquenda domus et placens uxor*,' but I hope to contract a marriage bond some day. My bride is lovely, pure, immortal; and our marriage, celebrated

[1] Lettres aux Jeunes Gens, p. 60.

on earth, will find its consummation in heaven." And again, " One night I was at my window watching the moon, her rays falling mildly on our house, one solitary star sparkling above at what seemed an incredible distance. I don't know why I began to compare the smallness and poverty of our abode with the immensity of the vault of heaven, and then thinking of the little band of God's servants in their lowly cells, who have worked such wonders, albeit counted as fools by other men, I was seized with such an irresistible mind to weep over this poor world which does not even know how to look upwards ! "

The system of Saint Sulpice was precisely what he needed, and he threw himself heartily into it. A friend who followed him there, but was not so amenable to discipline, remembers how Lacordaire used to say to him, " Depend upon it, *mon cher ami*, the priest who does not pass through a seminary will never attain the true priestly mind."

But he was not without his difficulties. He had left the world, as he himself said, so brusquely, without any interval to mould him to the lowly reserve suitable to a theological college, that he found himself involuntarily unlike the ordinary seminarist; he was so certain of his own entire sincerity in joining them, that he did not put sufficient guard over the impulses of his intellectual capacity, which had been trained to so much of discussion and argument; and his vocation became soon a matter of suspicion among his surroundings. But of this he was unconscious, and gave himself up to the life of devotion and study which he delighted in. The routine of Issy was acceptable to him. At five A.M. the students rose, and after an hour's meditation, met in the chapel, which was in the garden. Lacordaire delighted in the long, silent procession of white surplices through the bright, sunny gardens of early summer. Returning at seven to his cell, he made his own bed, and then the hours of study were thorough happiness to him. At this time he read the Bible largely and prayerfully, and henceforward it never ceased to be part of his daily life. "What do I do in my solitude?" he writes. "I give myself up to study and the meditation I always loved. I see more and more daily that there is no truth without religion, and that it only solves the endless difficulties before which philosophy is helpless. My powers of thought ripen from not being obliged to disperse and scatter what little they attain. My mind is like a field lying open to the ministering dews of heaven."

Recreation-time was one of his perils, as seen by the worthy directors of the college. His lively, original, impulsive nature, full (as his friend Père Chocarne says) of "French liveliness, seasoned with Burgundian wit,"[1] burst out from time to time in

---

[1] "Cette *gallica levitas*, assaisonnée de malice bourguignonne."

sallies of wit and fun, which astounded his superiors, and which they were prompt to repress. On one occasion he took special umbrage at the ugly, square cap worn by the seminarists, and after a war of epigrams there began a war of extermination ; Lacordaire seized the obnoxious articles from his companions' heads and burned them ! Tumult and innovation ! two things held in the utmost horror at Saint Sulpice ! but a quiet word from the Principal, and the storm lulled instantly. Not that Lacordaire ever showed the smallest lack of subordination in spite of his liveliness and impulsiveness, so that the good Superiors were often perplexed by the seeming contradictoriness of his character. All his fellow-students liked him ; the freshness and poetry of his nature, the free, loving warmth which had now found full vent, made him infinitely attractive to the young men surrounding him, and if the authorities did not always understand or appreciate him, his fellow-students evidently did. However, the Superior-General of the Congregation, Abbé Garnier, saw farther than some others could, and towards the end of Lacordaire's first year of theology he took his hand one day, saying, "*Mon cher ami*, I shall summon you next year to our Paris house, and make you *maître de conférences ;* for you must study theology thoroughly, without it the most splendid talents want foundation. And I shall make you a catechist, that you may exercise your gift of speech." Then with a sudden movement of fatherly kindliness, the venerable old man patted his shoulder, adding, "And I should like to be your confessor too." This was the beginning of an unfailing, lifelong friendship.

Unquestionably the sudden plunge from public life into one almost monastic was a trial, but to Lacordaire it was a trial of infinite value. Face to face with a great reality, he set himself to consider the true object of his life—his aim, and that which would be his chief hindrance in accomplishing the same. "My aim is to make known Jesus Christ to those who know Him not, to contribute to the perpetuation of a divine religion, to alleviate as many sorrows and avert as much sin as is possible; and my danger is the desire of fame—of being spoken of." But few letters of this period remain. In one of these, only dated "Issy, 1825," we find him saying:—

"You do not know one thing that delights me, a sort of renewing of my boyhood, I mean that age which comes between childhood and youth, with moral powers which belong to a riper age. While at school one is still too childish, one doesn't sufficiently appreciate the value of men and things, one is too wanting in perception to know how to choose and bind to oneself friends. The higher links of friendship escape such feeble minds, such unformed intellects. And then later on, in the world, one has no longer the power of creating solid ties, either because men do not live in such close contact, or because interest and self-love slip in even to the purest unions, or because the heart is less free in the midst of social stir and action. Friendship has a better chance amid a hundred and forty young men who see each other constantly, and are in perpetual contact; who are all like chosen plants transplanted into solitude. I take great delight in winning affection, in retaining somewhat of the world's courtesy in a seminary, in snatching some worldly grace. Simpler, more communicative, more accessible than I was; free from that desire to shine which had such hold upon me, untroubled as to my future, with which I am content, be it what it may; dreaming of poverty as I once dreamt of fortune, I live quietly with my companions and with myself."[1]

There is another letter written to a friend at the same period, which we must quote as bearing strikingly on his mental position :—

" Issy, 27th May 1825.

"We are accustomed, *cher ami*, to speak unreservedly of all that interests us, and I use this freedom to-day to say that I should very much like to know whereabouts you are as to the grandest subject of human thought. When I left you, your religious belief was almost *nil;* but neither of us had then sufficiently

[1] Lettres aux Jeunes Gens, iii.

pondered those weighty questions which sooner or later fix the attention of all men who are capable of understanding and discussing them. It appertains only to very weak minds to give themselves up to the stream of life without once asking whither it is leading them, without feeling surprise at what they do, without imitating the savage, who, hearing of the arrival of a missionary, hurries to him to ask, 'Men say you know where the Great Spirit is? Point me to Him!' Doubtless, *cher ami*, you have often thought of that Invisible Spirit Who made all we behold, and Who has given to us our little corner in the infinite course of ages; you have often sought after the object of His work and of your own existence. You have not imitated the men who eat, drink, and sleep, gather a few hundred pounds together yearly, and call that life! Like all noble souls, you realise the vanity of human things, you lift your eyes to the countless worlds which surround us, and teach us how small we are in His Eyes Who has created these limitless regions as a finite image of Himself; and the silence of those endless generations who have already fretted the earth disgusts you with the noise our own would fain make in the world; you look into your heart and find there a void which nothing can fill save the truth. Is not this the condition of your soul? But where shall truth be found? Men have ever chased this phantom which continually escapes them, the first intellects of every age have devoted themselves almost in vain to the glorious search, and they have barely handed down to us as a certain heritage the existence of God, natural law, and the immortality of the soul. Philosophy is a subject of endless disputes, and its empire over morals practically nought; you know it as well as I do. But, *cher ami,* we have a resource—Religion. We say that there is a religion, that is, a body of truths which God has revealed to men, which contains all their duties, and likewise the secret of their origin and their destiny. We say that this religion is completely stored in a book which is itself the history of the oldest people in the world, and that they remain to this day bearing witness to this book. For eighteen hundred years this has been so; the greatest men have lived and died in this belief. Moreover, never was there a religion more pathetic, more sublime, worthier of God; and the whole world admits that if there be a true religion, it is assuredly this. Consequently the search after truth is reduced to two points : Is an external divine revelation possible? Is the Christian revelation true? The first embraces all general difficulties as to revelation considered in itself and *à priori*, that is to say, independently of this or that fact; the second includes whatever can be raised against the reality of revelation as given to earth by Christ, the Son of God. If it be true that God can-

not reveal to mankind things which He has hidden
from human reason; if it be true that Christianity is
a tissue of sublime imposture, no need to seek
further; rather we must sit down and weep that
man has been thus cast upon the earth by an unknown
force, and with destinies so uncertain. No, *cher
ami*, such is not our lot; you will not reach this
dreary result if you love truth, if you seek it ardently
and heartily, if you are resolved to obey it when
found. For these three conditions are indispensable
to success in this all-important undertaking, and
nothing is rarer than their combination. Men do not
love the truth, they do not seek it honestly, they are
not resolved to practise it. Hearken to Him Who
knew all things: *Hoc est autem judicium*: 'That light
is come into the world, and men loved darkness
rather than light, because their deeds were evil. For
every one that doeth evil hateth the light, neither
cometh to the light, lest his deeds should be re-
proved.'[1]

"O *cher ami*, you are still, like myself, young,
still full of youthful simplicity of heart, you have not
the weight of fifty years of faults and mistakes upon
you, you are worthy to love and know the truth.
Are you certain that the Christian religion is false?
If you fancy yourself certain, ask yourself what are
your grounds of certainty, on what you rest; you will

[1] S. John iii. 19, 20.

see that your mind has nothing precise, positive, connected, nothing that can assure your conscience against the charge of temerity. If you are not absolutely certain that it is false, surely you are bound to study it, not only in the writings of enemies, but in those of its defenders. We will talk the subject over as often as you please. Happy the friends who are of one mind in religious matters. Adieu ! " [1]

Meanwhile some sort of a cloud seemed to hang over the ardent, intellectual seminarist. His eagerness in discussion, his readiness to admit all manner of pleas on behalf of reason, the bold, original form in which his questions were put, not unfrequently somewhat to the embarrassment of his professors ;— all these things frightened the worthy men who were at the head of the college. A custom prevailed by which the students in turn preached in hall during dinner, and here it was that the future orator of Notre Dame delivered his first sermons. But although they excited the enthusiasm of his fellow-students, these discourses were not quite akin to the respectable dead-level approved of by the authorities. Lacordaire narrates the tale of one of his discourses. " I preached, that is to say, I made my voice heard through the clatter of plates and forks in a refectory where one

---

[1] Lettres aux Jeunes Gens, iv.

hundred and thirty persons were eating. I can hardly conceive a more unfavourable position for an orator than speaking to men at dinner; and Cicero would never have achieved his orations during the senators' dinner unless he had made them drop their forks at his first phrase! how much less if he had had to speak to them of the Incarnation! Yet this is what I was obliged to do, and I confess that, at the air of indifference on every face, the sight of men who did not appear to be paying the smallest attention, but were fixing their whole energy on their plates, I was strongly tempted to shy my square cap at their heads! So I came down with a firm persuasion that I had preached atrociously. I swallowed my own dinner hurriedly, and going out I speedily found that my discourse had been effective, and that the men were struck with it. I confine myself to this phrase, which is quite sufficiently conceited, and will not record the opinions, judgments, flatteries, counsels, and so forth given me."

It was all very well for his fellow-students to pass so favourable a judgment, but Lacordaire's superiors were less indulgent; nor can it be wondered at. One of his greatest friends has remarked that if Saint Sulpice had not the grace to appreciate the future *facile princeps* of sacred eloquence, at least it had the wisdom to warn his contemporaries against a style of preaching, imitation of which would have been fatal.

D

Anyhow, two years and a half passed by, and Lacordaire was still not ordained. His quiet patience under what must have been a great trial is very remarkable ; but at length, when he fairly took in the hesitation of those set over him, he turned his thoughts seriously to the religious life, and began to prepare himself for joining the Jesuits. Who can tell how materially his career would have been altered had he been permitted to carry out this intention? Lacordaire actually took some steps towards its accomplishment, but the venerable Archbishop of Paris, Mgr. de Quélen, who appreciated the young orator more truly than his Saint Sulpice superiors, quashed the idea, and then M. Garnier came forward and explained to the Council his more penetrating views as to the seminarist. These worthy men were ready to admit their mistake, and to lay aside their doubts : he was at once ordained deacon, and on September 22, 1827, the Archbishop gave him priest's orders in his private chapel. On the 25th he wrote, "My desire is achieved, three days since I became a priest. *Sacerdos in æternum secundem ordinem Melchisedeck.*"

It was between these two eventful periods of his life that Lacordaire wrote a letter to a friend which foreshadows his future work, and in which we seem to see the preacher of Notre Dame girding on his sword for the battle of Christ before him :—

"*Aug.* 14, 1827.

"I have heard you say several times, *cher ami*, that you fully realised the importance of a serious religious study; but at the same time you felt yourself so distracted by the work which was indispensable to your daily needs that you must await a more timely and free opportunity. Now God's Providence has given you this, and at twenty-five, without any great exertion, you find yourself free from the too often painful solicitude concerning your career which besets many a man. So you will not be surprised if I call to mind, if not your promise, at least your former longings.

"From an earthly point of view, *cher ami*, it matters little to me whether you are a Christian or a sceptic : in this life it makes no difference to me. Our friendship is not bound up with any creed; it began in the wilderness of irreligion, when we both looked at the heavens with alike doubting eyes. That origin has created points of contact which can never be obliterated. And if voluntary error in what concerns religious belief had no ultimate consequences, I should give little heed to lead you to an examination which would merely tend to your intellectual perfecting. But if so be that there is a true religion, that is to say, one which comes from God, clearly those who deliberately reject it without cause will be called to give account for their contempt. 'Are we blind also?'

the Pharisees said to Jesus Christ when He reproached
them with their unbelief.   'If ye were blind, ye should
have no sin,' was His answer: 'but now ye say,
We see; therefore your sin remaineth.'   So who-
soever might see and yet has shut his eyes, his
sin remaineth.   Suppose then that there is such a
thing as a true religion, which at all events is possible,
there are but two answers available before God, '*I
have seen,*' or, '*I could not see.*'   Any man who is not
certain as to one or other reply is obviously casting
himself headlong over the precipice, unless he be sure
that religion is an impossible thing.   But how can he
be sure?   Surely it will be a sorry plea to say, ' Lord,
I never examined the question, because I was convinced that no religion was worthy Thee'?   The very
least one owes to the multitude of men who have believed is to look on it as possible, for otherwise they
have believed what of necessity was false, a thing that
could not be true.   And is that to be supposed?
So I repeat, at the Judgment Day there will be two
answers only available—'I have seen,' 'I could not
see.'   So far you cannot give the first.   Could you
give the alternative? could you give it a few years
hence? and when into one scale God puts the mental
power, the leisure, the opportunities He has given you,
what will you produce as counterbalance?

" Perhaps you will reply, Is religion to be studied
thus?   Is it a mere question of books?   I do not

see why it should be unworthy of God to require that every man might come to the knowledge of truth by means proportioned to the development of his moral powers, so that the Tree of Life, on its various levels, should be nearer in proportion as the hand stretched out is lower down. This would only be in accordance with Divine Goodness, and worthy of His Justice. What matter either to God or to men if generations go on to meet Him by one same path or by many? There is order wheresoever we find concord between the end and the means, however varied these may be. All the same, I am ready to grant that books and deep learning did not form part of God's primitive design, and that He had chosen the line of a powerful, unassailed general tradition. But observe that possibly nothing at the present day is precisely as it might have been. For instance, God created men for a social life, the individual feeble, society all-powerful. If a man separates himself and goes to make his own life amid the forests of another world, has he a right in his old age to accuse his Creator of the ills he endures, and for which his solitude affords no remedy?

"But this is what the unbeliever does. He has overthrown the ordinary providential lines in general teaching, he has raised up school against school, he has darkened the sun with clouds, and his children complain that they cannot see. Everything to which man has put his hand is no longer God's work only; the moral world has become like Corinthian ore, in which gold and silver were melted down with vile metals. To call Him to account for all that has thrust itself into religion, is an error and an injustice. At the last day we shall see what was His design, and comparing it with the result, we shall justify Him by our shame at having substituted our wretched imaginations for His Will.

"If you had been born three centuries back, with your present intellect and position, you would have been a Christian, and an enlightened one; you are only not so actually because for three hundred years men have toiled to bring about your unbelief. Is that God's fault?

"'Anyhow, it is not mine!' you will perhaps say. No, not if you have profited by the grace given you, not if you make use of the means He has supplied to you in reparation of your forerunners' faults. There is one such which must be combined with study, for study rarely converts any one: La Harpe admits it in a discourse on the study of the Psalms, in which he records the fresh impressions made upon him by reading Holy Scripture; pointing out how different these are when a man studies from a literary point of view, and from a sincere desire to know the truth. We only find what we wish to find because we only seek that which we desire. Fénelon and

Voltaire were both highly intellectual men; one wept and adored as he read Holy Scripture, the other only found material for scoffing. Let me say it with all Christian frankness, there is nothing but prayer which can fit the heart to accept the Faith. Why should you be ashamed to pray to Him Whose Omnipotence and Infinite Light you acknowledge? I have seen you seeking to worship Him after your own fashion. Why not say bravely, 'Lord, I have fallen upon times in which truth is clouded by strife: mighty subjects are questioned on all sides, while I cannot disentangle truth from falsehood. I can see nought save darkness, division, doubt. Teach me what to do, give me a hearty desire to know Thee'? *Cher ami*, he who prays and seeks will never perish. When God foresaw all the strife that would rage against Christ, and the dark veil which impiety would drop between Himself and men, He gave them prayer as their safety. So long as men can pray, they can be saved; and every man who has refused to pray will be without excuse before God's tribunal, inasmuch as every man knows that He Is, and knowing that, it is childish and unreal not to pray to Him. Believe me, this is a universal experience; conversion is only the effect of prayer, and that fact is a proof of the divinity of our religion. Truth is the work of silence and of reflection. Argument teaches nothing. Adieu."

III.

DE LA MENNAIS—THE *AVENIR*—ROME—
LA CHESNAIE.

THE great step was taken, and Lacordaire was a priest. But he did not at once decide upon his future course. That ambition was not his ruling influence may be emphatically asserted in view of an offer made to him shortly after his ordination. The Abbé Boyer, a learned and saintly Sulpician, the friend and counsellor of Mgr. Frayssinous,[1] one day addressed Lacordaire with the somewhat startling announcement that he wished to make him a cardinal! On explanation it appeared that Mgr. Frayssinous had asked the Abbé to find a suitable young priest to be appointed in the place of Mgr. d'Isoard as *Auditeur de Rote* at the Vatican, a post which invariably led on to high ecclesiastical position. The minister required a man

[1] M. Boyer himself refused the important post of Vicar-General of Paris. Charles X. once asked Mgr. Frayssinous who the friend was to whom he so often referred for counsel. "Sire, he lives in a garret at Saint Sulpice," was the reply. "Oh, then, that is why you never suggest sending him up any higher!" the king answered with a smile.

of solid learning as well as brilliancy—one who would represent France creditably—and M. Boyer knew no one whose gifts better suited him to fill the office than Lacordaire. Startled by the sudden proposition, the future Dominican was not carried away by it, and quietly answered that he had taken Orders with one only aim, to serve Christ's Church by his gift of speaking, which he felt to be his true vocation. If he had sought honour, he would have remained in the world, he said. His wish was to remain an obscure priest, probably some day to become a Religious. The good Abbé was proceeding to argue the point, and prove that in an important office at Rome there was a larger sphere of work to be done for God; but Lacordaire entreated him to say no more, referring him to the Superior-General, M. Garnier, who knew all his mind, and would confirm his resolution.[1] Shortly afterwards he accepted the Archbishop of Paris's offer of the chaplaincy to a convent of Visitandines. This office involved little more than the religious and spiritual teaching of a girls' school, but Lacordaire devoted himself to doing this humble work as thoroughly as possible. His pupils had to write out the substance of his instructions, and he took the pains to read all

---

[1] The appointment was actually given to Mgr. de Retz, who died holding it. His successors were Mgrs. de Ségur; de la Tour-d'Auvergne, Archbishop of Bourges; Lavigerie, Bishop of Nancy; and Mgr. Place, Bishop of Marseilles.

these childish papers, and to correct them himself. The good nuns were not especially satisfied; they complained that the Abbé Lacordaire was too metaphysical, and they were probably right. His instructions were quite over the children's heads; and though they admired him very much, they could not understand him.

The time, however, was very valuable to him; he led an exceedingly quiet, almost solitary life, so much so as to almost frighten his mother, who came to live with him. "She knew my nature to be affectionate," he wrote, "and she used sometimes to say plaintively, 'You have no friends here!' It was true; I had none, nor was I to have them until things had happened which were to change all around, my own lot included." But the consequence was that he was able to give himself up to study.

"Strength comes from the fountain-head," he wrote, "and I mean to seek it. It will be hard work, the rather that I mean to gather as I go everything which will be of use in that defence of Catholicism which has not yet assumed its definite shape in my mind, but the materials for which surround me in Holy Scripture, the Fathers, history, and philosophy. Everything which so far I have read in the shape of a defence of religion seems to me feeble or imperfect. Modern theologians cannot move independently of a guide. It is just like tourists in Switzerland : if some famous traveller has taken any particular road, every-body follows him, and men pass by paths which lead to unnoticed beauties simply because they have not been made historical."

It is remarkable to find Lacordaire thus from the very first contemplating that career which he so wondrously filled as time went on. The strength of judgment and absence of vanity (in spite of that love of fame which he spoke of as his great peril) which enabled him to put aside present brilliant prospects in stedfast pursuit of his true aim were strongly displayed now. His friends were anxious to see him put his mark, which they knew he was so capable of doing, on the time, and pressed him to make himself heard, speaking or writing.

"No. I am at present studying," he replied. "I am growing older, it is time to be reasonable, and to face life with steady gaze, undazzled by sunshine and youth. Let us be just towards God : He has not made men for celebrity, which few attain, and still fewer value when attained. He sees the littleness of this world too entirely to give His children so frivolous a task ; He has made the stars to turn us from such delusions. Glory is the illusion of childhood, and of those who never get any further ; but he who attains to it is heedless thereof, he has got beyond that. The wise man is self-sufficing, he has not to wait thirty years to know how much the great *coteries* we call nations are worth : he seeks the welfare and honesty of those who are dependent on him, he cleaves to that corner of the earth where Providence has placed him, and if he is endowed with one of those vast geniuses to which the world barely suffices, he craves yet more for solitude. He appreciates his contemporaries too well not to count it a happy thing to eat his onions and his wood-cherries far from them. The mania to be something great is the destruction of modern men, and if we should ever have a really great man, he will come forth from some fisher's hut or some charcoal-burner's hovel. The greatest of all glories, that of God, was born in solitude."

Towards the close of the year 1828, Lacordaire was made chaplain to the Collége Henri IV., and in its work he found a more congenial sphere; still persevering, however, in his studious and solitary life. He was earnestly occupied reading Saint Augustine, Plato, Aristotle, Descartes, Church history, and the writings of M. de la Mennais, with whom he was to be so closely allied ere long. It was in the spring of 1830 that he suddenly resolved to go to la Chesnaie and see the man of whom he said that he was "the only great man in the Church of France." They had only met twice for a few moments, but those clergy with whom Lacordaire was intimate were de la Mennais' friends, and he felt powerfully drawn to him.

"Having reached Dinan," he wrote, "I plunged

alone into the by-paths of the wood, and occasionally asking my way, found myself at a lonely sombre house, the mysterious fame of which was untroubled by any tumult. This was la Chesnaie. M. de la Mennais, who was prepared for my visit and my co-operation, received me cordially. The Abbé Gerbet, his most intimate disciple, and some dozen young men who had clustered around him, were there, the seed with which he hoped to fertilise the world with his ideas and projects. This visit, while it gave me many a shock, did not sever the link which bound me to the illustrious author. His philosophy had never taken a distinct hold of my understanding, his Absolutist politics had always been repulsive to me, and his theology filled me with a dread that he could not be reckoned upon as safely orthodox. But, nevertheless, it was too late; after eight years of hesitation, I gave myself up voluntarily, though without enthusiasm, to the school which up to that point had failed to subject my sympathies or my convictions."

The idea of devoting himself to foreign missions had at this time taken great hold of Lacordaire, and it was strengthened by the Bishop of New York, whom he met at la Chesnaie, and who offered him the post of his Vicar-General. He had a great desire to visit America, and to study her liberties, social and ecclesiastical. It must be borne in mind that, as he himself has said he had come at his religion through his social creed. Society was a necessity. Society could not be without religion, nor religion without Christianity, nor Christianity without the Church. Thus society and the Church were the two ends of the chain, how were they to be united? And this problem, he believed, might best be studied in America. His advanced Liberalism was already in straits. He felt that the inalienable and divine right to speak all that he held to be truth was " cribbed, cabined, and confined " by the political circumstances of his country. " The word of truth was committed to me," he said a little later, " and I was bound to carry it to the end of the world, no one having a right to seal my lips for one single day. I came forth charged with this mighty commission, and on the very threshold of God's temple I encountered legal slavery. The law forbade me to teach the youth of France under a most Christian king; and if I had resolved, as my ancestors did, to plunge into a solitude, there to build a peaceful house of prayer, fresh laws would have been routed out to drive me thence." Since his ordination he had seen the Jesuits' colleges suppressed, and various other aggressions upon religious liberty on the part of the Government. Gallicanism, that Ark of the Covenant, was imperilled, and must needs be fenced, while his spirit wearied under what he felt to be injustice and oppression. " Weary of the scenes which I confronted on all sides in France," he said a little later, " I resolved to seek that hospitality which the laws of America have never refused to the traveller or the priest." The Revolution of 1830 only served to give point to his perceptions as to the subjection of the Church to the State. Accordingly Lacordaire sought and obtained the consent of both his mother and the Archbishop of Paris, and he had actually gone to Dijon to take leave of his family and friends before leaving France, when a letter from the Abbé Gerbet completely changed his plans. This letter set before him the proposed establishment of the famous *Avenir* newspaper, calling upon him to give his adhesion and co-operation in a work intended to be at once catholic and national, set on foot with the object of freeing religion from the trammels under which it was fettered, and thereby of bringing about a complete and happy change in the social life of France. M. de la Mennais was prepared to throw over the Absolutist party to which he had hitherto adhered, and to accept the Revolution of 1830. Lacordaire's satisfaction was great, and he threw himself enthusiastically into the movement. All feeling of isolation passed away; fascinated already by de la Mennais' great personal gifts, he beheld in him the saviour of religious liberty in France; whatever was to be found in America seemed about to be brought to pass at home, and he was not the man to desert his country when there was a battle to fight. Without a moment's delay he threw up all his plans of travel, and took his unflinching stand beside de la Mennais and his little band.   The founders of the *Avenir* professed respect for the Charte and the law, but beyond that the most entire independence as regarded the powers that be. Liberty of the press and war to the knife upon arbitrary privilege, freedom of education and abolition of a university monopoly, liberty of association and war upon the old anti-monastic laws which had been revived in an evil day; liberty, *i.e.* moral independence for the clergy, and war against the *Budget des Cultes.* The only limitations assigned to these liberties were vague and general, and even these were not unfrequently outstepped in the eagerness of discussion. " It must be confessed," writes one of Lacordaire's friends, "that they were more keen to obtain their object than to forestall its abuse.   Too radical in its principles, their doctrine became still more so in practice.   ' Liberty is not to be given, but taken,' was their cry, and they carried out the precept.   Every morning they charged their foes afresh, every day they recorded new victories.   They addressed the clergy as an army ready for battle; they lashed out furiously, goading on the dilatory, pillorying deserters.   The enemy was given no quarter : philosophers, iconoclasts, ministers, *ombres de proconsul*, universitarians, bourgeois, Gallicans, all found themselves attacked at once. Resistance only kindled their fire ; the sun was for ever going down too soon upon their warlike ardour ;

patience and consideration found little favour in their strategy. To-morrow was nowhere in their calculations, everything must be had to-day; they were prepared to wrest forcibly and at the sword's edge whatever was not readily conceded. This haughty, antagonistic attitude, this want of experience of men and things, more excusable in the younger disciples than in their leader, seems to us the great evil of the *Avenir.* Error and exaggeration would have been corrected by time, counsel, and the practical teaching of facts. But these haughty, intolerant utterances, specially coming from the lips of clergy, disturbed even their friends. The responsibility of this false position fell chiefly upon de la Mennais and Lacordaire. It was the latter who wrote the fiercest diatribes, and faced the most burning questions. The articles on the suppression of the *Clerical Budget* were written by him. It is true that later on Lacordaire sought to refute himself in the *Ère Nouvelle*, taking up the opposite side of the question as to the suppression of the *Budget des Cultes;* but if law and justice are to be found in the newspaper of 1848, assuredly all *verve* and warmth are in that of 1830." [1]

Still, amid these outbursts and excesses, the writers of the *Avenir* were possessed with the most perfect *bonne foi*, purity of purpose, and uprightness of inten- tion; and the universal chaos of opinion, the division

[1] Chocarne, i. 115.

of parties, the strange and unascertained position of the clergy, together with the too obvious enmity of Government, questionable episcopal appointments, and the many sensational events which were daily occurring in consequence of the sort of guerilla warfare between Church and State, must be taken largely into account in judging them.   And unquestionably they were a bulwark and a protection to the Church.   The *Avenir* often brought to bear a powerful weapon upon some act of gross oppression or insult to the Church, and her oppressors often winced under the stinging scourge which descended so vehemently upon them. Lacordaire was generally the author of these pungent inflictions.

It was at this period, just a month after the *Avenir* was started, that Montalembert saw the man for the first time who was to become his dearest friend.   The *Ordonnances* of Charles X. of July 1830, published without consent of Parliament, and so seriously affecting the freedom of elections and the liberty of the press, were followed by the famous Three Days, the overthrow of the Legitimate dynasty, and Louis Philippe became king.   Montalembert was at this time in Ireland, whence he hastened at once to throw himself impetuously into the cause, to him so sacred, of God and Liberty.[1]   The young men met in de la Mennais' study, where a few laymen and a few priests gathered

---

[1] The motto of the *Avenir* was "Dieu et la Liberté."

round their leader. None among them was intimate with Lacordaire, who had never put himself forward as a disciple of de la Mennais. Montalembert's own description of the meeting is too striking to change a word : " I saw both men then for the first time ; dazzled and impressed by the one, I felt more pleasantly and naturally attracted by the other. If I could but describe him as he struck me then, in all the charm and brilliancy of youth ! He was twenty-eight, dressed as a layman (for the condition of Paris made it unsafe for priests to be canonically clothed), his height, his regular, well-cut features, his statue-like brow, the noble poise of his head, his dark sparkling eyes, the something indefinable that was proud and refined as well as modest in his whole person,—all this was merely the wrapping of a soul which seemed ready to overflow, not only in the free field of public oratory, but in the intimacies of private life. His fiery glance sent forth treasures both of fierceness and tenderness, seeking not only enemies to overthrow, but hearts to win. His voice, naturally clear and *vibrante*, often fell into accents of the most intense sweetness. Born to fight and to love, he already bore the stamp of a double royalty—that of soul and intellect. He struck me as full of charm, and yet terrible ; as the very type of all holy enthusiasm, of goodness armed on behalf of truth. He seemed to me one of the elect, predestined to all that young men most worship and desire

—genius and glory.   But more attracted by the calm pleasures of Christian friendship than by the distant echoes of fame, he taught me that these great external struggles only partly touch us; that they leave us the power to seek the heart's life foremost, and that the day begins and ends in proportion as some cherished memory rises or sets in the soul.   Such was the tone in which he spoke to me, adding, ' Alas ! we should love nought save the infinite, and therefore it is that when we love, the object of love takes such hold upon the soul.'   The day after this our first meeting, Lacordaire took me to hear his mass, which he used to say in the chapel of a small convent in the Quartier Latin; and we began at once to care for one another as pure and generous hearts do care when they meet beneath the fire of a common enemy." [1]

Lacordaire's version of the meeting is not less characteristic.   " He is charming, and I love him as if he were a plebeian.   I am positive that if he lives, his future will be as pure as a Swiss lake amid the mountains, and as famous."

He was never attracted in the same way to de la Mennais, whose genius excited admiration rather than won the heart, although Montalembert has said that there were moments when he knew how to be "the most caressing and paternal of men," adding, however, that he never displayed any tenderness towards Lacor-

[1] Le Père Lacordaire, p. 13.

daire. But the one overpowering need of Lacordaire's heart was confidence. He could imagine no friendship without the most absolute, unrestrained outpouring of heart ; so much so, that if he had a friend who was a priest, it seemed a necessity to him to place his whole heart before him in confession, and it is significantly remarked by one of Lacordaire's most confidential friends that he never sought de la Mennais in confession.

Montalembert must himself describe the events that followed :—

" He was not satisfied with writing, he spoke as he wrote. He had thoroughly taken in the fact that in free countries, or such as aspired to freedom, all great causes must, as at Rome and in England, be heard before the tribunal of public justice. A series of contests, all touching upon the emancipation of the priest and the citizen, brought him several times before the Correctional Police, either as accused, as accuser, or as advocate ; for he chose more than once to plead himself, and I well remember the amazement of a Président de Chambre, on discovering the priest, whose name was beginning to be so well known, wearing the advocate's gown. One day, in a reply to the King's Advocate, who had ventured to say that priests were the ministers of a foreign Power, Lacordaire exclaimed, ' We are the ministers of One Who is a stranger nowhere—God ! ' Whereupon the bystanders, albeit those 'men of July' who were so antagonistic to the clergy, applauded vehemently, exclaiming, '*Mon prêtre, mon curé*, who are you? You are a brave fellow!'"

He always rose to the occasion in these strifes. "I am confident," he wrote after some such, "that the Roman Senate could not overawe me."

The strife was about to thicken. Louis Philippe exercised the prerogative given him by the Concordat for the first time, and appointed three bishops. Lacordaire wrote concerning these appointments with a copious intemperance which he acknowledged and regretted afterwards, and the Government, not altogether unjustifiably irritated, summoned him, as well as the editor, de la Mennais, to answer for exciting the public to contempt of authority and disobedience to the law. They appeared before the Court of Assizes, January 31, 1831. De la Mennais had Janvier as his counsel; Lacordaire was his own advocate. We must quote some passages of his speech, which was never reproduced save by Montalembert in his political recollections of his friend.

"I rise," he said, "with an impression I cannot lay aside. Formerly, when the priest rose amid the people, an instinctive kindling of affection arose with him. Now, albeit an accused man, I know that my title as a priest is silent in my behalf, and I accept the fact. The multitude has cast aside the affection it once bore the priest, since the priest has himself cast aside a noble attribute of his calling, since the man of God has ceased to be the man of Liberty. . . . I am but a young man, an obscure Catholic, my acquaintance with public life is of the briefest, and yet I would fain speak to you of the hidden thoughts of my heart. . . . I was young, God had died out of my soul, and my country was not free. God had died out of my soul, because my cradle was rocked in the dawn of this nineteenth century, amid storm and tempest: my country was not free, because after great tribulations God had raised up to France a man greater even than her tribulations. . . . I was still very young; I beheld this capital, where curiosity, imagination, the thirst for knowledge, all led me to believe that I should un-riddle the world's secrets. Its weight crushed me, and I became a Christian; once Christian, I became a priest. Suffer me to rejoice therein, sirs; for never did I more realise what liberty is than the day when with holy orders I received the right to speak of God. The whole universe opened before me, and I saw that man possesses an inalienable, a divine, an eternally free gift—that of speech! The priest's word was intrusted to me, and I was bidden carry it to the world's confines, without any human being having the right to silence me for a single day. I left God's temple full of this mighty trust, and on the threshold I stumbled against legal servitude! . . .

"If I have excited disobedience to the law, I have been guilty of a great crime, for the law is sacred. After God, it is the country's safety, and no man is more bound to respect it than the priest, whose commission is to teach the people whence comes life and whence death.   Nevertheless, I must own that I do not experience that veneration for the laws of my country that men of old bore to theirs.   It was written on Leonidas' tomb, 'Go tell to Sparta that we died to maintain her holy laws.'   But I would not have such an epitaph on my grave : I would not die for my country's laws ; for the time has ceased to be when law was the sacred expression of the tradition, the customs, and the gods of the people : all that is changed.   Manifold periods, opinions, tyrannies, the axe and the sword all clash in our complex legislation, and the man who dies for such a law must worship both glory and infamy. . . . We have spoken of our oppressors, and you stumble at the word. . . . That which is myself, is my thought, my speech, and these are oppressed in this my country.   You might fetter my hands, it matters little ; . . . but though you do not that, you fetter my thought, you forbid me to teach, I to whom it has been said, *Docete.*   The seal of your laws is on my lips, when will it be broken ? And therefore I call you oppressors, and I fear to accept bishops at your hand.   .   .   .

"My task is accomplished ; yours, gentlemen, is to

acquit me. I do not ask it for my own sake. There are but two things which create genius—God and a prison. I need not fear one or the other. But I demand my acquittal as a step towards the union of faith and liberty, as a pledge of peace and reconciliation. The Catholic clergy have done their duty,—they have cried out to their countrymen, they have offered them words of loving-kindness; it is your part to respond. I demand it, moreover, that the petty despots, offspring of the Empire, may learn in their far-away provinces that there is justice in France for Catholics, and that they can no longer be sacrificed to antique prejudice and the hates of a bygone age. Therefore, gentlemen, I call upon you to acquit me, Jean Baptiste Henri Lacordaire, inasmuch as I am not guilty, as I have acted like a good citizen, as I have defended my God and my liberty, and that I will do all my life, gentlemen."

De la Mennais and Lacordaire were both acquitted. The verdict was not given till midnight, and they were immediately surrounded by a crowd of enthusiastic applauders. "By degrees they left us," Montalembert wrote, "and we walked along the Quays in the darkness. As we parted at his door, I hailed Lacordaire as the orator of the coming day. He was neither excited nor overcome by his triumph; and I could see that these little triumphs of vanity were less than nothing to him, as mere passing mist."

This unforeseen victory led the conquerors to fresh efforts. They resolved to concentrate their energies on freedom of instruction. Government had not taken any active steps towards promoting public education and freedom of instruction, as they had promised in the *Charte* of 1830 to do without delay. The Université (a body of Government officials at the head of all public instruction and private education, which maintained its position until the passing of M. de Falloux' new law in 1850) opposed all free instruction, and the editors of the *Avenir*, under the title of *Agence pour la défense de la liberté religieuse*, announced their intention to open a free, gratuitous school in Paris. Notice was duly given to the Prefect of Police, and the school was opened, May 7, 1831, and Lacordaire, de la Mennais, and Montalembert set to work, after the first had made a brief inauguration speech, with a class of some twenty children each. The next day but one, a *commissaire* came to put a stop to the proceeding. He addressed the children first: "In the name of the law I bid you disperse." Lacordaire immediately spoke: "In the name of your parents, whose authority is delegated to me, I bid you stay." The children all cried out, "We will stay." Upon which the *sergents de ville* turned every one out at once save Lacordaire, who asserted that the room which he had hired was his legal domicile, and that he would sleep there unless forcibly ejected. He was, however, put out, the premises placed under seal, and the school-keepers prosecuted. During the first legal proceedings Montalembert's father died, and as he succeeded to the peerage, while the action against the accused could not be separated, they were both brought before the Cour des Pairs, and, September 15, 1831, convicted, and sentenced to a fine of 100 francs.

Lacordaire was again his own counsel, and he seems to have addressed the ninety-four Peers of France who were his auditors with as much force as the jury of a former period. He began with a startling *Tu quoque* addressed to the Procureur-Général, who had lately prosecuted the Prince de Polignac and three other ministers on the strength of a law not as yet sanctioned. His concluding sentences were as follows :—

" If time did not fail me, I would have granted all that is demanded ; and supposing us to be guilty of the violation of a decree, I would have proved our innocence from that very fact. For, noble peers, there are holy faults, and it may be possible that the violation of a law should prove only the fulfilment of one yet higher. In the first trial of liberty of instruction, in that famous trial wherein Socrates was condemned, he was clearly guilty as regarded the gods, and consequently the laws of his country. Nevertheless posterity, alike that of heathen nations and of the ages which have followed Christ, has condemned his accusers and his judges : they have absolved only the guilty man and his executioner—the first, because he had disobeyed the law of Athens that he might obey a greater law; the second, because it was with tears that he proffered the fatal cup to the prisoner. And I on my part would have shown you that, while trampling under foot this decree of the Empire, I deserved well at the hands of my country, that I had done good service to her liberties, as to the cause and the future of all Christian nations. But time forbids my utterance. Enough. When Socrates, during that first and famous cause of free instruction, was about to leave his judges, he said, 'We go forth; you to live, I to die.' It is not thus that I leave you, my noble judges. Whatsoever may be your verdict, we go hence to live; for liberty and religion are immortal, and neither can those thoughts which you have heard springing from a pure heart perish." [1]

Writing in 1862, Montalembert appealed to the five or six peers of France still living who had heard the trial, whether the whole Chamber, which had listened "patiently and coldly" to the other pleadings, had not been carried away by Lacordaire's eloquence and personal presence? "The present generation," he says, "cannot form any adequate idea of the earnest

[1] *Moniteur* du 20 Septembre, 1831.

vehemence which kindled men's hearts at that time. There were many fewer journals, and many fewer readers than now; postal communication was far more difficult; railroads and telegraphs did not exist, and we performed our propagandist journeys by means of three days and three nights in an atrocious diligence between Paris and Lyons! But what life there was in souls! what energy in minds! . . . To understand the outburst of pure disinterested enthusiasm which took place among the younger clergy and many large-hearted young laymen, one must have lived through those times, one must have read their glances, hearkened to their confidences, held their quivering hands; one must have formed those ties during the heat of battle which death alone could sever. . . . A month later Lacordaire wrote, 'However cruel the state of things, it can take nothing from the charm of the past year, which will abide for ever in my heart like the song of a virgin departed.'" [1]

The cause was lost as far as technicalities were concerned, but every one felt that it had been won before the weighty tribunal of public opinion; and it was, to use Montaigne's words, "a defeat more triumphant than a victory." But the days of the *Avenir* were numbered. All the press waged war against it; the cause was seriously compromised with the Bishops and clergy in general by de la Mennais' advanced

[1] Montalembert, p. 49.

philosophic opinions and his extreme U ltramontanism;[1] and moreover, what was much to the point, financial reasons made it almost an impossibility for the editors to continue their work; and November 15, 1831, thirteen months after its first appearance, they announced the cessation of the newspaper, and simultaneously the intention of the three editors to go to Rome, there to submit the controverted questions to the Pope, promising absolute submission to his decision.   This was Lacordaire's idea.

"No one had the smallest inclination to hinder them," wrote Montalembert; "and it was unlucky, for the journey was a mistake.   It was, to say the least, an unusual piece of pretension to force Rome into an utterance concerning matters she had left open to free discussion for more than a year; while not to be wholly thankful for her silence was altogether to misunderstand the requirements and the advantages of the situation.   Such an aberration may be pardoned in young men of no experience in the ways of the world and the Church; but it is hard to account for in a priest of position and of ripened age, such as M. de la Mennais, who was more than fifty years old,

---

[1] A phrase of Montalembert's on this subject is curious to read now : "For we must add, on behalf of those who have not fathomed the depths of French *mobilité*, that at this period ultramontane doctrines met with precisely the like unpopularity among the immense majority of the clergy that Gallicanism excites at the present day" (p. 50)

and had been at Rome before, Leo XII. having received him with the utmost distinction."

On their arrival at Rome the agitators were asked for an explanatory document, which Lacordaire drew up, and then for two months they heard no more about it. At the end of that time Cardinal Pacca wrote to de la Mennais, saying that the Pope, while doing justice to their past services and good intentions, regretted to see them stirring up controversies and opinions which, to say the least of it, were perilous. He would cause their doctrines to be thoroughly examined, and meanwhile, as this might take some time, the Holy Father recommended them to go back to France. After this the Pope received them with his wonted courtesy, not conveying the slightest reproach, but at the same time not making the slightest allusion to the object which had brought them to Rome.

It was not a brilliant or flattering conclusion, as Montalembert observes; but he truly says it was all they could expect. Lacordaire was fully prepared for it. He saw nothing save a kindly, fatherly warning, deciding nothing, compromising no one. Those ten weeks in Rome had had a very calming, softening influence upon his mind. "I can see him now," says Montalembert, "wandering for whole days among the ruins and monuments, pausing in rapt admiration —full of that exquisite feeling for true beauty which never deserted him—for all the unrivalled treasures of Rome ; above all, revelling in the charm of her calm, lovely distances : then coming back to our common room to preach reserve, resignation, submission—in a word, reason, to de la Mennais." His keen sense of duty bore him triumphantly over all the temptations which pride, energy, and genius threw in his way, and, as Montalembert says, the penetration which sprang from humility and faith enabled him to fore-shadow the wise judgment which time so fully ratified. Unhappily it was not the same with the elder man of the three friends. De la Mennais lost his temper, and broke more and more with all his best and happiest antecedents, refusing to hearken to counsel. After receiving Cardinal Pacca's letter, Lacordaire put strongly before him that either they should never have come to Rome, or having come, they must be silent and submit. De la Mennais refused to accept the alternative, and persisted in remaining where he was to urge an immediate decision. Thereupon Lacordaire unhesitatingly took action, and, grieved to the soul, returned to France, March 1832, to wait in silence for the Pope's decision. "Silence," he said, "is the next strongest thing to speech."

De la Mennais saw him depart without regret, feeling merely relieved by the absence of an inconvenient critic and a faithless disciple. Montalembert, in an excess of generosity, held by his leader, and remained in Rome. He speaks in touching language of Lacordaire's earnest efforts to draw him thence. "There is no spiritual disunion between us," Lacordaire wrote as soon as he had reached France; "all my life I shall fight for liberty, and before de la Mennais had said a word, liberty was the moving power of my thoughts and my life. If he carries out his new plan, bear in mind that all his most earnest fellow-workers will forsake him, and, dragged by false Liberals into a line where success is impossible, no words can describe what may ensue. Do not let us subject our hearts to our ideas, for men's ideas are often as bright and as fugitive as the clouds which flit across the sun." Montalembert remained obstinate. "You are younger than I am," he pleaded again, "and that is the only reason why you are more mistaken." For four months they remained waiting in Rome, and then, losing patience, de la Mennais left Rome pettishly, making known his resolution to return to France, and at once without further ado begin the publication of the *Avenir* anew. On hearing this, Lacordaire, determined to separate his course distinctly from de la Mennais, went immediately to Munich to study there. Curiously enough, Montalembert and his companion travelled home that way, and the three men met again. Lacordaire had scarcely entered his hotel when Montalembert appeared, having seen his name, and they went together to de la Mennais, who received him coldly and resentfully. But they began at once to discuss the great question, Lacordaire endeavouring to convince the elder man that in attempting to renew the *Avenir* he was committing not only a fault, but a blunder. De la Mennais admitted it at last. The next day a great dinner was given to the three friends by the literary and artistic world of Munich. Towards the end of the meal de la Mennais was called out, and a messenger from the Apostolic Nuncio gave him a letter containing an encyclical letter from Gregory XVI. dated August 15, 1832. A glance showed him that it was not favourable to the doctrines of the *Avenir.* His line was instantly taken, and without studying the document he whispered to his companions that they had no choice but submission ; and returning to their hotel, he wrote a few but clear lines expressing his obedience, which satisfied the Pope. Their submission was speedily made known, and the three returned together to Paris, "*en vaincus victorieux a eux-mêmes,*" as Lacordaire said.

Characteristically, his generous feeling of sympathy for de la Mennais' discomfiture (believing as he did in his absolute good faith) led Lacordaire to return with him to Brittany, where he took up his abode at the lonesome, dreary country-house of la Chesnaie. "I believed," he wrote, "that I was bringing back a noble mind saved from shipwreck, a master more revered than before. . . . The illusion was great. Soon some of his young disciples gathered round him; the house resumed its former tone, a strange mixture of solitude and animation; but if the skies had not changed, the master's heart had. His wound was open, and every day he plunged the sword in deeper, instead of tearing it out and pouring in the balm of God's love. Terrible storms passed over that brow whence peace had fled. Broken words and threats would escape those lips whence formerly the words of evangelic teaching fell. Sometimes he used to remind me of Saul; but none of us had David's harp to calm the outbreaks of the evil spirit, and day by day more fearful forebodings arose in my mind, already depressed." Each day alienated the two men more, all community of life and interests was destroyed by their utter disagreement on all that was most important in their present and future course; and at last, unable to bear it any longer, Lacordaire left la Chesnaie never to return, having written the following letter to his friend :—

"*December* 11, 1832.

"I shall leave la Chesnaie this evening. I leave it from an honourable motive, being convinced that henceforth I should be useless to you by reason of the difference of our minds as to the Church and society, which increases daily, in spite of my sincere efforts to follow the development of your opinions.

I believe that neither in my lifetime nor for long after it any republic will be established in France or elsewhere in Europe, and I cannot take part in a system founded upon the contrary conviction. Without renouncing my Liberal opinions, I understand and believe that the Church has had good and wise reasons, amid the utter corruption of parties, for refusing to go on as fast as we wished. I respect her thoughts and my own. Perhaps your opinions are wiser, deeper; and considering your natural superiority to myself, I ought to be convinced thereof; but reason is not the whole man, and inasmuch as I cannot tear out of me the opinions which divide us, it is but right that I should put an end to that community life which is entirely to my advantage and your cost. My conscience demands it as much as my honour, for I must turn my life to some account for God, and being unable to follow you, I should only weary and discourage you, put difficulties in your way, and ruin myself. You will never know in this world how much I have suffered during the past year from the fear of causing you pain. In all my perplexities, hesitations, and doubts I have thought of you only, and whatever I may have to go through henceforth, no heart-sorrow can ever equal what I have now felt. To-day I leave you at rest as regards the Church, more respected than ever, so much above your enemies that they are as nought; it is the best moment to choose for inflicting a grief upon you, which, believe me, will spare you greater ones. I do not know what will become of me, whether I shall go to the United States or remain in France, or in what position. Wherever I am, you will always have token of the respect and attachment I must ever bear you, and I entreat you to accept this expression of a wounded heart."

"I left la Chesnaie alone, on foot, while M. de la Mennais was as usual out walking after dinner. At a certain point on the road I saw him through the bushes, with his young disciples, and stopping, I gazed, for the last time, on that unhappy great man, and then pursued my flight, not knowing what was to become of me, or how far God would accept the act I was performing."

These strong expressions were no mere verbiage : the separation cost Lacordaire pain which he never could look back upon without a shudder, and he underwent very unjust handling from some of his most intimate friends, who disapproved of the line he had felt constrained to adopt. Montalembert himself was among these, and he bears witness to the trustful confidence in his right motives which upheld Lacordaire through the trying season. "No one," he wrote, "can feel more deeply than I do the reverence due to past links, and should M. de la Mennais at some future time leave the Church, should he become the greatest of heretics, there would always be an immeasurable gulf between his enemies and me, and no one would read what I should be constrained to write without acknowledging the painfulness of my position, the lastingness of my respect, or the fidelity of my conscience. These are the eventful hours of a man's life, when he is forced to struggle against contradictory circumstances and conflicting duties. In the next world it will be known whether I have acted with the heedlessness of a man who breaks the ties of years carelessly and without sorrow!"

It was not long before Lacordaire's course was fully justified in the eyes of the whole Christian world. It is curious to observe (and it is Montalembert who points it out) how "a series of tergiversations and retractations, of unreal submissions and contradictory affirmations, led the ultra-apostle of absolute and universal Papal Infallibility to the point of open rebellion against the simplest and most legitimate exercise of authority, invited by himself as it was."

We need not follow de la Mennais' downward course. In 1834 the publication of his "Paroles d'un Croyant" left no doubt as to his complete departure from the ancient paths of faith and truth. Lacordaire felt bound to reply in a pamphlet called "Considérations sur le Système philosophique de M. de la Mennais," to which he attributed all his master's errors, and which Montalembert considers as containing some of the most eloquent passages he ever wrote. Yet even this was disapproved by some old friends, such as the Baron d'Eckstein and Padre Ventura, who looked upon it as an assault upon his former teacher. Lacordaire was not disconcerted.

"I have fulfilled my whole duty now as regards M. de la Mennais," he wrote, June 3, 1834. "I have told what my personal experience of ten years has taught me concerning the school he sought to found, and if I had done nothing else in my life, I should die content. My conscience is at rest, I can breathe, after a ten years' oppression I begin to revive. . . . There are at least some who understand me, who know that I have not become a Republican, or a *juste-milieu,* or a Legitimist, but that I have made a step towards that noble priestly character which is superior to all parties, while pitiful to all weakness. They know that the result of my journey to Rome has been to soften me, to draw me out of the fatal whirlpool of politics, teaching me to concern myself henceforth only with the things of God, and through these with the future happiness of mankind slowly won. They know that I only separated from that celebrated man in order not to plunge any further into that unfortunate system of politics, and by reason of the impossibility I found of bringing him to the lines where the Church was waiting to applaud him, and where he would have done far more for the enfranchisement of humanity than he will ever achieve where he is." And again, "I am no saint, I know it too well, but I do feel a disinterested love for truth; and though I have sought to extricate myself honourably from the abyss in which I had fallen, no thought of pride or ambition has prompted my conduct on this occasion. Pride always whispered, 'Stay where you are, do not move, do not expose yourself to the reproaches of your old friends.' But God's grace spoke louder, 'Tread human respect under foot, obey the Holy See and God.' My sole skill has been my frank submission. If everything has turned out as I foresaw, I had only foreseen it by absolutely putting myself aside. I do not rejoice in the gulf which self-will has prepared beneath the feet of a man who has done good service to the Church—I trust that God may stop him while it is yet time—but I do rejoice that the Pontiff, who is Father of all Christians, should have settled by his authority questions which were rending my native Church asunder, which were misleading crowds of souls who were honestly deceived—questions the unhappy attraction of which I had experienced so long and so bitterly. If I have had any personal triumph in the matter, may it perish! and may the Church of France rejoice in a vigorous peace and unity after this memorable lesson! May we all forgive one another for our youthful errors, and join in prayer for him who caused them by an excess of imagination too full of life not to be deplored !"

As far as men can see, these prayers were not answered. De la Mennais went on drifting farther and farther from the truth, while it is a remarkable fact that he carried literally no one with him. Montalembert observes that he is a solitary instance in the history of Christendom of a man possessing all the qualities of the most "redoubtable heresiarch," who did not succeed in drawing one single acolyte after him. Montalembert himself, although he could not accept Lacordaire's view, still shrank from the opinions to which de la Mennais was daily committing himself deeper. Hoping to escape from the distracting doubts which beset him, he went to Germany, pursued by his master's appeals. De la Mennais congratulated him with bitterness on being a layman, bidding him retain his independence at all costs, and adding scornfully, " The Word which once could move the world cannot now move the smallest schoolboys !" Meanwhile the evil genius was counterbalanced by the good genius. Lacordaire wrote continually with " inexhaustible energy and perseverance. Sacrificed, misunderstood, repulsed, he continued to lavish his neglected warnings, his always true predictions, upon me with such force of reason, such powerful and touching eloquence, such a moving intermingling of

severity and humble affection, such salutary alternations of pitiless honesty and irresistible tenderness !"
He writes to Montalembert : " The Church does not
say to you, ' *See.* ' She has no power to do that.
She says, '*Believe.*' She says to you at twenty-three,
holding as you do to certain lines of thought, what
she said at your first Communion, ' Receive your
hidden incomprehensible God, humble your reason
before God and the Church, His instrument.' For
what has the Church been given us save to bring
us back to the truth when we mistake error for it ?
You are surprised at what the Holy Father requires
of M. de la Mennais ? Unquestionably it is harder
to submit when one has made public utterances than
when everything has been silent between one's heart
and God. This is the special trial pertaining to men
of great talent. The greatest Churchmen have had
to break their lives in two, and on a smaller scale
that is just what every conversion is. Listen to my
voice, however despised ; for who will warn you if I
do not ? Who loves you enough to treat you so merci-
lessly ? Who will cauterise your wounds except he
who kisses them so lovingly, and would fain suck out
their poison at his own life's risk ?"

Lacordaire even followed his friend to Germany,
and by the tomb of S. Elizabeth of Hungary (the
fruit of which is one of Montalembert's most charming
books) pleaded with him. The struggle ended at

length, as was probable, in the younger man admitting his error, and slowly coming round to the other's belief and course of action. Few more touching words were ever written than Montalembert's pathetic regret over the struggle, and over his own ingratitude, which assuredly was not meant for such. "In him" (these are the concluding words) "I learned to understand and revere the only Power in bowing before which man is himself exalted. The captive of pride and error, I was redeemed by him who then appeared to me as the ideal priest, like to his own definition, 'Strong as adamant, and tenderer than a mother.'"

IV.

CONFERENCES.

LACORDAIRE had scarcely returned to Paris when (April 1832) the cholera broke out there with terrific force. He at once devoted himself to ministering among the sick, spending his whole time at a temporary hospital established in the Greniers d'Abondance. The clergy were still looked upon askance, the local government declined the Archbishop's proffered aid, and no religious garb could show itself in the streets. " No Sisters of Charity, no chaplain, no parish priest," he writes ; " they barely tolerate me and one or two more. Each day I gather in some scanty fruits for eternity. The greater number make no confession, and the priest is merely a deputy from the Church, timidly seeking here and there some soul which belongs to her flock. Some one or two make their confession, others die deaf and silent. I lay my hand on their brow and speak the words of absolution, trusting in God's mercy. I rarely leave without feeling thankful to have been there. Yesterday a woman was carried in, her husband, a soldier, whispered the question whether a priest could not be found? (I being in a layman's dress.) 'I am one.' One felt so happy in being at hand to help a soul and comfort the man." When this immediate pressure was over, Lacordaire returned to his old idea of going to some quiet country parish. He writes, December 11, 1832 : "I mean to bury myself in the country, to live for a little flock, and to find my whole happiness in God and the fields. You will see that I am a very simple, unambitious man. Farewell to great things ! to fame and great men ! I have seen the vanity of all, and only want to live in goodness and obscurity. Some day, when Montalembert has grown grey amid ingratitude and fame, he will come to look back upon our youthful days with me. We shall mourn together by the hearth of my presbytery ; he will do me justice before we both die ; and I shall give my blessing to his children. As for me, a poor priest, I shall have no children to grow up beside me or to survive me ; no household, no church shining with holiness and wisdom. Born in commonplace days, I shall pass through this world as one of those not worthy to be remembered ; I will strive to be good, simple, devout, hoping in the future without any self-interested motives, inasmuch as I shall not see it ; working for those who may do so, and not finding fault with Providence, which might well lay heavier troubles on a life of little merit."

Of course this was not the view others took of him, and on presenting himself to Mgr. de Quélen, the Archbishop met him with open arms, as a son who had come forth unscathed from a great peril. He reinstated him in the Chaplaincy of the Visitation, where for a time Lacordaire was thankful to rest and study. His mother too returned to live with him, and the remainder of her life was spent there—a little apartment in a narrow street beneath Sainte Geneviève, which for three years he inhabited. "He comes before me there," says Montalembert, "greater and more remarkable even than in the Cour des Pairs, the Academy, or even Notre Dame. I can see him daily gathering himself together and calming himself in prayer, in work, in charity, in solitude, in a serious, simple, unknown life, truly hidden in God. That was the nest where his genius brooded, and whence the eagle which outshone all its fellows at length soared."

He refused all attempts to draw him into public action, declining twice over to become editor of the *Univers,* which was beginning then. He also refused a professor's chair at the University of Louvain. Solitude was his passion at this time. "My days are very same : I work all the morning and afternoon regularly; I see nobody save a few country clergy who now and then visit me. I delight in the solitude of my life, it is my very element. . . . Nothing can be done without solitude, that is my great axiom. One's heart is the loser by too much expansion among strangers, it is like a hothouse flower transported. . . . A man is made within himself, not without." Yet from time to time a presage of the future must have come over him, for he writes, " The hour always comes to the man; it is enough that he wait patiently, in nowise controverting Providence." And again, " I have no ambition, and can have none, for all high position among the clergy means pastoral charge or administration wholly out of my line. I neither shall nor will ever have such functions. But conscience constrains one to do something with oneself."

Conscious of his vocation for preaching, he was not unwilling to prove it. His first sermon was preached at Saint Roch, where he was, strangely enough, last heard in Paris, some nineteen years later. It was in the spring of 1833. Montalembert, Ampère, de Corcelles, and others who knew his capacities were present. It was an utter failure, and they all went away saying that he was an able man, but would never be a good preacher! He came to the like conclusion himself. " It is evident," he wrote, " that I have neither the physical power, nor the mental flexibility, nor the knowledge of a world in which I have lived and always shall live apart; in short, I have *nothing* to the degree required to be a preacher in the full sense of the word. But some day I may be called to some work for reclaiming young men, devoted solely to them. If I ever can make use of words on behalf of the Church, it will be only in the way of apology; that is to say, in the shape of gathering together beauty, grandeur, history, and polemics, to the exaltation of Christianity and the fostering of faith."

The call was soon to come. In January 1834, Lacordaire was asked to give a series of Conferences to the students of the Collége Stanislas, one of the least important in Paris. The first was given January 19th, and for the next the chapel was so crowded that a temporary gallery had to be erected—five or six hundred people flocked to hear him. The only notes of these Conferences are some very brief analysis, but Montalembert says that they contain the distinctive mark of the great preacher of Notre Dame, his " startling originality and searching, earnest passion, his impetuous bursts of thought and word, of tenderness, of irony." It is told that in reply to some listeners who were scoffing he observed, " God has given you cleverness, *messieurs*, great cleverness, in order to show you that He is not afraid of any man's wit." There were vehement partisans on both sides. "Some look upon me as a rabid republican," he wrote, "as a renegade, and I know not what. Some of the clergy accuse me, not of atheism, but of never having uttered the name of Jesus Christ. . . . I despise all these petty worries. I fulfil my duties as a man and a priest. I am solitary, busy, calm, trusting in God and the future."

This was no exaggeration of the atmosphere which surrounded him. He was denounced as a dangerous democrat, a preacher of perilous novelties, a fanatical republican, calculated to stir up the worst passions of men ; not only at Rome, and to the French Government, but with such persistent reiteration to the Archbishop of Paris, that Mgr. de Quélen (whose position at that time was so painfully difficult that it seems almost ungenerous to accuse him of timidity and weakness) first stopped Lacordaire's Conferences, and then forbade their renewal during the winter of 1834-35. Meanwhile he had one vigorous advocate in the person of the *Chanoine de la Métropole*, M. Affre, himself later on the Archbishop who met his noble martyr-death on the barricades of Paris. His calm, resolute mind was able to see the real greatness of the young orator, and he became his firm friend.

"I had read his retractation" (of the *Avenir* doctrines), M. Affre wrote, "and was struck with its candour. I admired his talent, and without being blind to his faults, I perceived tokens of a great soul and an intelligence of no common order. . . . Unfortunately his Conferences at the Collége Stanislas, which had produced the strongest enthusiasm among his young listeners, had a different effect upon some others, not wholly without ground, in the bold, unwonted thoughts, and the strong, at times unguarded, expression of the same. . . . The Archbishop took alarm, and desired that the future Conferences might be submitted to him before they were delivered. Lacordaire refused, on the ground that he would be altogether hindered if he might not improvise at least the expression of his thoughts. I undertook to plead his cause, not unalive to the difficulties of extempore speaking on such matters, but believing that they were mainly set aside by the upright, frank character of the Abbé Lacordaire, who is absolutely free from all sectarian spirit, and most ready to listen to advice. I spoke strongly on his behalf to the Archbishop, but for the time vainly." However, not a murmur escaped the preacher, even among his closest friends. " It costs me something to obey," he wrote to Montalembert; " but I have learned from experience that sooner or later obedience has its reward, and that God only knows what is best for us. Light comes to a man who submits, as to one who opens his eyes." And to Mme. Swetchine he wrote, "I am quite calm and happy, and leave all to Providence, Which has never failed me, and knows best what is good for me. From a spiritual point of view, this resignation is profitable before God : perhaps I had judged M. de la Mennais too severely, and God sees fit to make me feel by personal experience how difficult a thing submission is when it touches oneself directly. But from an earthly point of view, persecution is always profitable to those who bear it worthily."

Even so. Shortly after, the Archbishop, who (as Montalembert said) had been mistaken in applying the words "*Vir obediens loquetur victorias*" to de la Mennais' fictitious submission, now gave Lacordaire opportunity of verifying it.

"Time went on," Lacordaire says, "and I did not know what to do, when one day as I was crossing the Jardin du Luxembourg I met a priest whom I knew. He stopped me and said, 'What are you doing? You should go and see the Archbishop, and come to an understanding with him.' A few minutes after I met an ecclesiastic much less well known to me, who stopped me again and said, 'You are wrong not to go to the Archbishop. I have good reason to believe that he would be glad to have some conversation with you.' This double expression of opinion took me by surprise, and being perhaps somewhat superstitious as to the dealings of Providence, I turned slowly towards the Convent of Saint Michel, not far from the Luxembourg, where the Archbishop was then living. It was not the ordinary portress who came to the door, but a Choir Sister who was kindly disposed towards me, because, as she said, 'every one was against me.' She told me that Monseigneur was at home to nobody, but she proposed taking in my name, on the chance that he might see me. He consented to do so. When I entered, the Archbishop was walking up and down his room with a preoccupied, troubled air; he received me coldly, and I began to walk beside him without his saying a word. After some considerable silence, he stopped suddenly, and turning to me with a glance of investigation, said abruptly, 'I am thinking of appointing you to preach in Notre Dame, will you accept the appointment?' This brusque proposition, which I did not understand, did not elate me. I answered that the time was very short for preparation, it was a solemn undertaking, and though I had succeeded in the presence of a limited audience, I might easily fail before some four thousand listeners. The end was that I asked for twenty-four hours' con sideration. After prayer to God and consultation with Mme. Swetchine, I accepted. . . . The Archbishop was surprised at the slender opposition he met with when his appointment became known. I believe it was because my opponents hoped it would be my destruction, convinced as they were that I knew no theology, and had no oratorical power, two things essential for such a work. They did not know that I had devoted the last fifteen years to the study of philosophy and theology, and during the same period I had practised myself in speaking under every kind of condition. Moreover, the orator is like the rock of

Horeb—until touched of God, it is a barren stone, but once let His Finger be laid upon it, and it becomes a fertilising spring."

Doubtless M. Affre's stronger mind had great influence with the Archbishop in this measure, and he was also subject to the urgent applications of a deputation of law students, led by Frédéric Ozanam.[1] The Conferences for young men, which had been inaugurated the year before, had not been over successful, and the Archbishop felt the need of a new start. Anyhow, the thing was to be. "The day arrived. Notre Dame was filled with a multitude of unwonted

[1] In 1833 a petition had been presented to the Archbishop by three law students—Ozanam, Lejonteux, and De Montazet—asking for Conferences in Notre Dame which might tend to Christianise their fellow-students, who were so generally impregnated with rationalism. In 1834 the petition was renewed by two hundred, insisting on a teaching somewhat beside the ordinary lines, touching upon the topics then urgent on all thoughtful young men, which should treat of the connection between religion and society, and should more or less directly be an answer to the rationalist German and French writings then in such extensive circulation. They pressed for the appointment of Lacordaire as preacher, as having forcibly enlisted the sympathies of the young men of Paris; and they held him more than any one to be capable of pointing out "that philosophy of science and art which would prove the Catholic faith the source of all truth and all beauty; that living philosophy which, plumbing to the depths of human existence, should instruct man as to his origin, guide his course, and help him to meet his end" (Petition, F. Ozanam, Vie, p. 261).

character.   The *jeunesse libérale* and the *jeunesse absolutiste*, friends and foes, as well as the crowd of merely curious men always abounding in every capital, all poured in streams to the venerable Cathedral. I went up into the pulpit, not unmoved, but with firmness, and began my discourse, keeping my eyes fixed on the Archbishop, who was the most important person present to me,—coming after God indeed, but before the public.   He listened, his head somewhat bent, in the most absolutely impassible manner, like a man who was not merely a spectator nor a judge, but who himself was incurring great personal risks in the solemn undertaking.   When I had once fairly got possession of my subject and my audience, when my heart fairly heaved under the necessity of seizing hold of this vast assembly of men, and when the first calm had yielded to inspiration, one of those outcries which never fails to touch men, when it is true and deep, escaped me.   The Archbishop trembled visibly, a pallor which even I could see came across his face, he raised his head and cast a glance of astonishment at me.   I perceived that the battle was won as concerned him, and it was so also with the audience. Directly that he left Notre Dame he intimated his intention of appointing me as an honorary Canon of his Metropolitan Church, and there was some difficulty in persuading him to wait until the end of the course."

This was the beginning of Lent 1835, and such was the first of those famous Conferences which have probably acquired greater celebrity than any church oratory of modern times, save that of Bossuet. Montalembert says that to his mind these first discourses were never surpassed by any that followed, except the series of 1854 given at Toulouse. The Archbishop was present at all : it was the first time since the Revolution of July that he had come face to face with the multitude, and he was intensely delighted at the success which so amply justified a move he had certainly felt some qualms in making. One day, rising from his throne, he apostrophised the young orator in the presence of his vast audience as " our new prophet."

Probably the venerable aisles of Notre Dame had never before embraced such a congregation. There was a nucleus formed by the Society of Saint Vincent de Paul, recently founded by Ozanam, one of Lacordaire's dearest friends, and in which foundation he himself had taken no small part ; and round this gathered, often hours before the Conference was to begin,[1] a vast crowd of men of every age, every position in life, every form of belief and unbelief, every kind of politics. There was a great majority of young men,

[1] Frédéric Ozanam's brother says that he often went to keep places in Notre Dame, for men who were unable to come early, some hours before the time appointed.

students of law and medicine, advocates, *savants*, soldiers, Saint-Simonians, republicans and monarchists, atheists and materialists. "New and strange scene!" writes Père Chocarne, "in which many a man, during the long waiting hours, must have marvelled what brought together so many men from such opposite quarters? the disciples of Voltaire hanging on the lips of a Catholic priest; the descendants of '89, meek listeners in the temple whence their fathers had driven Christ forth; seekers after a new religion before a pulpit whence the same creed has ever gone forth. What did they seek? how came they there?"[1]

There was much to account for the attraction beyond the mere lust of hearing. Singularly gifted by nature, Lacordaire had the additional attraction of knowing to the heart's core the difficulties he had to deal with. In the preface to the first published edition of his Conferences, Lacordaire says that they "belong wholly neither to dogmatic teaching nor to pure controversy. They are a medley of both, of the word of teaching and of discussion. Addressing a country where religious ignorance and intellectual cultivation go hand in hand, and where error is rather audacious than learned or deep, I have sought to speak of the things of God in a language which might reach the hearts and the circumstances of my contemporaries. God had prepared me for this task by

[1] Vie Intime, i. 199.

suffering me to live long years in forgetfulness of His Love, carried away in those same paths which He designed me one day thus to retrace ; so that I seemed to require little save my own memories, and some thoughtfulness, in order to bring myself into sympathy with a world which I had loved." And further on he says, " I have been asked what was the practical object of these Conferences ? What was the point of this singular preaching, half religious, half philosophic, which affirms and debates, and seems as it were to trifle on the borders of Heaven and earth ? Its object, its sole object, although it has often gone farther, was to prepare souls to receive the Faith ; inasmuch as faith is the principle of hope, of love, and of salvation, and inasmuch as this principle, weakened in France by sixty years of corrupt literature, now seeks to revive, and only asks the aid of a friendly voice ; a voice which rather entreats than commands, which spares rather than strikes, which rather expands the horizon than rends it asunder, which, in short, forms a treaty with the intelligence, and sets light before it with the same solicitude that we employ in handling a precious life when in peril by sickness. If this be not a practical aim, what is ? To myself, who have tasted alike the agony and the charm of unbelief, when I have poured one single drop of faith into a soul which suffers from the magic torture of its absence, I thank and bless God ; and had I done so but once in my life, at the cost and labour of a hundred discourses, I would thank and bless Him for ever." Animated with such a spirit, no wonder that when Lacordaire rose up pale and quivering with enthusiasm, his voice low and almost weak at first, but soon acquiring volume and power, his audience, "the most splendid audience of men that ever was," were speedily carried away. "Nothing could be simpler than his *début:* a brief, clear recapitulation of the last Conference, a rapid summary of the thesis about to be developed, this was how he set to work. Then he, so to say, let fly! It was grand to see the young apostle, still glowing with the grace of his conversion, surrounded by all those men yet in thraldom, burning to lead them to freedom, going freely with them into the hidden recesses of their minds, never blinking any difficulty, leading them by the paths he had trodden himself, overthrowing all antagonistic errors as he met them, and then, having reached the heights of asserted truth, bursting forth in passionate fervour, identifying himself with it, and crying out, My Church!" [1]

The great feature of his time was the absence of God from its daily life, and the need, the void, was keenly felt. "It may be," to use Lacordaire's own words in 1844, that "our old society had perished because God had been driven forth, and that our new

[1] Vie Intime, i. 201.

society is ill at ease because God has not as yet gained His rightful footing in it." [1]   His was a bright, hopeful nature ; he saw the wounds of his country plainly, but he believed they might be healed, and he believed still more strongly that the way to heal them did not consist in contempt and malediction.   Men were won by his large-hearted, loving Christianity, which strove to bring together the elements which half a century had divorced ; a Christianity which was ready to listen to the legitimate pleas of reason, to welcome fearlessly science and art, to claim liberty in all its least and fullest senses, above all to offer free-hearted genuine affection to all brethren in Christ ready to march under His banner.

When that all but inspired voice was stilled for ever, a Bishop of France said, speaking beside his grave, " The Conferences of Notre Dame are an epoch in Christian preaching, but also the epoch of a vast movement among the youth of our country.   Now, every year, each Easter Day sees thousands of men kneeling in Notre Dame at their Easter Communion. Ask them who made them Christians ? Many will tell you that the first spark which kindled their faith reached them from his lips." [2]

The course of Conferences this year and the following Lent of 1836 were upon the Church : the

---

[1] Funeral Sermon on Mgr. de Forbin Janson, Bishop of Nancy.
[2] Mgr. de la Bouillerie, Sorèze, November 22, 1861.

necessity of a Church, and her distinctive character; the constitution, authority, teaching, and power of the Church occupying the first series; and the second, upon her doctrine, tradition, Holy Scripture, reason, faith, and the means of attaining that faith. Where all are powerful and remarkable it is hard to specify any, but perhaps at the present day the Conferences which will strike readers most are the eighth, twelfth, and thirteenth, on the doctrine and faith of the Church. They are full of striking passages, riveting one by their beauty as well as by the power of their teaching. The veil of playful irony, which not unfrequently appears, carries irresistible force sometimes; *e.g.* when speaking to rationalists he says, "Do you know what you are about when you pronounce sentence against Christianity in the name of reason? I will tell you. You have studied some rudiments of science, some Latin and Greek; you have picked up a few notions about physics and mathematics, read some fragmentary ancient and modern history; you have enjoyed turning over the pages of more or less clever attacks upon Christianity, and with this little stock-in-trade [*ce petit bagage*], carried by men from twenty to twenty-five years old, you plant yourselves boldly in the face of Jesus Christ and His Church, in order to show them that you consider them without the pale of human reason. Do you think that Christianity, which is certainly older than you, has read more, has seen more, has lived with mankind more than you ?—do you think it might not with quite as much right look upon *you* as without the pale of reason ?" [1]

[1] Conferences, xi.

V.

MME. SWETCHINE—PREACHING ORDER.

IT is time to speak here of one who had a more than common interest and share in Lacordaire's life; one for whom his affection and respect were unbounded, and to whom he turned for sympathy and counsel as long as her life was spared : "I never took any weighty step without consulting her," he wrote.

Mme. Swetchine, whose name is almost as well known in the Church literary world as Lacordaire's own, was born at Moscow, November 22, 1782. Sophie Soymanof's father was a man of high position at the Russian Court, where he acted as confidential secretary to the Empress Catharine, and when Paul I. came to the throne, Mdlle. Soymanof became *demoiselle d'honneur* to his Empress Marie. Politics were in so excitable and uncertain a condition at this time, that her father thought it prudent to place her in a secure position, and when only seventeen he married her to General Swetchine, a man of forty-two. Her conduct as a wife was from first to last irreproachable, and no shadow of gossip ever presumed to touch her in days when such immunity was scarcely common. That the General was no ordinary person may be inferred from one anecdote told of him. He was intrusted by the Emperor with the execution of a barbarous and unjust sentence upon a colonel of the Russian army. Going to the square where the condemned man was waiting, General Swetchine gave him back his sword, bidding him leave Petersburg instantly, as reprieved by the Emperor. Then returning to the palace, he entered Paul's apartment, saying, "Sire, here is my head. I have not fulfilled your Majesty's command. Colonel —— is free. I have restored him to honour and life. Take mine instead." The Emperor, after a moment's frenzied passion, forgave him. But such a man was certain to fall into disgrace, and before Paul's death he and his wife had retired to his country estates, where Mme. Swetchine, whose tastes were cultivated, read enormously, and while eminently unaffected and unpretentious, she became probably one of the best informed, most truly intellectual women of her century. De Maistre, on his arrival in Russia, became one of her closest friends; and every one, of whatever nationality, of any mark, was sure to be found frequenting her *salon*, which, after the accession of the Emperor Alexander, was restored to Petersburg. We must not yield to the temptation of lingering over Mme. Swetchine's most interesting life, or the story of her departure from the Greek Church to join that of Rome. It was in 1816 that the Swetchines first went to Paris, though they only settled there in 1825, and from that time her *salon* became in all Paris that most remarkable for the talent, originality, and personal piety of those who frequented it. She was not handsome—quite the contrary—though there was an attraction about her face and manner which won everybody; it was her boundless power of sympathy which so irresistibly drew all ages and temperaments to her. Unlike many women of powerful intellect and gifts, she won the hearts of her own sex as she did those of men. Rivalry with any one never seemed to enter her head, and, as M. de Falloux says, "her disinterested loving-kindness won forgiveness for her superiority."[1]

Revelling in study of the gravest kind (she said of herself that she liked " plunging into metaphysics like a bath!"), she was all brightness and charm directly that a young or pretty woman entered her *salon.* Her younger friends delighted to come and exhibit their pretty toilettes to her before their balls; no less to come and pour out the griefs, or ask counsel in the perplexities which had arisen in those festivities. There was no sorrow, no anxiety, no care, moral or material, to which humanity is subject, to which Mme. Swetchine ever turned a deaf ear. It was but

[1] Vie, i. 280.

natural that when the young editors of the *Avenir* were making their devoted efforts on behalf of freedom of thought and education, they should find a warm friend and sympathiser in her. Montalembert had made her acquaintance on the strength of his devoted admiration for de Maistre, and he, as he himself says, had the blessing of making Lacordaire known to Mme. Swetchine soon after his return from la Chesnaie, "who quickly saw in him a *fils de prédilection*, and concentrated on his head, already storm-beaten in spite of his youthfulness, all the force of tender solicitude and close sympathy which her noble, upright soul contained. . . . For a quarter of a century she continued to be the guide, the counsellor, the healer of his struggling, agitated temperament, which grew calm and self-possessed beneath her softening influence. Nothing ever marred the blessed union of those two hearts, of that mother and son, who were so worthy of each other; a union so characteristically defined by Lacordaire when he said, 'I never met any one with such a thoroughly bold spirit of freedom confined within so solid a faith.'"[1] Speaking of his first introduction to her, Lacordaire says, "Mme.

---

[1] It is told how bystanders at Notre Dame pointed out an elderly lady sitting behind a column, evidently absorbed in the keenest, tenderest interest for the preacher, as Lacordaire's mother, the lady in question being really Mme. Swetchine, whose devotion to him was hardly less than that of a mother.

Swetchine received me with a friendliness quite unlike the ordinary world's ways, and I soon grew accustomed to tell her all my troubles, my anxieties and plans. She used to enter into them as though I were her son, and her door was open to me even at those times when she rarely received even her most intimate friends. What could have led her to devote her time and counsels to me thus? Doubtless some hidden sympathy moved her at first; but if I am not mistaken, she was confirmed in the course by the consciousness of having a mission to fulfil in me. She saw me surrounded by dangers, guided so far by my own inspirations, without worldly experience, without other compass to steer by than my own pure intentions, and she felt that in becoming a second Providence to me she was doing God's work. From that day, in truth, I never made any decision without discussing it with her, and I owe it to her that I have stood at the edge of many a precipice without falling over."

There seems little reason to doubt that during the trying period between his first Conferences being stopped and his appointment to Notre Dame, Mme. Swetchine was pleading his cause with the Archbishop with all her winning force and warmth.

One day, after a conference, Mgr. de Quélen took him in his own carriage to Mme. Swetchine's house, and led him into her room, saying, "See, here is your giant!" One of the most interesting volumes remaining in connection with Lacordaire is a collection of his correspondence with her,[1] which enables us to trace his inner mind at almost every stage of his public and private life. Another intimate friend with whom he became closely united about this time was Mme. de la Tour du Pin, of whom he says that "for twenty years she was one of the powers of my life, through the elevation of her mind, her sympathy with mine, and the admirable self-devotion which actuated her."[2]

In March 1835, knowing how limited his means were, and probably feeling that an unfailing sympathy always at hand would be the greatest assistance that could be offered him, Mme. Swetchine proposed that Lacordaire should take up his abode in her house. He declined solely on the ground that his mother, who was then living with him, might feel hurt if he left her, although she had a married son at hand. His mother died in February 1836.

His life was becoming very crowded. "I lead the life of a gladiator," he writes (July 1835) from Dieppe, "fighting against engagements to preach.

[1] "On ne connaîtra vraiment le Père Lacordaire qu'après la publication de ses lettres," Mme. Swetchine often said (Vie Mme. Swetchine, i. 475).

[2] Lettres à Mme. de la Tour du Pin et Mme. de ——, Lettre 63.

. . . My life is rather secular here, but it makes me feel all the more the necessity of working for God and living to Him. Absence is a good touchstone for real attachment. It makes me feel that I love Paris, which was for so long merely a vast heap of stones to me, but which now is inhabited by a soul, made up of some few souls there that I love." This went on for two years, during which Lacordaire's success as a preacher grew daily : the Archbishop could not make enough of his "young prophet," and what was more to him, he began to enter upon the fruits of his teaching in dealing with individual souls, which was ever the most profound delight and interest of his life—one to which we find him perpetually recurring, as the great point, the one object of a priest's career. "Up to this time," he writes, " my life had been spent in study and in polemics, but through my Conferences I entered upon the mysterious work of the apostolate. Intercourse with souls began to open to me, that intercourse which is the true happiness of any priest who is worthy of his mission, and which takes away every shadow of regret at having given up earthly ties and hopes. Through the pulpit of Notre Dame these bonds of affection and gratitude, which could spring from no ordinary gifts of nature, arose—bonds which unite the man and the apostle with as much of sweetness as of strength. I feel like a traveller in the desert to whom some unknown friend conveys the refreshing draught he pines for. When once one has become initiated into these delights, which give one a foretaste of Heaven's joys, everything else disappears, and vanity ceases to touch one save as an impure blast which cannot deceive one with its bitterness."

He was only thirty-three, and was surrounded with everything that could satisfy and intoxicate him, when, "through one of those marvellous intuitions which possessed him more than any one I ever knew," says Montalembert, he realised that silence, solitude, work, and recollection were needful to him; and acting with his usual decision and promptness, he resigned his post at Notre Dame, electrifying his hearers in his last Lenten Conference, April 1836, by its closing words: "May I at least have inspired you with the blessed thought of turning to God in prayer, and of reviving your intercourse with Him, not through your intellects only, but by your very hearts' impulse. This is the hope I take away, the prayer I utter in leaving you. I leave this pulpit of Notre Dame in the hands of my bishop, a thing created henceforth; created by him and by you, by the pastor and the people. For a moment this double commission has rested brightly on me: suffer me myself to lay it down, and to retire a while into solitude with God and my own weakness."[1] Nothing could shake his resolution, he was deaf even to Mgr.

[1] Conferences, xiii.

de Quélen's entreaties, and without loss of time he started once more for Rome. Much has been said as to the cause of this, as it seemed, uncalled-for and hasty retirement. But in truth it was neither one nor the other. Speaking of it many years later, Lacordaire's own expression was, "I felt myself not ripe enough for the work." He had for long looked upon such teaching—a teaching the object of which was to reclaim the strayed faith of his countrymen—as his vocation, and he had studied and prepared for it diligently; but once embarked therein, while others were simply fascinated, and in the burst of admiration which his eloquence and his intellectual gifts produced, forgot, or failed to see any imperfection, he himself became conscious of what was wanting, and felt forcibly—for whatever Lacordaire felt or did was forcible—that he needed more study, more concentration of thought and power on the work. He was well aware that there was another group of listeners who were not admirers. Some among his clerical brethren could not away with his entire departure from all conventional stereotyped lines; they talked profusely about striking out new paths, risk of creating rather than allaying doubts, above all, about Liberalism and "*idées lamennaisiennes*," as it became the fashion to call them. A letter addressed to the clergy and congregation of Notre Dame was widely circulated, in which it was asserted that "the Abbé

Lacordaire's sermons are neither more nor less than newspaper articles which would furnish very suitable material for a new *Avenir*. We regard them as the most absolute degradation of speech, the most thorough anarchy of thought, and that not even theological but even philosophic thought." All this conduced to determine Lacordaire to bide his time, and wait for that justification of his teaching which was sure to come. The idea of a Preaching Order had already presented itself to his mind, although it had not yet taken definite shape. But as he said on another occasion, " Through all important epochs in my life I have always heard God's Voice within me bidding me how to act ; I have always followed that secret warning, and I have always had reason to rejoice that I did so." So to Rome he went in May 1836, Montalembert returning there at the same time ; and the two friends led a happy, peaceful life together. Lacordaire used to say his daily Mass at the Gesù, having a small apartment near it (56 Via di San Nicolò a Cesarini); he was cordially received by the Holy Father, and by the Cardinals Lambruschini and Zuria, then at the head of affairs. The Pope reminded him of a former gathering in his apartment, a "*belle chambrée,*" pointing out the spot where Lacordaire, de la Mennais, Montalembert, and the Cardinal de Rohan had each been placed. The Jesuits paid him every attention, and he was welcomed heartily by the French Ambassador, the Comte de Latour Maubourg, the Borghese family, and many more. In one of his letters to Mme. Swetchine, July 25, 1836, he gives a good idea of his mind and actual position : " There is enough in me that is false, incomplete, exaggerated, of evil and even of good, to sink ten thousand men : God's goodness preserves me, I know not why. I am thirty-four, and it is a fact that my education is not finished in any respect. I am conscious of a crowd of thoughts waiting for fresh light, not unlike the incomplete works which surround one here with ruins. Born in an age which was steeped in error, God gave me an abundant grace, the ineffable stirrings of which I felt from my earliest childhood ; but the world prevailed over this Heaven-sent gift, and its illusions got possession of me beyond what I can express, as if nature were jealous of grace, and resolved to surpass her. When, contrary to all probability, grace won the day, some twelve years since, I plunged into Seminary life without having had time to cast aside a thousand false impressions, a thousand ideas inconsistent with Christianity ; and I found myself committed at once to the world and to faith, belonging to two worlds, with equal enthusiasm for both ; an incomprehensible medley of a nature as strong as grace, and a grace as strong as nature. No learned and devout hand took hold of mine ; some condemned me, others pitied me, but He Who repenteth Him not of His gifts did not fail me, and He is working out His design by slow degrees. .   . My days pass very uniformly. I get up at 5.45, the Holy Eucharist at 7 ; from 8 to 11 work, then *déjeuner*, then I read newspapers and magazines, take a siesta, and waste my time till 3 ; work again till 8, unless sometimes I go out at 6 for a walk ; dinner or supper at 8 ; and between 10 and 11 bed. This is only interrupted by a few visitors. Rome is a wonderful place for seeing people from all quarters of the world, and for becoming *au courant* of everything."

In the November of this year M. de la Mennais published a book called " Affaires de Rome," which seemed to Lacordaire to demand an answer, or rather a refutation, on his part. He discussed the matter by letter with Mme. Swetchine, who on her part consulted with the Archbishop of Paris on his behalf. But he, surrounded as he was by Lacordaire's enemies, was opposed to the publication, which the Pope, and those immediately around him, desired ! It was a curious sort of dead-lock, and certainly tended to make him glad that he had left Paris ! He had been hesitating whether to return, but, as he wrote to Mme. Swetchine, " I owe much to the Archbishop, but not enough to make myself over to him, bound hands and feet ! He has been sublime on my behalf occasionally ! but I am a burden hard to him to bear, which the future may make heavier. . . . I must wait, and grow older, and become better. My first ten years of priestly life have been too full, and too full of excitement. I owe myself a long solitude. . . . Let us offer to God the sacrifice of not meeting for some time. Your heart will tell you that God has wise reasons for keeping me from Paris, and that it would be foolish to return now."

Mme. Swetchine's wise counsels would bear reproduction at length, but we must only quote her opinion that "solitude may be good for you, useful, perhaps necessary ; solitude with its companion calm, freedom, self-possession ; but not isolation, which sweeps away support as well as difficulty, which would make you lose the precious habit of human contact—most precious to those whose lot is to live among men, and for them, and which would at once deprive your imagination of all the warnings of strict reason and of sympathy. Everywhere, in all conditions, the Divine precept, ' It is not good for man to be alone,' recurs." The ultimate publication of Lacordaire's " Lettre sur le Saint Siège " did not take place till 1838.

Meanwhile he was pressed to give Conferences at San Luigi de Francesi, and the chaplaincy there was offered him by the French Chargé d'Affaires. He also made a Retreat at San Eusebio, and shortly after, being invited by one of the chief ecclesiastics of Metz, who was passing through Rome, to go and preach there, he took counsel, as was his wont, with Mme. Swetchine and Mme. de la Tour du Pin, and the result was that he decided to accept the offer, and others of a similar character flowed in. "France is a large country," he wrote, "and her needs immense; why should I give up everything because Paris is closed to me? Elsewhere I should not be beset by unfriendly newspapers and the persecuting coterie of the capital." M. Affre meanwhile always stood his friend with the amiable but vacillating, easily-influenced Archbishop; and after much deliberation Lacordaire resolved to return to France in the summer of 1837 with his friend Montalembert. But just as they were about to start the cholera broke out in Rome with great violence, and with his usual impulse of self-devotion Lacordaire immediately determined to stay when most men were flying the contagion, and he put his services at the disposal of the Cardinal-Vicar forthwith. Writing to tell Montalembert of this decision, he concluded with the words, "If I die, you will cherish my memory; it will not be necessary to defend so insignificant a thing."

He writes, August 21, 1837: "Here we are, *chère amie*, in the thick of cholera. After three weeks' uncertainty, it showed itself unmistakably last week. Yesterday there were a good many sudden cases: Princess Massimo is dead; Sigalon, a well-known French painter, was carried off the day before. . . .

For myself, I was never better. . . . The Abbé de Solesmes wants me to go with him, but although I had fixed to go September 15th, I think I must wait until the cholera is on the wane. I do not like to fly before it, especially as so many people here are such utter cowards."

And September 16th : " My ignorance of Italian hindered my usefulness among the natives, and beyond M. Sigalon, to whose deathbed I ministered, there has been no cholera among the French and Belgians. I offered my services to the Cardinal-Vicar, and he appointed me to our parish of San Luigi ; but there have been few cases in this part of the town. It is now subsiding everywhere, and my poor heroism, as you call it, becomes a very small matter. The Abbé de Solesmes was taken ill, and in danger for twenty-four hours ; but, thank God, he is all right now, and is to leave shortly in a merchant boat now lying off the Ripa Grande. For I would have you know all roads have been closed for a month, and nothing passes save the post on horseback. All towns and even villages are armed ; they threaten to shoot you at the gates, and would not throw you a bit of bread for ten crowns ! The whole country loses its head at the idea of contagion, and though the cholera is lessening so much, and will soon be gone, I don't know when we shall be suffered to travel again. My health has continued excellent, thanks to unbroken tranquillity of mind. .... I am engaged for all next winter at Metz, in consequence of a most gratifying letter from the Bishop, and the Archbishop of Bordeaux has also written very kindly. I am obliged to refuse him this time. But in spite of all this, which promises me greater liberty and security hereafter in France, I thought that before returning thither it behoved me to write simply and respectfully to the Archbishop of Paris. This time in Rome, so useful in many ways, has added many years to my life in eighteen months! I leave it better, more detached, and without regret."

It was in September 1837 that Lacordaire left Rome, important projects working in his mind. Writing from Dijon, November 8th, to Mme. Swetchine, he says, "My one ambition is to establish in France that system of instruction which she lacks. Every cathedral ought to possess such a school. It is the crying need of a period in which our young men are not taught religion anywhere, while nevertheless they have an immense desire to learn it. I should count myself happy if I spend my life in creating such a system, which indeed I have already largely promoted, since there is not a diocese where it does not depend upon myself whether I shall be called upon to give instructions which M. Frayssinous had limited to Paris, and of which indeed he had a very rudimentary notion. It matters little what becomes of me, and, moreover, God's Providence will find me bread as He sees fit.[1] But I will never sacrifice a necessary work, which has gradually arisen in spite of endless obstacles, and for which He has been pleased to use me as an instrument, for any worldly prospects."

In December he writes from Metz, where he had "preached yesterday (December 3rd) in the Cathedral, before a numerous assembly. A large enclosure was reserved for men, and was full. The Bishop could not be present because of his great age and infirmities. His *grands Vicaires* were satisfied, although the sermon was rather abstract for a beginning. I have been received at Metz and in the four dioceses through which I have passed with a cordiality which took me by surprise, and which proves that my journey to Rome has not been unprofitable, even as regards France. I am quite satisfied, and I believe that all will be well."

"*Metz, January* 5, 1838.—I am surrounded here by unexpected consolations. The ground grows firm beneath my feet with a marvellous rapidity and solidity. I feel as if I had attained a point of emancipation, of self-possession, and of influence over others,

---

[1] "Je suis soldat ou curé de campagne avec la même facilité, et la vie douce, naïve, me recherche toujours plus que l'autre" (Lettre à Mme. Swetchine).

such as I had not dared to look for under less than ten years." "*January 29th.*—I was to have been at this moment on my way to Strasburg, but I learned by a letter from M. Chéruel that a rumour had been spread that the clergy of Metz had petitioned the Bishop to stop my preaching, and that I should be obliged to leave the place. This made me resolve not to go before Easter, and I am most glad of it. Practice has given me strength; my voice was never stronger or fuller: I shall be able to go on till Easter without the smallest risk of over-exertion, and that being the case, it is far better not to interrupt my mission." "*March 22nd.*—Directly after Easter I shall go to Liège and Brussels. . . . My course here is ending even better than it began. . . . Since I wrote last I have been asked to go to Liège, Grenoble, and Aix by their respective Bishops. I have refused Lyons and Marseille. . . . I have only engaged myself to Aix and Bordeaux, so you see I have resolved to keep to the provinces. I had come to that conclusion when I learned that M. de Ravignan was engaged to preach at Notre Dame till 1840 inclusive, so it seems I had done wisely."

"*Abbaye de Solesmes, June* 25, 1838.—What a pity, *chère et bonne amie*, that you cannot come and see us here; it is a charming place, where nothing is wanting save your presence. I am perfectly happy and content. I have already in one week devoured ever so many big books upon one matter,[1] and am more and more clear about it. Strangely enough, an ecclesiastic, a most excellent man, has been here to see me, in order to suggest the very thing which I have before me; this also occurred at Metz. The only consideration which sometimes frightens me is my own unfitness. I can see certain good points in myself, and specially a real progress during the fourteen years I have spent in God's service. I think I am disinterested, temperate; not too proud; much more detached from the world and its stir than I was; more ready to die to myself, more drawn to God by the mind and heart, easily touched by heavenly influences, and yet all the while my life seems so commonplace at best! But never mind, God will do with me as seems best to Him. I take courage because I never went to work more calmly or deliberately. You cannot think, *chère amie*, how quiet and patient I am. I am in no way feeling hurried, which is unusual with me."

The allusions in these letters are of course to the project which had gradually been taking shape in Lacordaire's mind, not only of devoting himself to preaching the Faith in his native country, but of becoming a Religious, and of reviving in France the extinct order of Preaching Friars. It was only on his deathbed, years afterwards, that, amidst acute suffer-

---

[1] The Dominican Order.

ing, he spoke at length upon this subject, dictating a paper from which we must take a considerable extract in order rightly to comprehend the great work of Lacordaire's life.

" My long sojourn in Rome," he says, " had given wide scope for reflection; I studied myself, and I studied the general needs of the Church likewise. As to myself, having already reached my thirty-fourth year, for twelve years in Orders, and having twice borne a not wholly unsuccessful part in the efforts made for the defence and advancement of religion in France, I found myself still solitary, not bound to any ecclesiastical institution, while Mgr. de Quélen in all kindness had endeavoured more than once to point out to me that a parochial sphere was the only one in which he could look to advance me. But I felt no vocation for that kind of work, and I also saw plainly that in the actual condition of the Church of France there was no other door open to that natural desire every reasonable man entertains for stability and security.

Turning from such personal considerations to the Church and her needs, it seemed plain that she had lost one-half her strength since the destruction of the Religious Orders. In Rome I saw the splendid remains of these institutions founded by Saints, and a Religious from the illustrious Cloister of S Gregory the Great actually occupied the Pontifical throne. . . . History recalled to me the names of SS. Antony, Basil, Augustine, Martin, Benedict, Colomba, Bernard, Francis of Assisi, Dominic, Ignatius, the founders of those countless families which had peopled the world with their heroic graces.   And beneath this shining track, the milky way of the Church, I beheld as chief factor the three vows—poverty, chastity, and obedience—the keys of the Gospel and of the perfect imitation of Jesus Christ. . . . Could one believe that the time had come when these mighty monuments of faith, these heaven-sent tokens of love to God and man, were to disappear from among us? . . . I could not think it; whatever God does is necessarily immortal, and no good work is lost in the world any more than any star is lost in heaven!

"Therefore it was that as I walked about Rome, and as I prayed in her basilicas, I became convinced that the greatest service to be rendered to Christianity in our times was an effort to revive the religious Orders. But while this conviction was as plain within me as Gospel truth itself, I was fearful and undecided when I considered how poor an instrument I was for so great a work.   My faith, thank God, was thorough : I loved our Lord Jesus Christ and His Church before all else. I had no ecclesiastical ambition, I never had any for the common aims of worldly men, before I turned to God.   I had loved glory before I loved God, and nothing else. But still, when I cross-questioned myself, I could find nothing in me that seemed to answer to one's idea of the founder or restorer of an Order. Whenever I contemplated those giants of holiness and Christian power, my heart sank within me; I was prostrate, discouraged, afraid. The mere idea of subjecting my liberty to a rule and to superiors was terrible to me. The child of an age which has little notion of obedience, independence was life to me. How could I suddenly acquire docility, and seek light for my steps in submission only? Then I began to reflect upon the difficulty of gathering men together, their varying characters and diverse minds, which have ever made a religious community at once the most cheering and painful of burdens even to saints. And from moral perplexities I went on to material ones. I had no fortune; I was consuming the last remnants of a slender patrimony in Rome. How could I buy large houses and provide for a number of men as needy as myself? Had I any right to incur such risks in the name of Providence? Nor was this all: external hindrances rose up like mountains before me. Could I expect to be even tolerated by the French Government? . . . No association, even literary or artistic, could be formed in France without the sanction of authority; and this utter bondage, acquiesced in as it was, gave shelter to prejudice under the garb of law. What could be done in a country where religious liberty, accepted by all as a sacred principle, yet could not protect the invisible act of a promise to God within a man's own heart, and where such a promise, dragged to the light by oppressive interrogation, was enough to cut him off from the privileges of his fellow-men? When a nation has come to such a pass that all liberty seems to be the privilege of those who do not believe as opposed to believers, can one hope ever to see justice, peace, stability, and any civilisation beyond mere material progress flourish?

"On all sides I found breakers ahead, and less fortunate than Columbus, I could see no plank on which to reach the shores of liberty. My sole resource was in that boldness which inspired the primitive Christians, and in unshaken faith in God's Omni-potence. . . . The primitive Christians did not merely die; they wrote and spoke, they strove to convince the people and the rulers of the truth of their cause; and S. Paul, when preaching Jesus Christ in the Areopagus, made use of every wile of eloquence to convince his hearers. There is always a resting-place for God in man's heart; in the con-dition of minds, the course of opinion, the laws—in all things and in all seasons. The great secret is to perceive it, and to make use of it, not the less making God's own hidden Grace the foundation of one's confidence and strength. Christianity has never defied the world, it has never insulted nature or reason, it has never used its light to blind and irritate men ; but at once bold and gentle, calm and energetic, tender and firm, it has penetrated the mind of generations, and those who are found faithful at the last day will have been won and held by the like means.

" I took courage from these thoughts, and it came into my mind that all my previous life, even my very faults, had paved my way after a fashion to the heart of my country and my age. I asked myself if I should not be wrong to reject such openings through a timidity which would only further my own ease, and whether the very greatness of the sacrifice were not a reason for undertaking it ? . . . Nevertheless, on my return to France in 1837, I had not come to a decision. After preaching a successful mission at Metz through the winter of 1838, I returned to Paris, and there I opened my mind more or less to those who cared for me. I met with no encouragement. Mme. Swetchine let me go on, giving little support to my opinions. Other people looked upon my project as purely chimerical. . . . But it was necessary to come to a decision. I had lost my mother in '36, and there was no use in returning to Rome. Urged on by the position of things, and stimulated by grace, which was stronger than I, the decision was at last made ; but the sacrifice was terrible. Whereas it had cost me nothing to leave the world for the priesthood, it cost me everything to add to that the burden of the religious life.   Nevertheless, in the last case as in the first, when once I had made up my mind, I knew no further weakness or vacillation, and I went boldly on towards the trials which awaited me."

He had been preceded by the Abbé Guéranger, who had restored the Benedictine Order in France ; and Lacordaire spent two months with him at Solesmes, where his Abbey was, on the way to Italy, in the summer of 1838.

Before leaving Paris, Lacordaire thought it due to the Archbishop to take leave of his Grace, and place before him his intentions.   Mgr. de Quélen was living at the Sacré Cœur.   He listened somewhat coldly, and observed, " These things are in God's Hand, but He has not made His Will plain so far as I see." Just as Lacordaire was taking his leave, however, the Archbishop changed his manner entirely, and told a dream he had had in 1820, which rather curiously foreshadowed events which had since come to pass, and in which certain Religious bore a part.   " There is nothing wanting to the complete fulfilment of my dream," he said, "but the arrival of these white-robed men who are to convert the people.   Perhaps it is you that are to bring them !"

From Florence, where Lacordaire occupied the same quarters he had inhabited six years before with de la Mennais, he wrote to Mme. Swetchine, " Do you know, *chère amie*, I am a better man than I was then! The nearer I draw to Rome, the more calm and contented I become. I believe that I am truly fulfilling God's Will, and I am full of gratitude for all He has done for me in France. . . . But you are possessed with the demon of *more* (*le démon du mieux*), you are never satisfied. Indeed I have great grievances against you! First of all, you have not enough confidence in me, you think me too mobile, you would not have me guided by the course of events. . . . You are logical, *chère amie*, and the Abbé Bautain says that logic is a terrible cause of error! . . . Fortunately I am going to be a monk, and you will get rid of me."

August 25, 1838, Lacordaire had a satisfactory audience of the Cardinal Secretary of State, and the day following he was warmly welcomed by the General of the Dominicans, Ancaroni by name. "I cannot tell you," he writes, "what a delightful conversation I had with this good and venerable old man. It was like Simeon and his *Nunc dimittis*. In a word, they give us Santa Sabina for our novitiate, sending the actual novices elsewhere, so that we shall be all Frenchmen. The novitiate will be for a year, after which the colony will return to France, I being the Provincial or Vicar-General of the Order, with *carte blanche*. We can found colleges for the instruction of youth, and we shall thus have three manner of houses—novitiates, professed houses, and colleges—uniting the life of regular clerks with that of a monastic order, an entire novelty, but a necessity, granted us. This alone is the security of our life and its usefulness. And lastly, I have obtained even more than I asked for without contest, and with a goodwill and kindly feeling which rejoice me unspeakably. . . . So as soon as I have had my audience of the Pope I shall return to France, and spend the winter looking out for fine, brave, stedfast young fellows, capable of mutual self-devotion and true humility. That is the great point. After Easter we shall return, and probably take solemn possession of Santa Sabina in May 1839."

A little later he writes to Mme. Swetchine, "I have had but one struggle in this matter, that of weakness face to face with a great self-devotion. I was happy, contented, free from anxieties, and I am going to take upon my shoulders, not so much a hard life and a serge gown, as the heavy burden of a family to bring up and feed. I am voluntarily going to surround myself with those whose bread I must provide. Selfishness said, 'Be still.' Jesus Christ said, 'When rest and glory were offered Me, I chose the life and death of the Cross.' My whole soul is uttered in these last words. And now I have conquered the enemy, I have laid aside every vestige of earthly cowardice, and that gives me a stronger confidence in success than all the facilities given me. It was pre-cisely the same thing, fourteen years ago, when I entered the seminary—first a struggle, in which I held the same argument with myself, then my decision once made, a firm certainty which has never once been for a moment troubled. At both these important epochs of my life I have sacrificed a certainty to an uncer-tainty, a condition with which I was satisfied for one which I feared."

Lacordaire returned through Bologna in order to visit S. Dominic's tomb,[1] and directly that he arrived at Dijon, co-operation began to offer itself both in respect of money and men. With respect to these last he was earnest, but not eager; he would have no one enter upon the life proposed to them hastily.

"Dear friend," he writes to one aspirant, October 18, 1838, "I am no way surprised, be sure, at the in-ward struggle you are undergoing. It is natural. No saint ever contemplated any great sacrifice for God's sake without misgivings. Only give yourself up to the

[1] "I arrived yesterday at Bologna, where one sole object was my attraction," he writes, September 19, 1838, "the resting-place of S. Dominic. . . . His tomb is in white marble, quite unlike the modern style, in a church at the extremity of the town, in a sort of desert. It was there that S. Dominic died, there where so many Religious have lived, and where some of the greatest men from all ends of the world have met. Now the monastery is almost empty, and the greater part turned into barracks, and where once saints prayed and wrote, now soldiers drink and swear."

leadings of grace without haste, without insisting on to-day or to-morrow. For my own part, I spent nearly eighteen months in resolving, and several times seemed almost to have given up my plans. . . . I am not aware of your precise age; but S. Augustine was not a priest till he was six-and-thirty, which did not prevent his writing ten folio volumes on religion, nor his being a great and powerful bishop. The only difficulty, my dear friend, lies in knowing how far you love Jesus Christ and His Church, and what sacrifice you are capable of making for Him. All else matters not. Think this over before God, and write to me when you have decided."

Meanwhile there were anxieties afloat among his friends in Paris and in Rome, especially the latter, owing to the openness and publicity with which Lacordaire spoke of his intended work. He wrote, November 3, 1838, to calm these anxieties: "All Romans make a mistake when they have to do with France; they always put the Government foremost, whereas public opinion is the thing to be considered first of all. Without that, nothing is done; with that and patience, we always end by obtaining the needful concurrence of Government. Consider my position. My journey to Rome was beginning to be known; it was talked about, and my motives in going. In another fortnight some of the newspapers would have taken it up; what should

I have gained by silence? My friends were before-hand in saying openly and sincerely what could not be ignored; they fired a moment before they were fired on, and so have gained for me the merit of not fearing publicity. . . . My present position is good as regards the public; it has passed no hasty con-demnation, it waits; and I shall take good care not to go back to Rome without having told it anything. As to Government, my position is neither better nor worse. Possibly the silence of the newspapers has struck them, so that they are not afraid of any general explosion. I shall do whatever is necessary to conciliate them, without subjecting my work to their approbation. Time is in our favour, and were thirty years required to re-establish the Dominicans in France, I hope that in the natural order of things these thirty years may be given me. If it is neces-sary that I should be the only French preaching friar, I *will* be the only one, and take my habit into our pulpits, and win for it all the friendliness which may possibly be shown to me personally."

And November 21st he wrote, "I believe it is being pressed at Rome that it is very dangerous to tolerate an Order which may become a stronghold of de la Mennais' former friends. I have not written to Cardinal Lambruschini on this matter, because I think I am sufficiently known at Rome for no heed to be given to such rubbish. . . . An age has already

passed over de la Mennais' tomb, and he is a terror
to no sensible man."

During this winter Lacordaire wrote his "Mémoire
pour le rétablissement en France de l'Ordre de Frères
Prêcheurs." In this he begins by telling his country
in straightforward words what he intends doing.
"We live in times," he says, "when a man bent on
becoming poor and the servant of all finds it more
difficult to carry out his desire than it is to create
himself a fortune and fame. Nearly all the Powers
of Europe, kings and editors, partisans alike of
absolutism and of liberty, are leagued against voluntary self-sacrifice, and never before was the world so
afraid of a man going about barefoot and clothed in
shabby serge! The only bondage is for those who
seek to serve God generously. . . . We, the children
of the nineteenth century, have demanded liberty to
believe in nothing, and it is granted; we have asked
liberty to seek all office and honour, it is granted; we
asked freedom to influence its highest destinies by
dealing with the weightier questions, in our extreme
youth, and it is granted; we have asked means of
luxury and ease—welcome. But when now, filled
with the Divine kindlings which are moving this our
century, we ask liberty to follow the inspirations of
our faith, to seek no fortune, to live in poverty with
a few like-minded friends; then, forsooth, we are
pulled up short, laws innumerable hurled at us, and

Europe itself is ready to fall upon us and crush us,
if called upon!"[1]　He goes on to point out the in-

[1] At the present time, when worse oppression than in Lacordaire's time is being practised upon the Church under a Free
Republic than was known then under a Monarchy, it may be
well to call attention to some of his words: "I ask protection
from public opinion; I ask it against itself, if need be. . . .
Is it conceivable that a country which has been proclaiming
liberty for the last fifty years, that is to say, the right to do
what harms no one, should pursue *à outrance* a mode of life
which suits many and hurts none?　What is the good of shedding one's blood for the 'rights of man'?　Is not a life in
common a right of man, even were it not a need of humanity?
. . . What is right and liberty, if it is not permitted to citizens
to live in one house, to get up and go to bed at the same hour,
to eat at the same table, and wear a like garment?　What becomes of property, what becomes of freedom of domicile and
individual freedom, if citizens can be driven forth from their
own hearths because they carry out domestic life as a Community? . . . It would not have been a mockery if the Revolution had said to Religious, 'There may be some among you
who did not enter the cloister willingly; henceforth the doors
are open to them, let them abide by their conscience.'　Neither
would it have been a mockery to add, 'The nation takes away
the property which your ancestors and ours formerly gave you.
She believes this sacrifice to be necessary to the welfare of our
country, and while leaving you enough for subsistence, she asks
you to bear the blow with the dignity of men who have re-
nounced the world from love to God and man.　Now that the
ancient order of things is abolished by this extraordinary and
terrible act, go where you will, build fresh shelters beneath the
protection of our common rights, and trust yourselves fearlessly
to the future.　Providence suffers revolutions for purification, not
destruction.'　Such language would have been injustice, but not

consistency of those who, seeking after liberty and equality, would hinder a Community life in which the prince and the peasant are alike, and share the same table.

The desired result was in a great measure attained. Public opinion, the value of which Lacordaire did not over-estimate among his countrymen, was taken with his boldness, his frankness, and the vigour of so gifted a man who had made his gifts so widely felt. There was no attack made on the book either by the press or the Government, and the first visible result was that Hippolyte Réquédat, reading the " Mémoire," came and unreservedly threw himself into Lacordaire's plans. Of this, his first associate, the leader said that though others, noble, pure-hearted as he, joined the little company later, there was none gifted with a purer, deeper beauty of soul, or on whom God's Hand was more visibly laid.

mockery. What is mockery is to pretend, in the name of liberty, to undo knots which cannot be undone, because they depend upon men's inward minds, and to sanction such a curious deliverance by the spoliation of the most venerated rights. When the Trappists were driven forth from the Abbey of Melleray, did they not take their vows as well as their faith with them? and what were they deprived of save peace, home, the fruit of their labours, and all those liberties which had been watered with the blood of their ancestors and their contemporaries?" The whole pamphlet, for it is little more, is well worth attentive reading under the light of the Republic of the present day.

VI.

THE NOVITIATE—LA QUERCIA—SANTA SABINA —NOTRE DAME—ROME—BOSCO—THE PRO-VINCES—NANCY.

EARLY in March, Lacordaire, together with Réquédat and the Abbé Bontaud, returned to Rome. Of the former he says that he is "a real saint." Their reception was most cordial. "I see true Christian fraternity for the first time," he writes to Mme. Swetchine of the Dominicans, "the true likeness of Jesus Christ in men. We might have lived together fifty years, and they could not have been more simple or more cordial." Cardinal Sala, in his official capacity, saw reason to desire that the French Novitiate should be out of Rome, and accordingly after taking the habit on April 9, 1839, at seven P.M., in the Chapel of S. Dominic, in Santa Maria Minerva (when Lacordaire, according to established use, took the name of Dominic), they proceeded a few days after to la Quercia, a convent at Viterbo. Lacordaire writes as follows to Mme. Swetchine :—

"April 15, 1839.

"It is a week to-day, *chère amie*, since we took the habit, and this is the fourth of our abode at la Quercia. It would be difficult to tell you all the feelings of tenderness and joy which filled me on the night of April 9th. The remembrance of my Ordination is very fresh, with all its happiness, but that which was then lacking I now found in the most ample abundance,—I mean the sympathy and welcome of a brotherhood. . . . On Thursday, at eleven A.M., we entered the Convent of Gradi at the gates of Viterbo, where we dined with the Provincial of Rome and all the Fathers. In the evening the Provincial took us to la Quercia, about half a mile off, where he initiated us with a short address in the presence of the Community, after which we retired each to our cell. It was cold, the wind had changed to the north, and we had only summer habits in fireless rooms; we knew nobody; all the excitement, the *prestige*, was over; friends were no longer at hand, though bearing us in mind. We were alone with God, face to face with a life which as a practical matter was yet unknown to us. At night we went to Matins, then to the refectory, and at last to bed. The next day, it was colder than ever, and we only half understood the course of devotional exercises. I had a passing moment of weakness; my mind reverted to all I had left—my formed habits, certain advantages, beloved friends, days filled up with profitable intercourse, warm hearths, the thousand joys of a life which God had filled with so much happiness external and internal. It was a dear purchase, the pride of a powerful action, to lose all that for ever! I humbled myself before God, and implored the strength I needed. By the end of the first day I felt that my prayer was heard, and the last three days comfort has been ever growing within me, as gently as the waves of a summer sea creeping slowly over its shores. Our daily life is as follows: The bell calls us at a quarter-past five, a quarter of an hour later we are in a little interior choir, by the Novitiate door, where we sing Prime, hear Mass, and make our meditation. After that we say our own Mass. Before midday we go to the choir of the church to sing Terce, Sext, and None, and on great days High Mass. We dine at noon; all meals are *maigre*, without special dispensation, and every Friday is a fast. On other days we eat some bread in the morning, but from September 14th to Easter the fast is continual, dispensation excepted. After dinner we either join the general recreation or take a siesta as we will. At three o'clock, Vespers and Compline. From four to eight we are free, and can go out for a walk if we think fit. At eight we sing Matins and Lauds, at a quarter to nine supper, followed by conversation in the Community-room, and to bed at ten. We have a little chapel in the Novitiate, where morning and evening we can make a short meditation when it suits us; the other exercises are with the whole Community, save such Fathers as are kept from the choir by the nature of their occupation. At other times we can assemble in the general room for study or conversation. Every one is kindness and generosity itself to us. The Sacred Office does not occupy more than two hours a day for the Fathers. The house consists of professed monks, of whom several are Spaniards, eight or nine students, and lastly us three, and two Italian novices. . . . La Quercia is a splendid convent; . . . a magnificent avenue reaches from the church to the gates of Viterbo; . . . the environs are delicious. To the south, close to the convent, rises Monte Cimino; on the north Montefiascone stands on its hill; on the east the Apennines; on the west the lower heights, which slope away to the sea, which can be seen by going a little way on rising ground; beneath, a rich valley. . . . It is a very paradise, and here we are for a year. You remember Réquédat's fine saintly face, it has acquired a new beauty of devotion which makes me delight to gaze upon it. He is an admirable fellow, and were I to die now, I should count upon him safely for the re-establishment of the Dominicans in France. . . . Now, *chère amie*, it is your business to give me abundant and welcome news. Remember that I am in profound solitude, and know nothing. Have you got my letters? Tell me about Montalembert, and all those I love. Give me all important political news too; they are quickly told, and it is important to me not to lose sight of France. I appoint you my 'own correspondent' at a hundred *Ave Marias* per month. Go on loving me, *chère amie.* If I have ever grieved you, this is the time for forgiveness. There is nothing of the old Adam left in me save the memory of your affection and my heartfelt return thereof. Your place is for ever marked in my life by the moment at which you took it, and all the good you have poured into it."

A month later Lacordaire wrote, "We are in a very earthly paradise, you could not find any one in a more flourishing condition;" and he goes on to say that he has written to the Archbishop of Paris, promising to preach in Notre Dame in the winter of 1841, on condition that it be in his Dominican habit. "If the Archbishop accepts, my object will be attained, viz. to show forth the religious habit in Paris, *en pleine* Notre Dame, without any legal power being able to interfere, and without anything to fear, from the people. The date I fix is sufficiently distant to leave a good margin after my novitiate. Montalembert is for ever preaching patience, and doubtless patience is an excellent thing, but one must likewise know how to take advantage of actual circumstances."

"La Quercia, *July* 3, 1839.

"The *Univers*, which I receive without difficulty, has kept me *au courant* of your *émeutes*, and your Ministries. These three governments which have been tried since the Revolution are curious enough. The first, founded on the sword, has perished by the sword; the second, founded on hereditary blood, has perished by relationship; the third, founded on industrial interests and a thousand mean little compromises, perishes through commercial interests and the alliance of mistaken ambitions. It is grand. God has worked in a truly Homeric fashion. In all epochs His Providence has made itself plainly felt, not less forcibly and urgently than to-day; one would almost say reverently, that He has become impatient. Through all this materialist muddle God works His way in France, each day brings a fresh proof. I receive incessant requests to join our work; an association of artists is forming in Paris and Rome with a view to the sanctification of art and of Christian propaganda through it. A young painter of three or four and twenty came to see me the other day. He was barefoot, going to Florence on an expiatory pilgrimage and to ask the gift of faith. He was a fine young fellow, so modest and humble; all those who saw him imagined he was a devout person come to join us. Réquédat receives letters from his former friends in Paris, once unbelievers and republicans, that might be written by nuns or anchorets, in the most definite Christian tone. . . . In a year's time our difficulty will be to select some fifteen novices from out more than a hundred aspirants."

" August 10, 1839.

"I have just received a kind long letter from M.——, who sees and will see nothing in the Dominicans but inquisitors and burners of men, and cannot imagine any other opinion of them! I am writing in reply to tell him that, after long study of S. Dominic's life, his Constitutions, and the history of his Order, it is perfectly evident that S. Dominic was a very gentle person, who never troubled his head about the Inquisition, and saw no other means whereby to save the Church than the apostolical lines of poverty, prayer, preaching, and the knowledge of God, which sublime view of the matter made him what he was. His Constitutions held the same language. His Order was scarcely founded when it was engrossed by missions in Europe and the West, by schools of theology, and later by its noble works in the two Indies. His saints, S. Pietro di Verona excepted, and the countless bands of his known and unknown holy men were all strangers to the Inquisition, and were merely gentle, charitable, penitent people. Throughout this history the Inquisition was a mere by-the-way accident, a function which the Dominicans of that day accepted, but in no sense their vocation, their principal business, or their official character. You know that M. de Maistre says all the harshness of the Spanish Inquisition came from the State, but this good man affirms the contrary. He is altogether a curious body, and I thought it good to tell him my mind plainly. I will tell you in confidence that I am writing a Life of S. Dominic. I daily give some hours to this work, and have already got over its chief difficulties. This will be my second battle. . . . I go on receiving letters from men wanting to join us. Yesterday two priests wrote, at the suggestion of their bishop, they tell me."

"*September* 22, 1839.

"We are offered a fine convent, with a church, cloisters, and gardens, which once belonged to our Order at Lierre, three miles from Malines in Belgium. It was bought by a certain Père Claes in order to preserve it for us, and now at his death his nephew offers it us for nothing, if we will go there. We accept it conditionally, that is to say, if we should not go to France, and secondarily as a great Novitiate after we have won the right to settle where we please by a primary establishment in France. Besides this, a wealthy Englishman, Mr. Lisle Philipps, offers through Montalembert to found a convent for us on his property. So we have made good way for six or seven months."

To Mme. de la Tour du Pin :—

" September 22, 1839.

" I am calm, laborious, rarely troubled with any thought of our opponents ; I see better the emptiness and pride of my past life; I think I am growing humbler; I understand better the general ruling of Christianity; I feel as though I were ripening, and may be guilty of fewer faults than in the past. Our enemies are very profitable for heart-purging, they bring our real penance. A few blows are soon forgotten, even when deserved and accepted ; but the incessant persecution of those who do not understand us, or who are envious, this is the Christian's true cross."

" November 17, 1839.

" I admire your audacity, *chère amie,* in asking whether the Life of S. Dominic will be a book, that is to say, a volume, as you call it ! Know then, Madame, that with the exception of two short treatises on the Republic and Law, Plato wrote nothing save dialogues of a hundred or so pages, which did not hinder his exhaustiveness; and that the greatest authors of ancient times did not write volumes ! But since a volume you desire, I beg to inform you that S. Dominic will make a volume, a big one too ! I have brought my great patriarch to the forty-sixth year of his life, which was only fifty-one, and neverthe- less but a third is done. The rest, however, is easy.

The work is very pleasant, though somewhat interfered with by our religious offices. But I give myself up to Providence, and take time as it is given me. Life is too short, *chère amie*, for hurry. It is a great misfortune that our authors write so fast. Men of old wrote slowly. They knew that a man's life is but a brief revelation, that there is always time enough to tell what is worth telling of it. I abide quietly at present, seeing clearly what I shall have to say at some future time, if it please God, and I wait His time patiently. I let my hair grow a little grey; I fear God and respect my fellow-men too much not to be willing to let my mental powers await their full maturity."

To another friend Lacordaire writes :—

"LA QUERCIA, *Oct.* 2, 1839.

" I see the advertisement of a reissue of your book, of which I am glad. Beware of laying down your pen. Unquestionably writing is a heavy vocation, but the press has become too important an agent to forsake one's post. Let us write, not for glory or immortality, but for Jesus Christ. Let us take up our pen as a cross. Supposing that nobody reads us a hundred years hence, what does it matter? The drop of water falling into the sea no less bore its part in filling the river, and the river ceases not. He who belonged to his own age, belongs to all ages, Schiller says; he has done his work, he has had his share in the creation of things which last for ever. How many books, now lost in our great libraries, have during the last three centuries brought about the revolutions which we behold! We do not actually know what our fathers wrought, but we live through them. . . . The close of your letter, in which you speak of the persistent drawings you feel to consecrate yourself to God, touches me deeply, and the hope of seeing you one of us would be very acceptable. . . . A week spent with us, when we open a Novitiate, would tell you more than much writing. For myself I am well satisfied, and regret nothing here save the lack of the vigour and severity which are necessary to us Frenchmen. When we become monks it is with the intention of going in for it thoroughly " (*jusqu'au cou*).

To Mme. Swetchine :—

"La Quercia, *Jan.* 9, 1840.

" The fulness of ocean comes from its receiving all waters that flow into it; if you let the chemists work their will, the ocean would be dried up in a hundred years. No one prizes purity of doctrine more than I do, and I may say that I grow daily more jealous over it as regards myself, but a charitable valuation of doctrine is the absolutely necessary make-weight of theological inflexibility. A true Christian's object is to find truth, not error, in a doctrine, and to seek urgently to find it, even as one gathers a rose from amidst its thorns. He who holds cheap the thought of any sincere man, any man who has made obvious sacrifices to God, he is a Pharisee, the only class of men pronounced accursed by our Lord. He who can say of any man whom he believes to be working for God's glory, ' What does he matter? does God need clever people?' is a Pharisee, who takes away the key of knowledge, and neither enters himself nor suffers other men to enter in. Is there any father of the Church who did not hold his own peculiar opinions, and sometimes erroneous ones? Should we throw their writings out of window in order that the ocean of truth may be purer? Oh, the man who fights for God has a sacred being, and until the time of his manifest condemnation, we must receive his thought with bowels of compassion ! "

As the year of novitiate drew near its close, Lacordaire came to the conclusion that instead of proceeding at once to begin his work in France, it would be well to remain for three years in Rome, studying theology, and he wrote a request to this effect to the General of the Order. " While apparently losing time," he writes to Mme. Swetchine, " we really save it, inasmuch as in France we should be obliged to begin both a Novitiate and a School of

Theology. I should have been overwhelmed beneath this burden, whereas now I shall bring at least five or six young men well trained, who will require only a year's novitiate to be effective Dominicans, and to take my place if need be." One consequence of this decision was that the Abbé Bontaud left Lacordaire reluctantly. His health failed altogether under the Italian climate and the Dominican *régime.* It was Lacordaire's earnest counsel which induced him to seek another sphere of work in Christ's vineyard. Writing in 1862 of the novitiate now closing, the venerable Padre Palmegiani, who had been Lacordaire's novice-master, says, "He was a very model of regularity and religious precision. Among the many virtues which stamped his life, the dearest of all to him was humility. He always counted himself the last of the novices, read at meals, swept the corridors, fetched water, trimmed lamps, performed every humble office, refusing every manner of distinction or exemption. He was never heard to speak of himself or his own affairs, nor could he bear to hear them alluded to. I well remember a novice asking him if the crowd attending his Conferences were really as great as was reported, and so forth, and how, pretending not to hear, Lacordaire turned round and began to talk about something else."

Before the two Frenchmen left Quercia, the artist Besson, who was shortly to join them, made a copy of the celebrated Madonna della Quercia for their future house.   It was on Palm Sunday, April 12, 1840, that Lacordaire and Réquédat took the vows in the presence of a somewhat remarkable and cosmopolitan assembly, which included Prince Borghese and his English wife, Mr. Augustus Craven and Albertine de la Ferronays ; and on Easter Day he was preaching at San Luigi di Francia in Rome, at the special request of the French Ambassador, before a crowded assembly. He was made much of, and caressed by the great world both of natives and visitors, and it was a relief to take possession of the quiet Monastery of Santa Sabina on May 15th.   They were seven in number. Réquédat has already been mentioned; his nature was described by one of his friends as being "steeped in the passion of self-devotion as some men are steeped in selfishness."   In a little society of young men who used to meet in Paris to discuss the loftiest questions of philosophy and religion, he had made acquaintance with a young architect, Piel, a man of remarkably pure life and high aspirations.   They became warm friends, and when Réquédat went to la Quercia, he told Piel that he would soon follow.   He took an active part in Paris in the confraternity of artists already mentioned—Besson, Cabat, and Cartier being its chief promulgators in Rome—and was greatly distinguished in a literary capacity—his style was said to recall that of Pascal—as well as in his profession as an architect; and it was not till after long and stedfast thought and prayer that Piel decided on following his friend, which he accordingly did this same Easter, together with Hernsheim, a promising pupil of the École Normale, where he was about to fill a professorship when a serious illness, and the reflections it produced, led him to join the little company of French Dominicans. The young artist Besson, whose history has been already made known to the English public, was the fifth. "We did not expect him at present," Lacordaire wrote, May 13th, "because of his mother, whose only child he is ; but it was she herself who besought him to follow his vocation, after she heard my sermon at San Luigi. For two days she urged him more and more pressingly. I went to see them all unwittingly on the Wednesday, and needed but to stoop to gather this beautiful flower. He is a miniature Beato Angelico, a wondrously pure, good, simple fellow, and with the faith of a great saint." The Abbé Jandel, who was the sixth, had made acquaintance with Lacordaire in 1837 at Metz, being then Superior of the Petit Séminaire of Pont-de-Mousson, and like most men, Jandel was deeply impressed by the earnestness and power of the elder man. In 1839 he went to Rome, intending to join the Jesuits, but was advised by them to seek his vocation with the Dominicans. He had been preaching in Rome that Lent, and was much thought of. Lacordaire mentions him as a " thorough " man.[1]　A young Pole, by name Tourouski, was the last of the little band.　A corridor and chapel apart were given up to them, and Lacordaire looked forward greatly to the opportunity for quiet and study, Thursdays from eight to twelve o'clock being the only time at which their privacy could be invaded.　" I have finished my visits," he writes to Mme. Swetchine, " and rejoice in the prospect of having no more.　Solitude is always a great power. Nothing frustrates intrigue and enmity so much as a man who keeps to his own room."

The first thing that occurred greatly to move Lacordaire after taking up his abode at Santa Sabina was the appointment of Mgr. Affre as successor to Mgr. de Quélen, who while loving him and feeling grateful for his personal kindness, Lacordaire had always felt to be a weak place in the Church of France.　He writes enthusiastically on the subject to Mme. Swetchine July 8, 1840, counting it a great act of God's Providence.　" Not that I deceive myself as to what we may expect from the new Archbishop," he says. " Mgr. Affre will only be just to us ; he will not give himself up, tied hand and foot, to any coterie ; he will feel the need for action, and consequently not to repulse zealous able men raised up by Providence ; he will not abhor his own times because of their troubles ;

---

[1] The Rev. Père Jandel is actually now General of the Order at Rome (see p. 157).

he will let himself be seen and approached; he will try to put an end to the disunion which exists among the Parisian clergy. But he is Gallican; he does not care for religious orders save under absolute submission to the Bishop, and possibly some day he may give me more ground for complaint than Mgr. de Quélen. But whatever he does, he will prepare the way for many good things, and that is quite reason enough for me to forgive him beforehand whatever he may do to me. I never measured Mgr. de Quélen with regard to myself, for I was one of the few he tolerated and even loved. . . . Now let us turn to S. Dominic. My manuscript will be taken to Paris early in August by the Abbé de Bouillerie. . . . Will your health and occupations allow of your superintending the printing of a volume of from three to four hundred pages, that is to say, of carefully correcting the proofs? Or would some one of your friends help you without your giving up the real superintendence? If you say yes, as I expect, you shall have the MSS., and I will give you details as to publisher, printer, paper, type, etc. A distinguished Catholic artist is at this moment engraving Fra Angelico's portrait of S. Dominic for the title-page."[1] The same letter mentions Réquédat's serious illness. He had been suffering from his chest

---

[1] M. Lavergne. "You know that he would take nothing for engraving the portrait? He is a clever painter, and a thoroughly good Christian" (Letter to Mme. Swetchine).

for a long time, and now he realised, as did his affectionate companions, that his work on earth was to be a brief one.   He went peacefully to his rest, September 2, 1840, and waits the rising of the dead within the walls of Santa Sabina.   "He is the first and the most valuable friend I have lost," Lacordaire writes, October 19th.   "No one had given himself to me with such self-devotion, no one promised better, or combined more natural gifts and Christian graces.   Truly God's ways are incomprehensible.   Nothing has touched me so nearly as this early loss, and the certainty I feel of my friend's invisible presence does not fill up the earthly blank he leaves."

Mme. Swetchine writes in return about the business matters connected with publishing the Life of S. Dominic, going on to say, "*Cher ami*, I have finished your MSS., and words fail me to say how it has gone to my heart, or how much beauty I find in it.   It is the best book of the kind I know, so complete, and as harmonious as the light which rises up in your own soul. . . . I boldly send you some annotations, for which your friendship will forgive me."

The Life of S. Dominic,

> " L'altro che per sapienza in terra fue
>   Di cherubica luce uno splendore," [1]

---

[1] " For wisdom upon earth
The other, splendour of cherubic light."

Paradiso, c. xi.

while written with enthusiastic warmth and brilliancy, and in many parts a poem in itself, will probably never be so attractive to English readers as Lacordaire's other writings—his Conferences, and above all his Letters. That "*santo atleta*," as Dante calls him, has had few nobler followers among the

> " Many rivulets since turned
> Over the garden catholic to lead
> Their living waters, and to feed its plants," [1]

than Lacordaire, and in some points it is impossible not to be struck with a marvellous resemblance between himself and the patron saint he is describing, as, *e.g.*, when he exclaims, "It is the privilege of certain souls to be prolific in vigorous affection to their last breath, and Dominic was continually acquiring new ties of love."[2] But the tone of panegyric is apt to be oppressive in hagiology, and not even Lacordaire's knowledge of the world and happy style can divest us of the feeling that the saint is undergoing his Academy laudation.[3] At the same time the

---

[1] " Di lui si fecer poi diversi rivi,
    Onde l'orto cattolico s'irriga,
    Si che i suoi arbuscelli stan più vivi. "

Paradiso, c. xii.

[2] Vie de S. Dominique, c. ix.

[3] Chateaubriand gave it the highest praise possible to Mme. Swetchine: " C'est immense comme beauté, comme éclat, je ne sais pas un plus beau style."

L

art-lover will find many of the legends with which he is familiar in the well-known frescoes at Florence and at Rome beautifully told, and the descriptions of Santa Sabina and San Sisto have all the charm of Lacordaire's personal attachment to the spot. The book was written in the Convent of Santa Sabina, of which he says, "Its walls rose on the loftiest and most abrupt side of the Aventine, above the narrow channel where Tiber brawls as it rushes forth, dashing against the remnants of that bridge which Horatius Cocles defended against Porsenna. Two rows of ancient columns supported an open roof, dividing the church into three aisles, each ending with an altar. It was the primitive basilica in all its glorious simplicity. The relics of Santa Sabina, who was a martyr for Jesus Christ in Adrian's reign, rested beneath the high altar, as near as possible to the spot pointed out by tradition as that of her martyrdom. The church joined the Palazzo Sabelli, then occupied by Honorius III., whence was dated the Bull approving the Order of Preaching Friars. From the windows of this dwelling, part of which was given to Dominic, the eye fell upon the Roman city and rested on the Vatican hill. Two winding lanes led to the town ; one going direct to the Tiber, the other to one of the angles of the Palatine, close to the Church of Santa Anastasia. This was the road by which Dominic was wont to go from Santa Sabina to

San Sisto. No pathway on earth retains so deeply the memory of his footsteps."[1]

S. Dominic was master of the Papal household, and to this it was owing that Santa Sabina was made over to him. No locality is, as Lacordaire says, more connected with his history. "Everything around reminds us of him," Père Besson wrote a few years later, when appointed to the Priorate of that house,[2] "and one seems still to hear the echo of S. Dominic's sighs, as he knelt here. . . . The spot where he was wont to pray is still pointed out. . . . There is one cell where he, S. Francis of Assisi, and the blessed Angelo de Carmi spent a whole night talking of heavenly things ; and it was in the Chapter-room that my patron, S. Hyacinthe, received the habit from S. Dominic." Besson was bent on the restoration of Santa Sabina, but the magnitude of the undertaking was too great, and he had to content himself with painting the Chapter-house of San Sisto, where his frescoes are a point of great interest.[3] An orange-tree planted by the saint still grows in the garden of Santa Sabina,[4] and in the church the faithful

[1] Vie de S. Dominique, c. xii.

[2] A Dominican Artist, p. 169.

[3] The frescoes represent S. Dominic's miracles. San Sisto is now annexed to the Irish Dominicans of San Clemente.

[4] It is said that the year before Lacordaire began his work of restoration this tree put forth a new and vigorous shoot, as though in sympathetic forecast of his success.

look with veneration on a rude black stone, said to have been flung by his hands at the devil, who sought to molest his meditations.

Some months of study and repose followed, but as winter drew on, it was decided that Lacordaire should revisit Paris. " Our General wishes it," he wrote to Mme. Swetchine ; " it is thought that a long absence from France would do us harm, and that it is well to be seen there, if only *pour faire acte de présence.* Moreover, I must gather in the harvest of my Life of S. Dominic; I shall bring back some select young fellows, and put myself in communication with many who will help us later on. The diocesan administration having changed, it is well to be *en rapport* with it, and know what one may expect for the future. I shall see other Bishops on the way; and this return will testify my entire freedom, the confidence of my Order, which sends me thus alone to France, and it will be a fresh proof that the establishment of the French Dominicans is no chimera. Our habit will be seen, and it will pave the way for next year, when I count on preaching in it. . . . I shall bring nothing but my Dominican habit and a cloak. I can wrap that around me when necessary, but I will not put off my habit."

Mme. Swetchine wrote highly commending the project. " I cannot tell you," she says, November 17, 1840, " how often I have mentally gone over the objections to an overlong absence on your part ; one's ignorance of whatever one does not see, or judge of for oneself; the dangers of a long self-concentration, and of an explosion when thought breaks lose at last, sometimes by an anticipatory process ! This applies to all natures, but especially to yours, which cannot live and develop without the adaptation of well-balanced activity and contemplation. The more I think of it—and I have done nothing else since yesterday—the more convinced I am that your proposed plan, wisely and carefully carried out, will have an admirable result. The pleasure of seeing you again will win the day for your Dominican habit ; you will attract all those who do not yet know you, and draw closer the links between you and those who are already friendly."

Accordingly Lacordaire started on November 30th, and visiting the various houses of his Order at Siena, Florence, Lucca, Genoa, etc., he reached Paris without hindrance before Christmas. His arrival was unexpected, save by his intimate friends, and as it has been observed, his former enemies had not time to think of their opposition—every one yielded to a lively spirit of curiosity. The new Archbishop, Mgr. Affre, received Lacordaire warmly, and without making the slightest difficulty as to his preaching at Notre Dame in his monk's habit, at once asked him to fix his own day. "So I appeared," he says, "at Notre Dame with my shaven head, my white gown, and black mantle. The Archbishop presided ; the Chancellor, Ministre des Cultes, M. Martin (du Nord), was determined ͺto be present himself at a scene the result of which no one could precisely forecast. Many other notabilities crept in amid the crowds, which overflowed from the porch to the sanctuary. I chose as my subject the Vocation of the French Nation, with a view to sheltering the audacity of my presence beneath a popular line of thought. I succeeded, and the day after the Chancellor invited me to a large dinner party. During the meal, M. Bourdeau, formerly a minister of Charles X., leaned towards a neighbour, saying, ' How strangely this world revolves !   If I had invited a Dominican to my table when I was Chancellor, the place would have been burned down the next day.' But now there were no incendiaries, nor did even any newspaper invoke the vengeance of secular law upon my *auto-da-fé*."

"He only alluded casually to his own monastic vocation," Montalembert says ; " but he fully intended, when he thus ascended the metropolitan pulpit, to inaugurate the monk's dress, which had been lost for fifty years in France. And so he appeared with his shaven head and white habit among some six thousand young men, as eloquent as ever, and there was no serious opposition. The Government manifested some timidity, and issued some trifling prohibitions, but Lacordaire displayed neither fear nor boastfulness.

He had some sort of negotiations with the Ministre des Cultes, and disarmed him by his simplicity, straightforwardness, and vigour. I acted as intermediary, and in one of the letters it was my office to read to the Minister he said, 'The stability of Government, the maintenance of those liberties which experience has proved necessary to France, the propagation of the Gospel, of which the Church is sole and infallible guardian,—these are my aim and object in things temporal and spiritual. Free from all party spirit, I have always sought, from respect to my faith, to keep it within the realm of justice and worth. Public opinion has rewarded me by placing me on a level far beyond my humble talents; and if the Government has not taken me at my true measure, I perhaps owe it to the fact that I have never sought their favours. Now that I can by no possibility aspire to anything, I have acquired the right to say so, and I use that right merely to reassure your Excellency as to my thoughts and intentions.'"[1]

Lacordaire only remained two months in Paris. In March we find him travelling by Lyons (where the Archbishop, Mgr. de Bonald, received him at the Archevêché, and congratulated him on his choice of a subject for Notre Dame, observing that it was well continually to remind France of her mission), Genoa, where the king, Carlo Alberto, the Minister of Foreign

[1] Le Père Lacordaire, p. 113.

Affairs, Conte della Margarita, and Cardinal Tadini, the Archbishop, all fêted the enterprising Frenchman; and it was a triumphal progress as far as la Quercia, where he was stopped by an attack of smallpox, which, however, coming after vaccination (thirty-nine years before), was not serious, and only produced further kindly demonstrations—the Pope sending anxious inquiries, the Cardinal Bishop of Viterbo, and the Governor Delegate visiting him, and so forth. Returned to Rome in April, the little French Community found itself transferred to San Clemente, where ten additional members were shortly expected to begin their novitiate. All seemed prosperous, and yet Lacordaire was anxious.

"Yesterday," he writes (April 28, 1841), "I went by summons to see Cardinal Fieschi. He charmed me by his frankness, cordiality, and enthusiasm; he quoted my sermon, and talked of Rome with the most delightful *desinvoltura*, as though seeking to give me the *carte du pays*. Yesterday the French Ambassador came to see me, and visited San Clemente as a French establishment. I must own, *chère amie*, that I am alive to all these tokens of esteem and affection; but what reassures me is that I never felt more ready to refer all to God, and to feel my own weakness. I see how little it would take to bring the whole thing crumbling about my ears, and how insufficient my natural and spiritual supplies are for the burden I

bear.   I am now father of an independent house ;
seventeen persons to feed and clothe, for whom I am
responsible to God.   Fourteen take the habit. . . .
Although the novitiate has not yet begun, I am none
the less occupied with it, and have two lectures daily.
This is absolutely necessary, not only that the Brothers
may learn what it befits them to know, but to keep
them occupied.   All this year will be devoted to
them, and I shall lose nothing by it, for it is surprising
how much one learns by teaching.   I take part in all
the offices, and am actually at last learning plain-song,
of which I did not believe myself capable.   It is
seventeen years since I used to despise *ut, re, mi, fa,*
at the Seminary, and now I am quite proud of being
able to *solfeggiar !*   How God changes men ! "

A great blow to his plans was indeed impending.
On April 29th the Congregazione informed Lacordaire
that a French Novitiate could not be sanctioned, as
no French Province or Community existed as yet ;
but they were authorised to choose any house in the
Roman Province for their Novitiate, and accordingly
selected la Quercia.   They had actually begun a
preparatory Retreat, when suddenly it was announced
that the Congregazione could not allow the Frenchmen
to take their habit in Rome, and that they must be
divided into two bands, and go to different Novitiates,
one to la Quercia, the other to Bosco, in Piedmont.
It was a great and unexpected blow.   To all human

appearance the work seemed crushed by its members being thus separated and divided from their head. But Lacordaire took calmly the trial; he intimated his submission, and gathering together his little band, reminded them that obedience was the first duty of a Religious, though at the same time they, who were as yet bound by no vows, were now free to reconsider their determination, bidding them weigh the uncertainty of their future conscientiously before God, and decide as they saw fit. All answered with one voice that they were ready, like himself, to obey, and that they had no idea of forsaking the vocation they believed themselves to have experienced.

"Our young fellows behaved admirably," he wrote to Mme. de la Tour du Pin : "if our enemies, whoever they may be, thought to dishearten them and break up our work, they have been greatly out in their calculations. On the contrary, their ready obedience proved the true religious spirit in them, and so far from losing credit in Rome, we have gained immensely. Every one is perplexed as to the real cause of this upsetting of our plans.[1] . . . Perhaps we shall never

[1] Mme. Swetchine expresses herself strongly convinced that the French Government had been at the bottom of the discomfiture : "Il m'est impossible de repousser ici ce vieil adage de jurisprudence, qu'il est naturel d'attribuer le délit à qui la profite. . . . Malgré cette visite de votre Ambassadeur à San Clemente, je n'en serais pas moins disposée à croire que c'est la diplomatie qui a tout fait ; non pas assurément que j'aie quelque raison de

know, but the actual result is to strengthen our hands by proving our stedfastness, and that the work does not depend upon me personally. Another advantage is that I am set free much sooner than I expected; I can return to France, travel, preach, and write as much as I wish. Those I leave at the head to represent me are thoroughly capable and worth more than I am: we shall only lose the exceeding comfort of living together. You cannot think how happy we were during our short time at San Clemente. It seems as if God had been pleased to give us a foretaste of the happiness we shall find when once we have a French convent, before our dispersal." By the middle of May this dispersal took place, five of the French novices and a lay brother going to la Quercia, while a similar party went to Bosco, near Alessandria. Besson was of the latter, and it was to him, with his artist's tastes and habits, no small sacrifice to leave Rome.

"SAN CLEMENTE, *May* 13, 1841.

"I write to you from our deserted San Clemente. This morning our Bosco brethren started; those destined for la Quercia departed thirty-six hours earlier. I am alone, after having been surrounded by a numerous and happy family. We parted with

douter de la bienveillance personnelle de M. de Maubourg pour vous ou pour votre œuvre, mais parce que son devoir n'en aura pas été moins de se conformer aux instructions qu'il aura reçues."

perfect calmness, full of mutual confidence, and in the loving hope of being gathered together again in France."

There can be little doubt that the move was a political one, and that the Roman authorities were induced to believe that the de la Mennais danger was not quite extinct. Cardinal Lambruschini said to one of the Frenchmen interested that they "might do some good in France, but it was a great calamity for that country that there was so large a party of young men formed with Lacordaire at their head, who had no idea of anything but the separation of Church and State." La Bouillerie began to deny the fact, but the Cardinal broke in with assurances that Lacordaire and de la Mennais—it was all the same thing !

Meanwhile Lacordaire remained a while at the Minerva Convent, his time divided between study of S. Thomas Aquinas and the preparation of his Conferences. " The transit from activity to contemplation, from family life to solitude, is less painful to me than to many, thanks to the habit of years which has used me to these alternations. The first day or two I suffer, then I fall into the old mould; but for this adaptability I should have been dead long ago. I have spent years without seeing anybody or taking part in anything, and think of them now with a shudder, for I am already greatly changed ; the waters have lowered, *chère amie*, and the time of rest among sons and brethren will come. I shall be astonished at myself in many ways then no doubt, like an old soldier who can no longer wield his sword."

In September 1841, Lacordaire left Rome, going first to la Quercia and Bosco, at which last place he found the young architect Piel dying of consumption. "His malady has made a tremendous advance during these four months," Lacordaire wrote, "and I find nothing of himself left save his still vigorous mind, which is calm, serene, resigned, and wondrously cheerful. Réquédat was as resigned as he is; he too had freely offered his life to God, but there was a certain austerity in his calmness, while Piel seems to welcome death, and to feel neither regrets nor temptations. He says he always expected to die thus, and at his actual age." Piel lingered till December 19, 1841.

"Bosco is a charming convent, built by Pio Nono in a splendid position. It contains the novices and students of the Piedmontese province; it is perfectly ruled, and this is the first time I feel quite *en religion.* I am about to give the habit to two new French novices." Lacordaire went on to Lyons and Bordeaux, at which latter place he was engaged to preach during the coming Advent and Lent. It was an event in the town, says Père Chocarne. Two immense tribunes were erected in the Cathedral, in order to increase the accommodation of the spacious nave, and every department—Government, the Bar, the army, etc.—was duly represented there. The enthusiastic excitement of this crowded audience wound Lacordaire up to a great pitch himself, and he often was forced to check the irresistible inclination of his hearers to burst forth in applause. It was a kind of frenzy; go where you would, the topic of the day was Lacordaire and his Conferences. A distinguished lawyer of the town wrote to the preacher some time after: "You have left as many friends as admirers in Bordeaux, for you have found the secret, so difficult nowadays, of conciliating opinion, of combining political differences, and of absorbing men's minds in the one subject, greatest of all."

One result of Lacordaire's Advent Conferences was that a house near Agen was given him for the use of his Community; and the Lent station, especially Holy Week, confirmed the work begun so satisfactorily. A charity sermon at Tours, and a week in Paris, and the active Dominican was on his way to Bosco again; but he arrived there weak and exhausted, after a somewhat difficult passage of the Saint Gothard, and an attack of fever at Vercelli, which laid him up there in a little inn for a week.

Among his letters of this period to Mme. Swetchine, there is one of especial interest, as it seems to me, replying to her earnest desires to bring him to Paris.

"I have always been surprised," he writes, July 14,

1842, "at the fixity of idea with which you draw me to Paris, as towards the sword destined to cut the knot of my fate. I could quite conceive that no reputation, and consequently no moral force, can attain its full development save in Paris; but such force once acquired with God's help, or rather by His Sovereign power, which lifts up and overthrows as He sees good, is one to condemn oneself only to live, to act, to do any good in Paris! If I study the traditions of the apostolic life, I see all the first teachers of the Word of God going from town to town like their Master, and followed by S. Paul, whose life, as I find it in the Acts of the Apostles, is but one continual journey from Rome to Jerusalem all along the Mediterranean shores. It is all very well to say that Paris is France. Not so: the greater part of our men do not see Paris more than once, passing through; and if they happen accidentally to hear some preacher, the recollection of his voice forms but a part of their general impression of the great things they beheld. I do not deny the good done, many proofs of it occur to me; only yesterday I got a charming letter from an unknown young Brettonais sending me a volume of poetry dedicated to me, and thanking me in the warmest terms for the good I had formerly done him. No doubt; but the same thing happens elsewhere, and what a difference there is between touching a whole town in all its various classes, and merely raising one's voice amid the vast whirlwind of the capital, a voice stimulated rather by outward fame than by inward grace!   Do you know what happened at Bordeaux during Holy Week?   In the big hotels, full of *commis voyageurs* from twenty miles round, the masters were expressly required to provide *maigre* food, and during all that week the Church's rule was carefully kept with but few exceptions.   If, again, I look at my private position, the sort of problem which I am to many, and the political enmities which surround me, I feel that Paris is murder to me; for it is the centre of all power, of all intrigue, of all those hidden forces which can never be grappled with by any religious success.   You might convert a thousand men on one day in Paris, and the public conscience would know nothing about it.   Then think of Notre Dame! eight or nine sermons in a year, taking away all possibility of anything else—like a few thunder-claps heard afar off in the darkness!   If you increase the number, by the end of two or three years you would become exhausted, and be forced to repeat yourself, which is impossible in such a position.   I should have liked my Saint Stanislas a little enlarged a thousand times better!   But Mgr. de Quélen was bent on making a show, and he succeeded, I grant you; still ask M. de Ravignan why he left Notre Dame for Saint Séverin. It was this feeling, joined to the need of recollection, which took me so quickly from Paris.   Later on, my experience of the provinces fully confirmed my impression. I saw that the gain was immense, visible, clearly defined, and, moreover, that one could conquer hatred and prejudice best on that ground. I did not leave one enemy at Bordeaux; scarcely had I arrived in Paris, and my mere presence stirred up passion.

"And from an altogether different point of view, I would ask you, have I lost in public opinion during the last six years? I will venture to say that I possess more true and real esteem than if I had not left Notre Dame for those six years. Fame is composed of many elements, victory and *éclat* are but a part; there is another side, without which it soon pales before men. I do not particularise, I would not seem too skilful in the secrets of glory. They are matters with which pride mingles swiftly, even when one seeks to deal with them from the side of cold, disinterested speculation."

Enclosed in this was the copy of a letter to Mgr. Affre, explaining why he was unable to comply with his recent request to preach at Notre Dame, the Bishop of Nancy holding him to his promise to go there. "I ought to confess, Monseigneur," he says, "that your request took me by surprise and unprepared. I had not leisure to prepare for what I did not in the least expect. . . . It is evident, by experience, that I can do a good work in the provinces, a greater and more solid work than in Paris. A few annual

Conferences given to a shifting audience cannot compare with whole months of consecutive teaching given every winter in some large country town to a fixed congregation, made up of all classes of society—at least I do not think so. There is more stir and credit in Paris, I grant, but what are credit and name? If I have been weak enough, which God knows, to desire reputation, I am satisfied. I desire no more than what God has freely given me, and it is but just that I should tend His affairs when He has so tended mine. Therefore, Monseigneur, I beg you to think no more of me for Notre Dame. If I am to preach in Paris again, I will ask you for a church some winter, as I might do elsewhere, and you will remember me kindly enough to be satisfied to grant it. My one regret would be if you thought me ungrateful. I am not. Your offers have given me genuine pleasure; they have linked the present to a past which will be ever dear to me. . . . . I am glad to think that some day when you think over all the ingratitude and injustice you have experienced, you will reckon me among the few of whom you have no cause to complain, and as one who has always been stedfast in affection for you."

VII.

LIBERTY—PREACHING.

LACORDAIRE spent some months of this autumn at Bosco, whence he writes that Père Jandel "is admirable. He is the very man I want; I shall be the outsider, and he the inner workman (*je serai l'homme du dehors et lui du dedans*); for although I do make some progress in the spiritual, the active, eager man still peeps out." That winter was spent, as promised, at Nancy, whence his letters tell, not boastingly, but thankfully, of a great success. His time was more than ever crowded. "The week passes like a flash of lightning, and do what I will, my correspondence is always in arrears." The congregations were large, attentive, and friendly; the Bishop full of kindness; no voice of opposition had been raised, and the Legitimists, who had begun by being irritable and defiant, were conciliated. The Archbishop of Paris, though he had not pressed Lacordaire to give up his promised course at Nancy, continued to ask him to come to the capital. Lacordaire answered frankly that he would do nothing which could in any way seem uncourteous to de Ravignan. Three winters were already bespoken by Grenoble, Lyons, and Strasbourg; after that he was willing to preach for three seasons in Paris, if the Archbishop still desired it. "Everybody in these days," he writes, "fails through hurry; they don't remember that good circus-drivers begin slowly, which is the real secret of all things. Thank God, I feel no jealousy, no desire to prove myself worth more than other people; I honour all the gifts which God sends His Church, and every day I marvel at my own undeserved share of esteem. Dear friend, ten years ago where was I? On the verge of want, shattered, lonely; having attained a dawning reputation together with a heavy burden of the hatred and prejudices of some men, the overweening enthusiasm of others, the mistrust and defiance of the greater part. I knew not what was to be my visible course, and in the bottom of my heart I saw but vaguely the limits of my own ideas. Now, with ten years' work, I have swept the ground, traced out my path, and created a work which seemed purely chimerical; or rather God has done all this for me, bringing success out of discomfiture, suffering me twenty times to totter on the brink of destruction, and continually bringing me out of danger. How can I ever forget that ten years ago you were given me at that painful hour when, in separating myself from a man who was still in the height of his glory, I lost every stay I most required in losing him? You have been, through God, to me like those rays of sunshine which come in spring-time to the poor labourer and comfort him for the winter's hardships. And so I am content, and feel at present much more longing to hide than to produce myself to the world. Pride would dictate such a course, even if Christian feeling did not suggest it. Nothing dignifies a man so much as not seeking fame, and not doing the commonplace thing which everybody would do in his position."

He was rewarded for his constancy to his engagement by the satisfactory establishment of the first Dominican house in France, a young man who was among his congregation, M. Thierry de Saint-Beaussant, being brought from his attitude of artistic agnosticism to earnest Christianity; and in gratitude he bought a house, of which the Community took possession at Whitsuntide 1843. A valuable library of 10,000 volumes was made over to them by the heirs of a late Cathedral dignitary, who had left his books to the first religious body that should be established in Nancy. De Saint-Beaussant further built a chapel, refectory, and other needful quarters, and himself became a Dominican. He died in 1852 at Oullins, and Lacordaire observed that he and Réquédat, both so early called to rest, were the first-fruits of the restored Order; Réquédat gave the first spiritual, de Saint-Beaussant the first material, corner-stone of the building.   During the summer Père Jandel was placed at the head of this Nancy foundation, and Père Besson undertook that of Bosco.

But in spite of all these encouragements, difficulties and storms were gathering. The Minister of Public Worship (that same M. Martin who had been so cordial in 1841) took fright at the prospect of a Dominican Convent in Nancy, and wrote to the Coadjutor Bishop, bidding him refuse his consent. Mgr. Menjaud stood his ground firmly, and declined to drive away a man whom he admired and esteemed, at the moment he was carrying out an excellent work, religious and social, in the town.

An attempt was then made on another side to overthrow Lacordaire's influence. The *Patriot* news-paper assailed him in gross terms, attacking him both doctrinally and personally; and as the authorities would not interfere, Lacordaire prosecuted the paper for defamation, which, as it was well understood, in-volved both the Minister of Public Worship and the Rector of the Lycée, who had taken a cowardly, time-serving line against the Dominican. Party spirit rose high; most of the inhabitants of Nancy were energetic in defence of their favourite preacher, who was thus calumniated. The leading advocate of Nancy under-took his cause, and Lacordaire proposed pleading on his own behalf in order to assert the rights of religious orders in France. Indeed he saw God's Hand in the whole matter, as bringing to light the truth, and asserting the freedom of such associations. But the Government saw that things looked unpromising for them, and that whatever might be the verdict, they would lose ground, and therefore they hastened a compromise. Mgr. Menjaud put out a strong letter against which there was no appeal, and Lacordaire, seeing himself amply justified, agreed to withdraw the prosecution.

There were gleams of quiet, happy privacy among these activities which are highly characteristic of Lacordaire's nature. Thus we find him hastening from Nancy to Bosco, living there in the greatest retirement, working in the garden, studying, going forth to preach to the Savoyard soldiers at Alessandria, putting aside the Superior, the politician, the leader, as far as possible. Padre Morassi, Master of the Novices, tells how on one occasion a distinguished ecclesiastical guest came from far in order to see the celebrated Père Lacordaire, and being introduced into the Superior's room, and having explained his errand, he was shortly placed, but without introduction, by Lacordaire's side at the dinner-table. Eager to see the object of his curiosity, the visitor soon whispered the inquiry to his neighbour, Which was Lacordaire ? " The priest sitting at the top of the table," Lacordaire answered slyly, and the visitor, apprehending no deception, took it for granted that not the speaker (who was at one end of the table), but the Religious at the other end, was the celebrity he wished to interview, and watched his every movement, to the brink of incivility, all dinner-time. As soon as that was over, he hastened to the person he supposed to be indicated, and began to speechify about his delight in making acquaintance with one so famous, etc. etc. Greatly to his dismay, the object of his eloquence only smiled, giving the unwelcome information, "I am not Père Lacordaire ; he was sitting by you at dinner !" But the real Lacordaire had slipped away and was lost !

It has been said that clouds were gathering, and here we must leave Montalembert to speak both of his friend and of the political aspect of things, which at that moment was so weighty, and which we contemplate with double interest under the complications of a still more aggravated character of the present period, 1882 :—

"The question of freedom of instruction, opened by Lacordaire twelve years before, in the *Avenir* and before the Cour des Pairs, after lying dormant a while, had now reawakened with new energy, and had laid vigorous hold on the public mind. There naturally arose together with this question that of freedom of association, inasmuch as the Communities alone could really supply the requirements of free instruction.

While the Bishops and Catholic editors claimed the liberty promised by the *Charte* with all its consequences, the far more numerous orators and writers of the University party maintained monopoly *à outrance,* and poured forth all the torrents of unpopularity which the legatees of perversion and persecution from the eighteenth century always know so well how to excite, especially against the Jesuits. 'We owe them nothing save expulsion!'—the cry of a deputy well known for his outbreaks—seemed to the crowd of so-called Liberals the best answer to the appeals raised on behalf of religious associations in the name of Liberty and equality. Government, which was more timid than unfriendly, and fully intended avoiding all persecutions, nevertheless let itself be overruled and carried away by the stream of anti-religious opinion. The Dominican's white robe seen in the street or the pulpit no longer encountered the anxious, but friendly neutrality of 1841 ; it caused a serious anxiety, which betrayed itself in protestations and threats, even before more serious demonstration. Under these circumstances Mgr. Affre invited Lacordaire to renew his Conferences, and, spite of the pressure put upon him by the Government, that prelate, who a few years later sacrificed his life with such modest composure, now upheld the liberty of the Gospel with invincible firmness. The pressure was great ; the King even sent for Mgr. Affre to the Tuileries, and there, in the Queen's presence, argued for an hour, endeavouring to induce the Archbishop to withdraw his resolution. But Mgr. Affre stood firm, and asserted that it would be a dishonour to himself and to Lacordaire were he to retract. The King ended by exclaiming, 'Well, Monseigneur, if anything goes wrong, remember that you shall not have one soldier or one national guard to help you!' In December 1843, Lacordaire once more took possession of the pulpit of Notre Dame, which he occupied for eight consecutive years, and until the *coup-d'état* of 1851."[1]

Clearly there was no vacillation, no overruling by pride or vanity of the opinions we heard him express so plainly a few months before. Then it was a question of accepting the more flattering invitations of the metropolis rather than of provincial towns, of taking the higher instead of the lower place. Now the call of duty was plain ; there was a great battle to be fought, and Lacordaire was not the man to refuse the post of standard-bearer, or voluntarily to keep out of the thick of the fight, when his commanding officer summoned him to it.

"That was the heroic age of our religious and liberal struggle," says Montalembert. "One might watch a Dominican and a Jesuit, both illustrious men, alike superior to the veriest shadow of jealous rivalry, teaching our young men how to tread human respect under foot and leading them at once to live up to

[1] Montalembert, p. 115.

their faith and to acquire the civic rights of Catholicism. Every winter Lacordaire gave seven or eight Conferences during December and January, after which he went for Lent to preach at some provincial town — Grenoble, Lyons, Strasbourg — leaving de Ravignan to replace him in Notre Dame, and to prepare those Easter Communions which have ever since been the glory and consolation of the Church in Paris, and which as early as 1844 induced the exclamation, 'We must bring Voltaire to bear on these people!'[1] And indeed they tried their best to do so, but with liberty we can afford to laugh even at Voltaire. This first station at Notre Dame, since the strife had become hot, did not end till February 1844. Lacordaire himself called it 'the most perilous and most decisive of his campaigns.' It succeeded beyond all expectation, kindling and strengthening hearts; a worthy prelude to the struggle in Parliament of that memorable year and the one following, when the Religious Orders, furiously attacked from the tribune, were defended as they had never been since 1789. Thanks to the union and courage of the Episcopate, thanks to the resolute attitude of Catholics in the elections, resistance to the mere passions and prejudices of incoherent Liberalism grew visibly stronger day by day. Catholic action was at once sensible and dignified ; its intervention in the conditions of

[1] "Il faut mettre la main de Voltaire sur ces gens-là."

modern society became daily more regular and more efficacious.

" This state of things lasted till the moment when the Revolution of February first precipitated, then led away, and finally annihilated this healthy effort.   No voice was raised within our ranks to criticise or hinder.   ' We both served Christian liberty under the flag of public liberty,' Lacordaire said with happy concision of himself and de Ravignan.   The latter, in a calm, dignified, and eloquent document, claimed the right to be and proclaim himself a Jesuit, as a citizen in the name of the *Charte*, in the name of liberty of conscience, thereby guaranteed to all men. And M. Dupanloup [since Bishop of Orleans] spoke as follows with the universal assent of the clergy and the faithful : ' What is meant by the spirit of the French Revolution ?   Do you mean free institutions, freedom of conscience, political freedom, civil freedom, indi-vidual freedom, family freedom, freedom of education, of opinion, equality in the sight of the law, an equal division of taxes and public expenses?   All this we accept deliberately and fully. . . . These precious liberties which men accuse us of not loving, we pro-claim them, and we demand them FOR OURSELVES AS FOR OTHERS.' "

They are wondrous discourses, even to read, those Conferences of 1843-44, on the rational certainty of Catholic doctrine ; the repulsion raised in the mind by it; above all, on the opposition of statesmen and men of intellect against it. The unflinching boldness and calm superiority of an invincible cause with which Lacordaire handles his subject is throughout something most unwontedly impressive. "One of the most powerful passions of man is the passion of sovereignty. Man will not be merely free, he must be supreme; he must not only be master of himself and at home, he would fain be master of other men and in their domain. De Maistre says that the rage of domination is innate in man's heart. But I do not accept the expression, for the crave of power is not a mere rage, it is a generous passion. A man possesses every gift of birth and fortune, he can enjoy at will the pleasures of family life, of society, luxury, honour, repose; but he rejects these. He shuts himself up within an office, and buries himself in the delight of toil and difficulties. He grows grey with the weight of business not his own, receiving no reward save the ingratitude of those he serves, the rivalry of others ambitious like himself, and the blame of the indifferent. The first schoolboy at hand takes his pen, and without talent, ancestry, past service, one to whom society owes nothing but forgiveness of his audacity, he attacks the statesman, who instead of enjoying his fortune and position, scarce has time to swallow down a glass of water between his prolonged anxieties. The statesman heeds it not; he issues forth from his

Cabinet to the battlefield ; he watches by the general's side to counsel him ; he signs treaties for which all posterity will call him to account.   And at last he dies, his career cut short by toil, care, and calumny; he dies, and while waiting for the decree of futurity, his contemporaries cast an epigram upon his tomb !"[1] Those who were present describe him as frequently electrifying his audience, carrying them away with irresistible force by the stream of his sympathetic influence.   "It was thus," says Montalembert, "that he saw his early dreams becoming realised.   He enjoyed the unexpected triumph, but without excitement or vanity."

" What we have gained of unity, of power, of future strength, during this last campaign is hardly credible," he wrote in June 1844.   " Even if free instruction were lost for fifty years, we have gained more than that, because we have gained the instrument which wins it, and therewith the liberties necessary for the salvation of France and of the world."

" His counsels were always on the line of prudence and that practical mind which characterised him," Montalembert says.   " He used to urge us not to want everything at once, to keep the ground already won patiently, not to plunge into boundless unfathomed theories, above all, not to give our enemies any pretext for proclaiming that we aimed at the total overthrow

[1] Conferences, xvi.

of French society.   He took no part in the controversy
either on paper or in act; and there was not a single
allusion to it in his Conferences.   It was during the
warlike year 1844 that he delivered his celebrated
Conferences on Chastity, which shut the mouth of his
most energetic detractors, their beauty remaining
above all criticism, like an exquisite pearl which no
breath can tarnish.   But the universal popularity of
his preaching, the immense audiences which gathered
wheresoever he appeared, were more eloquent arguments than anything politics or law could afford.   His
victory was proved by his preaching in Paris and
throughout France, and by the establishment of his
right to community life and to his habit, which no
one ventured to contest, whithersoever he went."   It
was on his deathbed, speaking of these times, that
Lacordaire said, " Directly that any nation realises the
true elements of liberty, these will work, even unconsciously, against all oppression ; and as truth appeals
to truth, justice to justice, so in the logical circle of
things human and Divine, liberty appeals to liberty."
'Wolves did not cease to be wolves," Montalembert
observes, "as we see too plainly even now; but
Lacordaire had put those to shame who would have
howled with them, and in the name of liberty he had
turned their strength against the oppressors."

It is curious to trace Lacordaire's perfect sense of
his own power, without any apparent self-satisfaction or

vanity. Some pressure was put upon him by the Archbishop (who induced Mme. Swetchine herself to back him) to forbear appearing at Notre Dame in the much-contested monk's habit; but he was immovable on that point. "The Archbishop knows that no one will insult me in the pulpit of Notre Dame," he writes, November 12, 1843; "he knows that an immense audience will shield me from any individual outbreak; he knows that I shall not give the multitude time to gather itself together, that at my third sentence I shall have penetrated their hearts, and found my safety there. Nothing can stand against popular impulse. Curiosity alone will keep hatred quiet, and the very boldness of the measure will move those who would fain not be moved; France has an instinctive feeling for honour, which enchants her whenever she comes within its shadow. If anything could damage me in Notre Dame, it would be a change of garb. . . . And on the personal side, I should altogether lower my character if I were to lay aside my habit in order to preach at Notre Dame. Who but would suppose I did it for the small glory of preaching there? . . . Let me show that I would never accept openings or fame at the cost of dishonour. Let me put duty and dignity foremost. The older I grow, the more I feel that God's grace is detaching me from this world; I care only to do His Will. If it is His Will that I should preach in Notre Dame, I will do so; if He closes those doors, I will preach elsewhere; if all the pulpits of France are successively closed to me, as may be the intention of Government, I will wait for better times, and do what good is practicable the while. Or I will be content to do nothing, if nothing is possible. The present matters little, the future is all in all."

Nevertheless the Archbishop was still so anxious as to the question of the monk's habit, that through the Papal Nuncio he obtained a formal authorisation for Lacordaire to preach in the secular priest's garb, and eventually he consented to wear the ordinary canon's rochet over his habit, and thus, on December 3, 1843, began his famous course. What he had said of his power to arrest and win all hearts by his third sentence proved most true. The opening was anxious. The Archbishop took his place, looking nervously around on the vast multitude which crammed Notre Dame's mighty nave; a body of young men with arms ready to defend their idol surrounded the pulpit in a serried mass. Lacordaire went into it; a silence, awful in such a crowd, occurred for a few moments, while the orator slowly and calmly looked round upon the masses of expectant listeners, and then began his sermon; perfect stillness continued, and, as he said, before another moment he had obtained full control of his audience. From this hour his royalty was confirmed beyond power of assault, and he never let go the hold then affirmed upon men's hearts and intellects.

The delicacy with which his half-playful irony sometimes touched things, the dignity and pathos which are found in every Conference, will hardly bear being demonstrated by quotations.   We may barely illustrate the former by such a passage as the following from one of the discourses of 1843 : "The war against Catholic doctrine is no war of *enfants perdus ;* it is a civil, a social war, and as this war has been the history of eighteen centuries, as it involves your destinies, and those of your posterity, needs be you must pause, and well weigh this public passion of statesmen and men of intellect against Catholic doctrine.   The question is serious, *messieurs*, it is delicate.   But be reassured, I will treat you even as Massillon treated Louis XV. in the royal chapel of Versailles.   Whatsoever be your needs and my goodwill, I can do no better for you than treat you as that great century treated its great king." [1]

Or take another passage from the Conference on Humility in the Soul : "Wherever we are, we would fain be foremost. The artist who reproduces with pencil or graver, the orator creating thoughts in the mind of the multitude, the general commanding his battalion and promising victory to it, the minister ruling an empire, the king beneath his purple,—we all aspire to

[1] Conferences, xvi.

primacy, and to a sole primacy. We are only content when, able to measure our surroundings with a glance, we find space, and beyond that space, as far off as may be, a kneeling world ready to worship us."[1]

The Effects of Catholic Doctrine on the Mind was the subject of the Conference of 1843; on the Soul, that of 1844; on Society, of 1845. In 1846 Lacordaire took for his subject Our Lord Jesus Christ, a course of which Montalembert says that to his mind it contains "the most striking riches of his eloquence;" 1848, of God; 1849, the Commerce of Man with God; 1850, the Fall and Restoration of Man; 1851, the Providential Economy of Man's Restoration,— a series embracing, as it is seen, all the mysteries of Creation and Redemption. Unquestionably it is as an orator that the world in general will remember Lacordaire, and class him among her great men, although to the inner circle it may be that, as his dearest friend says, "the orator will be lost in the Religious." But, as Montalembert seeks, and most successfully, to prove, his oratory was the fruit of his intense religious convictions more than any mere natural gift. "Before all else, he was the priest, the confessor, the penitent disciple of a crucified Master. While yet a seminarist he wrote, 'I would fain come forth from this mere natural life, and consecrate myself wholly to the service of One Who will never be jealous,

<hr>

[1] Conferences, xxi.

nor ungrateful, nor vile.' And all his words, as his life, were stamped with this love which passes all other love." Montalembert goes on to cite the burst of living tenderness with which he opened his Conferences on Jesus Christ, just at the moment of supreme excitement and burning external strife : "Lord Jesus, during the ten years which I have been speaking of Thy Church to this audience, it is indeed ever of Thee that I have spoken ; but now at length I come more nearly before Thee, gazing upon that sacred Face which is the object of my daily contemplation ; those holy Feet which I have kissed so often ; those dear Hands which have so often blessed me ; that Head crowned with glory and with thorns ; that Life, the savour of which I have breathed ever since I was born, which my boyhood forgot, which my manhood regained, which my riper age worships and proclaims aloud. O Father ! O Master ! O Friend ! O Jesus ! help me more than ever, forasmuch as drawing nearer to Thee, Thy Presence must needs be seen in me, and my words glow with the richness of Thy touch !"[1]

Or again, a little later : "Pursuing love all our life, we never attain it save in an imperfect state which wounds the heart ; and even if we won it in life, what would remain after death ? Grant that a loving prayer follows us beyond this world, a friendly memory yet whispers our name ; but ere long Heaven

[1] Conferences, xxxvii.

and earth have moved on, forgetfulness follows, silence shrouds us, no breath of frail earthly love lingers still about our tomb. It is over, ended for ever, and this is the story of man's love. Yet not so. There is One Man Whose tomb has been kept by love; One Man Whose grave is not merely glorious, but beloved. There is One Man Whose ashes are still warm after eighteen centuries; Who is daily born anew in the thoughts of a multitude of men, Who is visited in His cradle by shepherds and kings bringing in gold, incense, and myrrh. There is a Man Whose steps a multitude is found to tread in unweariedly, and Who, while out of sight, is traced by a crowd in every spot of His former dwelling-place—on His Mother's lap, on the lake's shore, on the mountain-top, in the valley beneath the olives, in the lonely wilderness. There is One Man dead and buried, Whose sleep and Whose rising is watched, Whose every word vibrates yet and brings forth more than love—the virtues that spring from love. There is One Man Who ages since hung from a gibbet, and daily millions of worshippers take Him down from that throne, kneel before Him, and without blushing at their humiliation, kiss His bleeding Feet with unquenchable love. There is One Man, scourged, crucified, killed, raised through His wondrous Passion from death and shame to the glory of an unfailing love, which finds peace, joy, and

ecstasy in Him.   There is One Man Who, pursued to
His death and the grave by undying hate, and Who,
requiring Apostles and Martyrs from every generation
as it springs up, finds them everywhere.   There is
One Man, and One only, Who has for ever established
His Love on earth, and that Man, O my Jesus, it is
Thou ! Thou Who hast vouchsafed to baptize me, to
consecrate me to Thy Love, and Whose very Name
at this moment as I speak burns within my heart, and
brings forth these tones which overwhelm me, and
which I myself knew not to be in me !"[1]

"Truly," says Montalembert, "he did not recognise
those tones, nor we either ! for none of us had ever
heard the like, and none who heard them that day can
ever forget them !   None can ever forget those days
when every high, and pure, and noble fibre of their
heart quivered beneath his living words ; when there
burst from the heart of the priest, as from the rock
touched with the rod of the Lord, that pure
impetuous torrent, overflowing, irresistible, as an
Alpine torrent ! . . . . How can we ever reproduce his
lightning glance, the magic tones of his voice, the
power of that action which filled up speech ?   Who
can venture to describe the unexpected turns, the
bold strokes, the tender touches, the sudden bursts
of a talent which has never been surpassed in France,
save by Bossuet ; which literally carried away his

[1] Conferences, xxxix.

audience, and left them under an emotion which can only be expressed by that word liable to so much commonplace degradation—ravishment, but which to the Christian suggests memories of S. Paul: *Quoniam raptus est in paradisum?* Yes indeed, like S. Paul and his two noble countrymen S. Bernard and Bossuet, this humble Burgundian priest of our own times was verily a prince of the Word—*Quoniam ipse erat dux verbi.* He knew the way to men's hearts; he assaulted, convicted, subdued them, not by the mere ordinary and transient admiration which genius excites, but by that mysterious power which belongs to human words when they spring from unearthly sources, and take shape in that priestly eloquence which Lacordaire carried to perfection, and of which he fathomed the most hidden secrets."

Montalembert, however, was no mere blind worshipper of his friend's talent. He gives force to his exceeding admiration by the vigour of the criticism, which he is not afraid to utter boldly. Lacordaire was sometimes incomplete, he says, and did not always keep sufficiently clear of declamation. At times, even Montalembert does not hesitate to say, he disturbed his more logical hearers by putting forward the objections he was about to deal with more forcibly than the answers to the same; he often lacked simplicity of style (a quality in which Montalembert's own beautiful writing is so pre-eminent), and his literary and historical resources were not extensive or always accurate. "His classical reading seemed limited to 'De Viris' and Cornelius Nepos," Montalembert goes on to say, " and to the slender stores of his childhood. Yet he was obstinately, persistently devoted to the classics; mythology, Greek and Roman history, were an inexhaustible treasury in his estimation. No one in our days ever so used and abused Brutus and Socrates, Epaminondas and Scipio! He had gathered to himself a little private literary stock,[1] from which he could never part, and which, indeed, he often put to a marvellous good use, though, generally speaking, he was not sparing enough in handling it. His taste, great and noble as it was, was not irreproachable." I purposely dwell upon these criticisms, because the very fact of their existence proves the genuine reality of the feeling which in spite of them Lacordaire's eloquence excited in one so capable as a judge.

One side there is connected with his most remarkable history which must never be forgotten while the wonders of his eloquence are before us, carrying away all before it. It is difficult to separate Lacordaire from his pulpit life, and yet there was meanwhile a man, so unlike the popular idea of the great preacher,

[1] "Il s'était fait ainsi un petit bagage littéraire, dont il ne se séparait jamais."

one so humble amid his overwhelming successes,[1] so prostrate with the sense of his own weakness, so sternly rigid to his own frail body and earthly mind, as almost to strike those admitted to look behind the curtain dumb with reverence and awe. Among the detractors always eager to soil the reputation of any real greatness, some were found who delighted to spread reports of Lacordaire's supposed vanity, of the eagerness with which he looked out for applause; carrying their inventions so far as actually to affirm that after his Conferences he would disguise himself and mix with the outer world, in order to drink in his own praise !

We will leave his companion Père Chocarne to describe how these days, these "grandes journées de Notre Dame," as he calls them, were really spent : "He used to remain during the morning in deep meditation. No one ever ventured into his room, except one or two of his most intimate friends, who might just look in to see that he wanted nothing; but they crept silently in and out, glad to do anything for him, but cautious not to disturb him. He breakfasted alone at nine o'clock, leaving off *maigre* diet on these exceptional days, but his meal was nevertheless most

---

[1] "Un jour, quand on me lira, si on me lit un jour, on cherchera curieusement dans les coins de phrases quelques allusions aux choses du temps, et on sera surpris de trouver si peu ce que le vulgaire aura cru si abondant " (January 10, 1850).

simple. In fine weather he would go into the garden and stroll quietly about, pausing before a flower, delighting in the greensward as it caught the light; refreshing his soul with the sight of God's glories in creation as a sort of prelude wherewith to kindle his soul. At eleven o'clock he used to go forth, generally accompanied by his friend Cartier. About three P.M. he would come back, broken down with fatigue, but his countenance shining, his brow lit up, his soul all akindle and overflowing with faith, love, eloquence. Sometimes he would recruit his exhausted powers by going to bed, letting a young layman for whom he had a special affection sit by him, and so they would talk at length of the love of Christ and the blessings of the religious life. At supper-time his meal was brought to him; precisely the same as that of the rest of the Community—two eggs and some salad. And then he would resume the conversation, which always turned upon the Love of our Lord, the love of suffering, and the like. He seldom if ever spoke of his Conferences, and if any one spoke of them in commendation, he did not answer, though sometimes he was ready enough to ask his intimate friends to tell him where they were defective. The young man alluded to above told him one Sunday evening that some people thought he studied effect in his action, and that he planned certain pauses with care in order to excite the thrill of admiration which was sure to ensue. The Father seemed surprised, and, after a moment's thought, owned that he had never thought about it. 'So I have very little exterior signs of humility,' he said; 'but after all, am I really as humble as I ought to be?' 'No, Father, not yet.' 'It is true,' he replied; 'but I will work hard to become so, and you, *cher ami*, must help me!' . . . The day always ended with severe scourging, notwithstanding his fatigue and exhaustion. . . . This was the energetic reaction of will by which Lacordaire kept himself from slipping downwards amid his dazzling success."[1]

Throughout it was the same. Perhaps no more touching incident in his brilliant, exciting career could be found than one told of his station at Lyons in the Lent of 1845, which was almost more successful, more wonderful in the enthusiasm it aroused than any previous occasion. Nothing of the kind had ever been witnessed in that busy city; it was described as a "very delirium." By five o'clock in the morning crowds gathered round the doors of the Cathedral, and the moment they were opened every seat was occupied, and there men, grave business men, intellectual men, artists—the very *élite* of the population, in short—were content to sit seven and eight hours waiting in order to secure the brief hour of Christian eloquence which at last was afforded them. One night, after such a scene as this, when even the reverence instinctive to

[1] Chocarne, Vie Intime, ii. 76.

God's House had scarcely refrained his listeners from clamorous applause, the hour of supper arrived, and Lacordaire did not appear. He was waited for a while, but as he did not come, he who was so notoriously punctual in all his habits, at last a messenger went to his room. He knocked, no answer; thereupon he entered, and found Lacordaire at the foot of his crucifix, his face buried in his hands, absorbed in prayer broken with many sobs. The friend went anxiously up to him, asking, " What is the matter, *mon Père ?* " " I am frightened," was the answer amid many tears. " Frightened, Father, of what ? " " I am frightened at all this success ! "

It was that same spring, May 1845, that Lacordaire made a pilgrimage to Ars, in order to see and hear the venerable Curé of that place, M. Vianney. A crowd surrounding the church hailed his white Dominican robe enthusiastically, and was soon edified at seeing him listening humbly and attentively to the aged saint of Ars, who himself remarked to a friend, " Shall I tell you what struck me when Père Làcordaire came here ? He who is greatest in wisdom has come to humble himself before the lowliest and most ignorant; the two extremes meet ! "

Lacordaire was exceedingly moved by the warmth and beauty of the old man's simple sermon on the Holy Spirit, and he spoke of it recurringly afterwards, adding, " Though our manner of expression might be different, I am thankful to know that we feel the same." The orator had heard the saint, but in his turn M. Vianney would fain hear Lacordaire, and accordingly he gave out that at Vespers "*on dirait mieux que lui.*" Lacordaire could not but do as he was asked, though, as he said, he came to hear, not to be heard; and in his sermon he spoke so lovingly and with such veneration of the grand old Curé, that the Ars people were quite proud and delighted. "Did you hear how the great preacher put himself down far below our Curé?" they went about asking one another. When Lacordaire left, M. Vianney accompanied him some distance, and at their final separation there was a moment of pathetic contest, each of those two remarkable men asking the other's blessing. It behoved the elder man to yield and bless the younger, which he did, Lacordaire kneeling in the road before him, the tears in the eyes of both. "I am quite shy of my own pulpit," the Curé d'Ars said afterwards; "I feel like that man who, having met the Pope and lent him his horse, never dared mount it again himself!"

VIII.

CHALAIS—PERSONAL INFLUENCE, 1848—THE REPUBLIC—POLITICS.

WE must return to the year 1844, when, during his Lent station at Grenoble, Lacordaire became possessed of an old convent, formerly the Chartreuse de Chalais. It was a large, rambling, dilapidated building on a sunny mountain plateau, looking on one side down upon the lovely valley of Graisivaudan, and on the other towards Lyons, the Rhone, and the Saone; originally founded by some Benedictines, who ultimately handed it over to the Carthusians, with whom it became a sort of *dépendance* to their great convent the Grande Chartreuse hard by. During the Revolution the property had been taken and sold in the name of the nation, and now, with the full consent and approbation of the Bishop of Grenoble, Mgr. de Bruillard, Lacordaire bought it for his rising Order. He describes his taking possession as follows : " Together with a few young Religious from Bosco we started for the dear mountain Chalais. We left our carriage at the foot of the hill, and it took us three hours' hard walking to get to the top. We arrived at sunset, weary, hungry, without any provisions or furniture, nothing save each his Breviary. Fortunately the farmers who were giving up the place had not yet left, indeed we reckoned on this. They made a good fire, and we gathered cheerfully at a table where some soup and a dish of potatoes satisfied our hunger. We slept soundly on straw, and the next morning daybreak enabled us duly to admire the magnificent retreat God had given us. The house was poor, the church, with its thick mediæval walls, had been used as a barn ; but what grand woods surrounded us, what rocks were lifted up above us, what meadows with their mountain flowers ! Time was wanted to get things into order, but it was easy to bear privation amid such natural beauty, and the recent ruin had not effaced the memories of olden times. . . . The bell which the Benedictines and Carthusians had used still hung in its pine-covered *flèche*, and the same clock which had struck their hours of prayer now summoned us to our offices." This establishment was not made without considerable difficulties. The Ministre des Cultes had a remarkable faculty for interposing his interference wherever Lacordaire struck root, and the impertinence of his letters to the venerable Mgr. de Bruillard might have produced a serious hindrance but for the Bishop's calm indifference. He was eighty-two then, but as vigorous as any younger man, and by the union of a judicious silence and resolution he defeated M. Martin's opposition. In fact the Government of that day was very glad to do whatever it could by means of intimidation, but it was not prepared for actual violence, and Lacordaire felt that he was at once strong with his footing on the *Charte*, and also as fighting the cause of all religious liberty.

Leaving Chalais for Nancy, Lacordaire passed, among other places, through his native town, Dijon, where for the first time he preached, to his intense emotion and pleasure. A gratifying circumstance befell him there, the Bishop of Langres, who had been one of his strong opponents, inviting him warmly to his house and his cathedral. "He received me with open arms, no reconciliation was ever more thoroughly and gracefully made." At Nancy Lacordaire was called upon to preach a funeral oration over his old friend Mgr. de Janson, August 28, 1844. The late Bishop of Nancy had always been one of his staunchest supporters, and deserved the encomium bestowed on him as "one of the first to build afresh the ancient Church of France on her fresh foundations."[1] It was at this time too that he for the first time printed some of his Notre Dame Conferences, having, as he wrote to Mme. Swetchine, "formed the monstrous resolution to bring out a volume every year, till I have gone

[1] Oraison Funèbre, p. 119.

through the whole doctrinal series, after which you
may do what you will with me as far as this life goes !
Perhaps you will be inclined to suppose that this work,
if it be one, will have neither head nor tail, but you
are quite as wrong as it is possible to be ! Be it
known to you, on the contrary, that it is systematic,
so systematic that I am surprised at it myself, for I
have not tried very much to make it so. The Conferences of 1835 treat of the Church : the need of her ;
her constitution ; her authority, rational, moral, and
infallible ; her headship ; her connection with temporal
things : this is the foundation. 1836 treats of the
sources of the Church's doctrine ; tradition, Holy
Scripture, reason and faith, as the natural results.
From the teaching authority we come to the question
of the doctrines taught. So going on, I shall treat of
its results on the soul, nature, society, and arrive at
last at the articles of faith. It is a beautiful course ;
it will be quite complete, a sort of little Summa for the
nineteenth century. I see what you are afraid of.
You remember the old newspaper reports, and ask if
all that rubbish is to be brought out again ? Pray,
give me credit for a little more sense than that. In
addition to those reports, I have my notes, my own
recollections, all of which blend together ; I polish up,
I renew the tints, perhaps I prune away some little
youthful shoots, and together with the greatest possible
faithfulness, you will have something respectable and

tidy. . . . I have long fancied that I should let all these *débris* take their chance, and then in my old age perhaps write a book about all that I have been thinking of through life. But as one grows older one finds out that we cannot shape our destinies at will, and that we must give ourselves up to the leadings of God. Since it has been His Will that my thoughts should touch the public by means of speech, why should I take away their simple natural character? Sooner or later these scattered pages would have been put together, and I was ashamed at the prospect, for reading them over, my self-merit was grievously damaged by their many faults. So in ten years, *chère amie*, I have unconsciously prepared a tolerably complete work, which I am now beginning to publish. Perhaps it may not be finished for another ten years, there may be many interruptions; but I have great confidence that God will suffer it to be completed. I feel His blessing this year like an overflowing ocean, everything succeeds. Yet all the same, holiness progresses slowly; the head is easier to perfect than the heart. I languish in the valleys, albeit every day the horizon of truth is opened wider before me. Oh, how hard it is to become holy! I am at a loss to understand why God makes the use of me He does, or seems to do, for I may deceive myself even about that!"

In 1845 Lacordaire obtained permission to transfer the French Novitiate from Bosco to Chalais, and, August 8th, the festival of transference took place. As far as was possible, henceforth the founder's time was spent there. " I wish I might never have to leave Chalais again. God knows that my happiness would be to pass my life with you there," he writes; " but it is necessary for the work that I should move, and whenever I make arrangements to stay at home, God is sure to overthrow them." When at Chalais, or indeed in any house of the Order, Lacordaire was foremost in the strict observance of every rule. His punctuality was always absolute. His brethren tell how once he and one other were the only occupants of the newly-opened Dominican house at Toulouse through Lent, all the other members being out preaching. The two kept all Community rules most precisely, but one day the other Religious overslept himself, and instead of calling Lacordaire at three A.M. for Matins, did not appear till four o'clock. Lacordaire remonstrated, " *Avant tout la règle !* " but when the same thing happened again the next morning, he exclaimed, " My dear fellow, the Community can never work at this rate! I must be wakesman myself in future !" Great men are apt to think themselves privileged to do things after their own fashion, and at their own time, but Lacordaire subjected himself to every detail of regular duty as a matter of course. He was fond of saying, " Do your day's work, plough your furrow, finish your own affairs;" and he certainly did so himself. Every day at ten o'clock he used to sit down to his letters for two hours, by the end of which a pile all sealed and directed might generally be found on the corner of his table; he never neglected this. Sometimes coming home after an absence, an enormous heap of correspondence would be awaiting him, and then that was always his first care. Without any rest he would sit down at his writing-table and give himself up to answering letters—many very long, and in his close, neat hand-writing, in which rarely a word was erased or altered —and by the next day the arrears were all cleared away. His habit of having a fixed time for every-thing, and of keeping accurately to it, enabled him to get through a most enormous amount of work, and any unwonted increase never seemed to worry him or make him irritable. He never infringed on the fixed hours of devotion or sleep for any pressure of work, he simply seemed to work harder and with more despatch; and at such times he used to join his brethren at recreation with a bright eye and cheer-ful smile, like one who sought refreshment after extra tension of brain. Those who assisted frequently at his Mass say they could not help being struck with the exceeding reverence and thoughtfulness with which it was always said; routine and daily custom seemed quite unable to deaden the solemnity of the act to him. He might always have been celebrating his first Mass, it was said by one of his brethren. Nor would he ever occupy himself with saying offices, or any other devotion than the Mass itself; and when during his busiest time at Sorèze he was asked why he did not say his office during the school High Mass, he replied that "Mass was too high and holy an act for anything save that which the priest was doing and saying to fill the mind." He always gave some time after saying Mass to the study of Holy Scripture, which with the Summa were the only books that might always be found on his table. At the close of his life he said to some of his Sorèze children, " I have been studying the Bible for thirty years, and every day I discover new light and new depth in it. Men's thoughts are soon fathomed and exhausted, but God's Word is a boundless fountain." And he writes, "How I pity unbelievers as they grow old ! Light grows so full, so precious, so piercing as one approaches death under the auspices of faith and holiness rooted in the Gospel. One ceases to *believe* merely ; one *sees*. Just as the mystery of darkness thickens round a soul that has not faith, and everything becomes darker and more doubtful to him, so light spreads and surrounds more and more the soul which habitually lives in God. When I read the Gospel, every word seems a light and a blessing on my path."

The New Testament was his favourite study, and S. John and S. Paul, the Apostle of Love and the Preacher of the Cross, his favourite teachers. He did not give much time, indeed he could not possibly have it to give, to general reading. Frivolous reading he despised, what he called "*niaiseries de salon.*" Homer, Plutarch, Cicero, Plato, S. Augustine, S. Teresa, Bossuet, and Pascal, these were the substantial authors in whom he delighted, and he used to say they were enough for any one! His love of order and neatness has already been alluded to. His room was always arranged in the most orderly fashion. He could not endure the slightest disorder. "Never mind whether anybody sees it or not," he used to say, "the angels see it." Then, when circumstances permitted, he would work for hours with a passionate enjoyment of the labour which was all done in and for God, so that he used to become so enrapt in it that those who entered were often awestruck, as in the presence of one very near God, in very close communion with Him. To those privileged to see him in this familiar attitude, he was full of the most tender, pathetic kindness, albeit to the outer world he often seemed cold and hard. No one could resist the charm of his personal intercourse who came into close contact with him. Whatever pleased him was instantly and thankfully referred to Him from Whom all good comes : whatever brought sorrow or indignation might for a moment bring a cloud over his fine face, and he would look inexpressibly sad ; but that soon passed away, and he saw God's Hand even in that which troubled him. No vein of bitterness or harshness ever crossed him. " He had none of that humility which refuses to see its own talent and merit, above all, that humility which is for ever producing itself in this respect to all comers," says Père Chocarne. " He had no hesitation in acknowledging the gifts he possessed, and considered himself as neither better nor worse for them." He used to say that " humility does not consist in hiding one's gifts or graces, or thinking oneself worse and inferior to what one really is, but in realising thoroughly wherein we are deficient, in not being puffed up by what we may be, remembering that it is all the free gift of God, and that even with all His gifts we are infinitely small and poor. It is noteworthy that great holiness inevitably produces humility." Lacordaire's conventual humility, if we may be allowed the expression, was like that of all his great forerunners in the religious life, founded upon His lowliness Who made Himself the Servant of all. He was always seeking to take upon himself little acts of service towards others ; in themselves nothing, but acquiring a meaning as expressing the feeling of brotherhood and perfect meekness. Many little anecdotes are told of his services in kitchen and refectory—how he would wash his brethren's feet or clean their shoes, or wait upon a stranger at table —trifling in themselves, but, as expressing a tone of mind, full of meaning. One of his great pleasures at Chalais was to go out on a woodcutting expedition with the novices, when with his axe Lacordaire would "do as good a day's work as any man, and marshal his forces like a general at the head of his army."

During all these years he was moulding many men to their Christian career with a downright severity, which was before all others lavished upon himself. We shrink from entering upon the details of his secret asceticism; such hidden things seem scarcely fit to be dragged into the light of day, and discussed by all —those who are utterly incapable of understanding the great soul which found strength and refuge in asceticism, as well as those who may look on in reverential wonder. But this is quite plain, that the only thing which enabled Lacordaire to keep the attitude of loving humility and self-abnegation which he so wonderfully preserved through the success which, as we have seen, "frightened" him, and in spite of a passionate, eager, overflowing natural temperament, was precisely that asceticism of which we, less gifted, weaker in every conceivable way, are altogether unqualified to judge. To such of his disciples as a similar dealing was applicable, to men of a like, or rather we should say of a far-off, resemblance to his vigour and power, he freely and heartily dealt out the same treatment, in many cases most successfully. The volume of his "Letters to Young Men," published by Henri Perreyve after his death, is itself a treasure-house of manly, straight-forward counsel, full of strength and power, often humorous and playful, always plain and practical. He did not by any means look upon the religious life as the one point towards which all men were to be driven ; witness the following letter to a young friend seeking counsel as to his course :—

" October 3, 1846.

"I will tell you at once what I think about the changed circumstances of your position. I do not think you can decide on quitting the world, and refuse the advantages offered you. Your duty to your family and the debt of gratitude you owe your friend are sacred. It seems to be God's Will to frustrate all your plans and keep you in the world ; and even if you cannot perceive what is His aim, it would be difficult not to perceive a proof of His Will in all these occurrences, to which you must submit. Perhaps you will serve Him better in the world than under the monk's habit. It seems to me evident that you must accept the offers made to you, and apply yourself steadily to your worldly career without persisting more in a plan to which God's Providence has set so many obstacles."

To another he writes :—

" *November* 7, 1849.

"Your letter indicates progress, at least in frankness and sincerity towards me.   It is only by dint of time, by earnest watchfulness over yourself, by prayer, reading, meditation, the Sacraments, works of penitence and charity, that you will succeed in uprooting the evil propensities of your character, pride especially.   Thus you need to watch yourself very particularly in recreation, and see whether you are really seeking to give pleasure or only to make a show and shine ?   Kindness in intercourse with other men is the brightness of life.   A mind which takes thought for others, avoiding whatever gives them pain, which sacrifices itself, never holds back out of pride or temper—such a mind is that of a Christian, and the delight of all who come in contact with it.   Make yourself to be loved, for men are only loved for their goodness.   As to meditation, I think your best course is to listen to what is read, and seek therein material for reflection.   The dwelling on truth, self-application, as loving as possible, this is the essence of meditation.   Do not be disheartened by dryness ; feeling is a consolation, but the strict fulfilment of duty is the true source of all interior gain. Meditation, even if ill performed, will at last bring about an increase of spiritual life if it is persevered in ; if you do not attain perfection in it, you at least may acquire the habit of its first essentials, which are reading and thought. . . . As to penitence, do nothing which will be noticed by others, not that one need fear to be known as penitent, but because whatever goes off the ordinary lines is not fit for all men, and also because we should not suffer ourselves to be thought more holy than we are. . . . You can easily practise some penitential observances without notice. . . . Make an interior offering of yourself to God for any humiliation and pain He may see fit to send you; think on Our Lord's Passion, and apply it to yourself, specially on Fridays. Meditation on His Sufferings is the groundwork of all holiness. . . . Read two chapters of Holy Scripture daily. . . . Kneel down a moment in preparation. You must learn to value every word of that Book before all else, and to prize human writings only in so far as they approach its tone. If you could learn the Psalms and S. Paul's Epistles by heart, it would be a great gain to your soul. I should not advise you to enlarge the circle of your philosophic studies, but rather to retrench and circumscribe it. The strength of knowledge is concentration. Learn to meditate upon a few lines of even a second-rate author, nothing is really useful unless it is fertilised by medi-tation. A wide field of reading often puzzles the mind, and if you happen to have a good memory, it may dazzle others, but it does not ensure depth or solidity Depth involves extent, but extent does not necessarily mean depth."

"Whatever you do," he writes to another young man, June 10, 1850, "do it steadily and perseveringly. I would rather that you read nothing than see you take to reading casually."

Lacordaire's element was among young men; with them he was easy, expansive, full of warmth and friendliness, and his power of attracting and preserving their confidence was great. He looked upon himself as "the Apostle of youth," and accepted the office as his appointed lot. Certainly it was not from sparing their foibles and weaknesses, with which he could deal in the freest possible way without hurting or giving offence. To one we find him writing: "You are lukewarm and careless towards God. Prayer, communion, penitence, devotional habits, all that gladdens and uplifts the soul is almost strange to you. You have no regular system; . . . you do not love Jesus Christ as your best friend, ready to seek Him everywhere, to give all for Him as He has given all for you. The Crucified Lord does not speak to your soul, and outweigh your sinful longings. And then what is left? Nought. You wander without light or warmth. . . . My poor fellow, this is your condition, and it will only cease when you give yourself wholly to God. It is not necessary for you to become a priest or a Religious. Not so; you will find it possible to love God tenderly and heartily everywhere. But you must really *will* it, and to that end you must have some fixed rule of intercourse with Him. . . . You are vain, *mon cher ami;* you like what is 'showy; you are proud of your horse and your groom ; you want to be a fine fellow, and admired; you are proud of your position ; in short, you are a small creature full of all manner of vanities, of which perhaps you yourself are unconscious ! Nobody needs to humble himself and to be humiliated more than you do. You see how I speak to you ; it is because I love you, and would go through a great deal to win you to the true Love of God. You are cold naturally, but there is something behind in your heart."

To Henri Perreyve, who was one of Lacordaire's most chosen friends and disciples, he writes :—

"*April* 22, 1852.

"You have dangers ahead; and it is in you to make many mistakes, but your faults will be generous ones, I hope, and God forgives these, for He loves generosity. During the last four years I have seen many things which have disgusted me with mankind, but you are a bright hope for the future. Nevertheless learn to be temperate if you would be stable. Impetuosity and exaggeration often lead to astounding falls, whereas temperate ideas and acts easily maintain their stedfastness. Above all things be kindly; kindliness is a grace very near the likeness of God, and one which disarms men above all else. You have its stamp upon your soul, but such furrows can never be ploughed too deep; your lips and your eyes are not yet as charitable as they might be, and no art can give them this gift save a culture of interior kindliness. Gentle, charitable thoughts of others gradually stamp the countenance, and help it to win hearts."

Except in his own Order and among these young men, Lacordaire undertook but little personal direction of souls. His life was too active and his journeys too perpetual to fit in well with that kind of work. In the few exceptional cases, he seems to have waged unremitting war upon indolence, self-indulgence, and vanity; and the few women under his direction were urged to read steadily and substantially, to undertake good works in a persevering spirit, and to seek their happiness without the world's code of pleasure. Distinguished birth or position were in his eyes only an additional call to humility of heart and practice, and little as we possess of his instructions to this class, there is enough to indicate that the women he directed needed brave, simple hearts and stedfastness of purpose. It was thus that amid his many duties, public and private, the comparatively calm years from 1843 to 1848 passed by. Another Revolution was shortly to open out new issues to him.

Advent 1847 found Lacordaire preaching at Toulon

and Marseilles, and on February 11, 1848, he delivered a remarkable funeral oration upon O'Connell. This was practically the beginning of what may be called his political life, and concerning it Montalembert himself puts the question whether his friend throughout that always displayed a safe and solid judgment? answering in the negative, while he adds, "When a political mistake or change of opinion has been wholly free of all unworthy motive, all selfish fear, all mean jealousy, and all sordid interest, a man need not blush to own it."

"He had foreseen the storm," another of his friends says, "and was neither astonished nor overwhelmed when the popular movement broke out in which not the throne merely, as in 1830, but the monarchy itself was overthrown. He was not a republican partisan, as many have thought and said : he always expressed his preference for a constitutional monarchy; like many others, he may have believed in the future triumph of democracy, but he was never a democrat. He was a Liberal from his birth, he lived and died faithful to this flag, which he carried independently of all parties and all forms of government."

"I intend to live and die a penitent Catholic and an impenitent Liberal," were his own words, addressed some years later to the *Cercle Catholique;*[1] and while

---

[1] "Je compte vivre et mourir en pénitent catholique, et en libéral impénitent."

never drawing back from this affirmation, he frequently protested against being called a democrat : " I have always been puzzled by the way some people persist in speaking of my political position, because I have never said a word or written a line which could indicate the smallest tendency to what is called the Republican party. All my political system may be reduced to this, that outside Christianity no society is possible unless it be a social state struggling between the despotism of one and the despotism of many ; and further, that Christianity can never regain its empire in the world save by a hearty struggle in which it is neither oppressor nor oppressed. There I take my stand, and I have nothing to say to anything else."   " But," he writes to a friend, January 10, 1850, " I might cry on the housetops that I am no democrat, and people would only insist the more that I am ! "[1]   Now, February 1848, he had little faith in the new Republic, but he did not feel justified in refusing such support as his adhesion might give, hoping to obtain from it at least that

[1] Yet even Montalembert says of him, " Né démocrate, il ne lui en a pas coûté de croire, avec tous les hommes sensés de ce siècle, au triomphe inévitable de la démocratie ; mais il n'en avait épousé ni les tendances outrées, ni les mauvaises querelles. Comme la plupart des vrais liberaux, il était assez indifférent aux questions dynastiques, et même, jusqu'à un certain point, aux formes gouvernementales ; mais ses préférences demeurèrent toujours acquises à la monarchie tempérée."

religious freedom which the recent *régimes* had failed to grant freely. And with this intention he suffered himself to be drawn into the struggles of the hour, and took part in the editing of a daily paper, the *Ère Nouvelle*, no longer out of youthful enthusiasm and hope, but as a duty which was out of keeping with his personal inclinations. He wrote to Mme. Swetchine, March 16, 1848: "My ideas, thank God, have taken full shape, and time will see them carried out. Above all things, one must lay aside fear, and not shrink back from any duty. This is perhaps the first time that I make any real sacrifice for God. Up to this time whatever I have done has been in sympathy with my tastes; but at the present moment I am laying aside my own inclination, and in the fullest sense of the words, I give my life up to God as opposed to my own will. This will be the consolation if I perish, and I look upon it as the plank of my possible shipwreck. Pray for me, and forgive me for coming so seldom to you. Time has clipped its wings to fall faster!"

Speaking of this time, at the close of his career, Lacordaire says :—

"It was difficult to know what to do, because it was difficult to see what was for the best. It was not possible to re-establish a tempered Monarchy after the catastrophes of 1830 and 1848; it seemed equally impossible to set up a Republic in a country which for thirteen or fourteen centuries had been ruled by kings; but there was this difference between the two positions, that the Monarchy had fallen and the Republic was standing upright. And that which is standing has a better chance of life than that which is thrown down; while even if there was little hope of establishing the new *régime* permanently, it might at least be used as a temporary shelter, and as a means of giving France some of those institutions the lack of which had been the evident cause of the overthrow of two thrones and two dynasties. This was M. de Tocqueville's view of the matter. He was not a Republican, but if the Republic were overthrown, and especially if it were overthrown at the actual moment, he saw no hope of anything but Absolutism. It was necessary to choose between these two extremes, and every sound politician had to work on one or the other side; everything else was mere delusion. It is easy enough to see it now, but few men saw it all plainly then, and one may almost say that the greater number of good men were deluded by the phantom of a restoration of Constitutional Monarchy after a brief reign of Republicanism. I was very undecided myself. Since my earliest days I had been a partisan of Parliamentary Monarchy, I had limited my hopes and longings to that; I had no hatred either for the Bourbons or the Orleans family, and had thought of nothing more than what hopes they held out for the future liberties of our country, ready to support the one if they had been faithful to the *Charte* of 1814, or the other if they had carried out the *Charte* of 1830 fairly. If you could imagine those two houses united in giving France a Monarchy solidly founded on institutions which involved no self-contradiction, no one would have been more hearty towards them than myself. But all that was a mere dream of the present as of the past. As a follower of principle, never of party, I had always been influenced by things, not people. And whereas it is easy to follow a party, it is difficult to follow principles when one cannot be definite as to their application. As a Parliamentary Liberal, I understood my own position perfectly; as a Republican, I was not so clear. And yet it was imperatively necessary to come to a decision.

"While I was yet hesitating, the Abbé Maret and Frédéric Ozanam came to me. They said that uneasiness and uncertainty prevailed among Catholics, that all rallying-points were getting lost in what might soon be irreparable confusion; that we might easily excite hostility in the new *régime*, and so lose the chance of obtaining from it that liberty which the late Government had obstinately refused. The Republic was well disposed towards us, they said, and we had none of those cruelties and irreligious deeds which stamped the Revolution of 1830 to reproach it with. The Republic believed and hoped in us, surely we should do well not to discourage it, else what was there in prospect but ruin, and what was this Republic save the natural government of a society which has lost all its anchors and all its traditions?   My friends had still higher ulterior views drawn from the condition of European society, and the powerlessness of the Monarchy to recover solid standing-ground.   I did not go entirely with them here; a tempered Monarchy, with all its faults, always seemed to me the most desirable of governments, and I could only look upon the Republic as a necessity for the time being, which must be honestly accepted, until ideas and realities should fall naturally into a different shape.   This difference of opinion was weighty, and made it difficult for us to work together under one flag.   But the danger was urgent, and it was a moment in which it behoved one to lay aside personal feeling, unless one was able to raise one's own standard openly, and bring other lights and power to bear upon the difficulties of the period. Hitherto I had taken my definite stand in all public events; was I now to fall back into a selfish, cowardly silence because the difficulty was complicated?   True, I might say that I was a Religious, and use my habit as a shield; but I was a militant Religious, a preacher, a writer, surrounded with sympathies which involved other duties than those of a Trappist or a Carthusian. These considerations moved my conscience, and, urged by my friends to take my line, I yielded to the force of circumstances; and although I shrank from renewing my career as a journalist, I joined with them in hoisting a flag which represented at once Religion, the Republic, and Liberty."

It was thus that Lacordaire found himself once more a newspaper editor, in conjunction with the group of fervently religious men, who, as Montalembert says, believed that 1848 was indeed the beginning of a " New Era." This was the name they gave their paper, " in which they upheld the new *régime*, professing the solidarity of Christianity and Democracy with an honest but intemperate eagerness, which Lacordaire, who had so eloquently combated the traditional belief in a solidarity of Catholicism and Monarchy, did not share, but could not sufficiently control." [1]

A few days before the *Ère Nouvelle* appeared Lacordaire resumed his Notre Dame Conferences. It was February 27th when a vast multitude flocked together to hear what the most popular orator of his day would say concerning the events which were passing around him. Mgr. Affre, who had given, so to say, his vote of confidence to the Republic already, by a Pastoral Letter of February 24th, in which he praised the people for their moderation and reverence in the day of victory, was present, and Lacordaire

[1] Montalembert, p. 204.

could not refrain from apostrophising him. "Monseigneur, the Church and our country unite in thanking you for the example you have set us all during these days of great and memorable excitement. You have called us together in this Cathedral immediately after a revolution in which all seemed lost; we obeyed the call, we are here beneath this great dome; we learn that there is nothing to fear for religion or for France; both will go on their way under God's protecting Hand; both thank you for having believed in their indissoluble alliance, and for having discerned these things which abide and are strengthened by the very movement of events from those which are but temporary."[1] The subject of his Conference was God—the Existence of God—and at one point Lacordaire burst forth with one of those storms of eloquence which from time to time wholly carried away every listener, and which can be but feebly rendered in any language apart from the glowing countenance and thrilling voice of the all but inspired speaker. "Let me tell you, *messieurs*, this is the first time since authority to preach God's Word was committed to me—it is, I say, the first time that I have approached this question—the existence of God —if indeed such a thing can be called a question! Hitherto I have always passed it over as useless; I thought it needless to prove to a son the existence

[1] Conferences, xlv.

of his Father, and that he who knew it not was unworthy to know it. But the course of thought constrains me to touch upon it; and yet while making such a concession to the logical order of things, I would not have you think that I held it a need for your hearts, or the heart of the people and the age to which we belong. Thanks be to God, we believe in Him; and if I could doubt your faith, you would rise up to thrust me forth; the very doors of this Cathedral would burst open to cast me out, and the people would need but one glance to confound me, that people who even now, in the midst of the excitement of power, after overthrowing generations of kings, yet bore in submissive hands, and as belonging to their triumph, the likeness of the Son of God made man."

At this point the popular feeling could not control itself, and there were loud bursts of involuntary applause. Lacordaire turned calmly to the people: "Do not applaud God's Word—believe it, love it, fulfil it; this is the only acclamation which will rise up to Heaven, or which is worthy to do so."

His allusion, so happily made, was to an incident of February 24th, when the mob had taken possession of the Tuileries, and was throwing furniture, etc., out of the windows. A young man, member of the Conference of Saint Vincent de Paul, hurried to the chapel, fearing that it would be profaned. He found it had already been invaded, and the vestments were tossed about, but the altar was untouched (Mass had been said there that mornfng). Summoning to his aid some National Guards and two students of the École Polytechnique, they took the holy vessels and the Crucifix, and proceeded by the Place du Carrousel towards Saint Roch. Attacked by some of the excited mob, one of the party held the Crucifix aloft, exclaiming, " You want regeneration—you can only have it through Christ ! " There was a cry, " Yes ! yes ! He is Master of all ! " And heads were bared to the cry of " Vive le Christ ! " while a procession followed the young men to Saint Roch, where the Curé came forth to meet them, and the mob asked his blessing. He spoke a few timely words, which were respectfully listened to, and the cry rose up, " We love the *bon Dieu*, we want religion ; it must be respected. Vive la Liberté ! Vive la Religion et Pio Nono ! " [1] Very different indeed was the religious aspect of things during this Revolution of 1848 to what we have unhappily seen since.

For a time the *Ère Nouvelle* prospered ; the circulation was between eight and ten thousand daily, a large number then ; the Archbishop publicly sanctioned it, and the talent of its editors made it popular. Lacordaire defended the *Budget des Cultes*, the suppression of which was sought in a series of powerful

[1] *Ami de la Religion*, No. du Mardi, February 29, 1848

articles. Frédéric Ozanam put forth some very remarkable papers on Divorce. "We sell as many as
ten thousand copies in the streets sometimes," Lacordaire wrote (June 30, 1848) to Mme. Swetchine,
"and fresh subscribers come in fast. At the same
time there is a vast increase of wrath against us,
and heaps of anonymous letters. It is a downright battle, the most amusing thing imaginable, albeit
very serious. One set of people write, 'Yours is the
best newspaper going,' and the others cry out, 'It is
atrocious, horrible, *sans-culotte!*' Let one do what
one may, there is no leading a quiet life here below,
chère amie!"

"The difficulty of this work," he wrote a little later,
"is to combine the religious and political spirit; that
is, the spirit of charity and peace with the thing which
of all others produces the most deadly hatred and
most terrible divisions. If you visit the sick, the
poor, the prisoner, Christianity is all right, everybody
understands it. But if you apply Christianity to
politics, a yell is raised at once; impartiality is called
weakness; pity, treachery; gentleness, a wish to stand
well with all the world. Nothing so easy as the *parti
pris* of faction; nothing so hard as justice towards
factions."

After a while Lacordaire saw that it would be well
for him to withdraw; his own interests and those of
his fellow-editors, who wished the paper to take a

more decidedly democratic line, required it.[1] He had never been prepared to go as far as they did, and now, when financial reasons involved a new arrangement as to the proprietorship of the newspaper, he gave up the direction. "Everything has been friendly," he said, September 7, 1848, writing from Chalais. "I never intended to remain at the head of the management, nothing would be more contrary to my tastes, I may say to my duties. So far from my withdrawal damaging the paper, I think it will give strength, by making its position more definite, and allowing of a more decided tone. In every case I am satisfied, being convinced that I have done my duty, alike in establishing and in leaving the *Ère Nouvelle.* I have considered the past six months as in God's Sight; and not to speak of the mere errors of detail, I think that under these trying circumstances I have done what religion and patriotism required of me. My vocation was never political, and yet it was impossible to avoid coming into temporary contact with these great perils, were it merely through a mistaken self-devotion, or to gain a sad experience. This I have now gained, and without any serious loss. You cannot think how restful it is to me, or how much more clearly I see what God requires of

---

[1] "Ce journal va bien au delà de mes pensées en fait de démocratie, et tous ses rédacteurs savent combien j'ai combattu pour le maintenir dans une ligne plus réservée."

me henceforward. Even if I should have lost ground in men's esteem, what does that matter if I have not lost ground in God's sight? This retirement cost me less than it would have cost many, because I have been so accustomed to live very much apart, in limited intercourse with a few souls, animated by intercourse with God." He left Ozanam, in whom he had such absolute confidence, although their opinions were not always precisely parallel, at the head of the newspaper, and hastened to leave Paris, in order, as he said, "to put the seal to it all. Rapidity is not precipitate hurry. I had consulted Montalembert and other friends, I had arranged every minutest detail, and it was easy, when the moment came, to depart like the swallows."

But the *Ère Nouvelle* was not the only startling political feature of this Revolution in which Lacordaire had his share. Three Bishops and twenty priests were elected members of the Constituent Assembly, and not unnaturally Lacordaire was one of the first representatives desired by the Catholic party. He never came forward as a candidate anywhere, but seven or eight constituencies put him forward. The *comité d'arrondissement* in which he lived asked him to be present at two meetings, and answer certain questions. "So I went to the amphitheatre of the École de Médicine and to the great *salle* of the Sorbonne, and at both places I declared freely that I was not a *républicain de la veille*, as the expression of the day is, but a simple *républicain du lendemain*.[1]   At the first place I had a great success; at the Sorbonne there was an excitement and commotion from without."

In spite of vigorous opposition, Lacordaire registered 62,000 votes in Paris, and also a very large number at Toulon, where he had lately been preaching an Advent course, and was known and liked; but it was Marseilles which had the honour of returning him as its member.   He had only once been there for a few days in the previous month of January, after his visit to Toulon; but the single sermon he had preached had aroused a paroxysm of sympathy, and several large deputations had brought him addresses.   The members of the Catholic Club had conducted him enthusiastically to the point of departure, and the Duc de Sabran, as their mouthpiece, urged his speedy return.   A little later he was invited to establish a Dominican house in the town.   Commissioned by such a constituency, Lacordaire took his place in the Assembly, May 4, 1848, seating himself at the upper end of the first left cross seats.   This, as he himself said afterwards, was a mistake.   " I was too young a republican to take so marked a place," he said, "and the Republic itself was too new to deserve so marked a token of adherence."   He quickly

---

[1] This may probably be best translated as not so much a republican by conviction as one of action.

perceived the error and altered his position. The *Univers* of the day wrote concerning this event: " Yesterday was a great day for Père Lacordaire, for the Church, whose minister he is, and for the religious Orders, whose most popular representative he is among us. The Dominican entered the National Assembly, whither he has been called by the free suffrage of two hundred thousand Frenchmen. He was clothed in the white Friar's robe which he has restored among us. His election was confirmed without the slightest opposition, and his monk's dress did not arouse the sound of complaint in the Assembly, where, notwithstanding, M. Dupin and M. Isambert were to be found. More than this: when the whole Assembly moved to the peristyle of the Palais Bourbon, there to proclaim the Republic in presence of the people and the Garde Nationale, Père Lacordaire went with the Abbé de Cazalés, Grand Vicaire of Montauban, down to the railing, which was besieged by the surging masses of the Parisian crowd, which crowd saluted the eloquent Religious with wild acclamations. He shook hands with numerous citizens and National Guards, and was brought back in a sort of triumph to the door of the Assembly. When the House dispersed, leaving it by the Rue de Bourgogne, the orator had to cross the ranks of a company of the Tenth Legion, who again raised the cry of ' Vive le Père Lacordaire ! ' From this day we may say the oppressive laws against which we have so long contended—laws which have been brought to bear on men's consciences, upon all freedom of self-devotion and penitence, by various successive despotisms—are practically abrogated. They have fallen to the ground, and have received their death-stroke from the monk's courage and the people's sympathy. The Second Republic has thus repaired one of the most odious iniquities of its predecessor."

Lacordaire's career as a member was of the briefest. Ten days only were his term of office. During those days he spoke twice, not successfully, Montalembert says. From the first he seems to have felt keenly that he was not in his right place, and that this surging ocean of political excitement was not the sphere in which his life ought to be dedicated to God. On May 15th an irruption of the mob told its own story as to the position of the Assembly relatively to the country, and "for three hours," Lacordaire wrote, "we remained defenceless in presence of a scene where no blood indeed was shed, and where it may be no great danger was incurred, but in which there was all the more loss of honour and dignity. The people (if the people it really was) outraged their representatives merely to prove that they had them at their mercy. . . . During those weary hours one solitary thought kept for ever repeating itself in my brain—monotonous, implacable—'The Republic is lost !' " " I saw him sitting motionless, imperturbable, in his place," Montalembert says, " pointed out by his white robe as a mark for insult to the mob. The next day he sent in his resignation; he had recognised that his temperament, at once so impetuous and so thoughtful, was not adapted to the daily storms of parliamentary life." [1]

He knew well beforehand that he would be accused of inconsistency, want of judgment, even want of courage; but these trifling annoyances were more than compensated by the sense of duty fulfilled. " One must learn," he said, " to be lowered in man's sight, that one may rise in that of God." His letter to the electors des Bouches-du-Rhone, who he felt might justly complain, is a striking one :—

" Yesterday I resigned the seat with which you had honoured me. I restore it after but a fortnight's occupation, and without having done anything of that which you expected of me. My letter to the President of the National Assembly will already have explained the causes of my retirement; but I must needs say something more detailed to you who selected me, and conferred upon me the highest mark of esteem it was in your power to give me. You reckoned upon me, and I have failed you ; you counted on my speaking, and I have scarcely entered the tribune ; you relied on my courage, and I have

[1] Montalembert, p. 205.

run no risks; surely you have every right to question me, and I feel a need to forestall your questions.

" I felt within me two men—the Religious and the citizen. It was impossible to separate them; it was essential that each, as united in me, should be worthy of the other, and that no act of the citizen should ever do any hurt to the conscience of the Religious. But, as I advanced in this wholly novel career, I saw parties and passions more clearly marked out. Vainly I strove to maintain my own line of superiority to their vibrations; the necessary equilibrium was beyond my power to preserve. I speedily realised that in a political Assembly impartiality eventuates in powerlessness and isolation, that one must needs choose one's side and throw oneself into it headlong. This I could not bring myself to do. Thenceforth my retirement was inevitable, and I have effected it. God knows, *messieurs*, that the one thing which hindered my determination was the thought of you. I feared to wound you, I grieved to break in this speedy and unforeseen manner links which I had so gladly contracted. My chief consolation is the remembrance that during the very brief term of my political life I have acted upon a conscientious inspiration akin to your own. Elected without my own seeking, I accepted in the spirit of self-devotion, I have sat without passion, I have withdrawn from fear of not being that which I would always be in

God's Sight and in yours. My resignation, like my acceptance of the seat, is a homage which I pay to you."

In a private letter of May 28th, Lacordaire says: "My position in the Assembly had become intolerable to me; I could not keep free of Democracy, and yet I could not accept such Democracy as surrounded me. All my own convictions and circumstances drew me one way, and the actual facts surrounding me forced me another. And after all, what is a man without any special standing-ground or clearly-defined line? Resignation has cut this Gordian knot, but not without a great inward struggle. It is very hard to seem inconsistent and vacillating, but it is harder still to resist one's own conscientious instincts. So at last I took the upper hand, and now I am writing quite calmly. . . . I should never have expected to have such a horror of political life; you would hardly credit the degree to which it has arisen. I found out that I was merely a poor ordinary monk, and not at all a Richelieu; a poor monk who delights in peace and quiet."

In reply to some criticism, he writes again, June 6th: "You may rely upon it that hereafter my retirement from the Assembly will be one of the things most approved in my life. But anyhow, however that may be, one must look at duty, not the world's

opinion.   One of the most real virtues a man can
perform is to do his duty subject to the risk of being
blamed.   Just now I feel like some one who was perish-
ing in an abyss into which he had fallen, and who has
been miraculously extricated.   I have received some
most touching letters from this point of view, but
generally my act seems to have caused an unpleasant
impression.   Few people look into the future.   I
have written a few letters in self-justification to some
friends, but it is better to wait and let time be my
justification.   How often I have been misjudged!
If you knew all that has been said of me in various
salons and other places, you would be dumbfoundered!
It is best to let all such storms pass by without letting
them disturb one.   Moreover, solitude is a safeguard
to me which increases in value as time goes on.   It
brings me untold peace.   I am never unhappy save
when I hesitate what course to take; at all such
times I suffer greatly from uncertainty first of all,
and then from apprehensions of what may occur; but
once my resolution is taken, I become calm and at
rest."

It was really the calm after the storm, and from
this time Lacordaire never mixed again in public life.
How confirmed he must have been in the wisdom
of his decision, as the events of that exciting summer
followed on!   There are but few letters of this period,
and only one slight allusion to the noble martyr-

death of Mgr. Affre on the barricade of June 25th.
It is in a letter to Mme. de la Tour du Pin, dated
July 2, 1848: "I go to-morrow to Chalais for a
fortnight, a necessary visit which I have delayed in
the hope of something like a tranquil state of things
in Paris. I must take advantage of this interval of
peace, which, alas! may possibly only be too short.
You know the terrible details of these last days.
God has preserved us, and the death of this good
Archbishop of Paris is a warrant that He will save
us in the future. Pio Nono living, and Mgr. Affre in
his martyr's death, are a forecast of future days of
mercy and resurrection. This is my firm hope."[1]

[1] It is almost too well known to need repetition how Mgr.
Affre went forth to his death. Ozanam, Cornudet, Bailly, and
others who were serving as National Guards during these days of
civil war, believed that if the Archbishop would undertake the
office of mediator, the strife might be allayed. They went to
him, he received them gently and kindly, replying that he had
already thought of the course himself, but he knew not how to
carry it out? Would Cavaignac permit such a step? and how
could he be reached? After a short discussion the Archbishop
said, "almost submissively," that he would go. At that moment
a priest came in, greatly excited with the terrible details he had
just witnessed. The Archbishop listened with emotion, but would
not be dissuaded from his intention. He was soon ready, but
then there was a further request made, that he would wear his
purple cassock and his archiepiscopal cross. Mgr. Affre assented
at once. His passage from the Île Saint Louis to the Assembly
is described as a sort of triumphal march : the troops, National
Guards, and Garde Mobile presented arms, every one uncovered ;

To Mme. de la Tour du Pin :—

"CHALAIS, *September* 10, 1848.

". . . It is with nations as with men ; misfortune is their education, provided their intelligence and their heart are worth anything. And France is too generous, too enlightened, possessing too much faith and charity not to profit by the teaching God is

there seemed an instinctive consciousness afloat that the Archbishop had come forth on a mighty mission. General Cavaignac received them "with respect and admiration ; " gave him a proclamation for the insurgents, and a promise to spare them if they would at once lay down their arms. At the same time he explained to the Archbishop on what a perilous mission he was entering, and how General Bréa, sent on parley, had just been seized by the insurgents. But Mgr. Affre could not be deterred from his work of mercy, and his heroic "*J'irai !*" will never be forgotten while the memory of good men lives. The three friends, Ozanam, Cornudet, and Bailly, wanted to go with him, but this he absolutely refused to permit; and as they still followed him at the Pont des Saints Pères he bade them leave him, as their uniform gave them the look of being an escort. They sorrowfully obeyed. The rest is soon told. Mgr. Affre went home, took a little food, made his last confession, as fully expecting death, and then set off for the Faubourg Sainte Antoine, accompanied by his Grand Vicaire, the Abbé Jacquemet. As they went he repeated several times the words, "The Good Shepherd giveth His life for the sheep." At the Place de la Bastille, M. Brèchemin, a young man who followed them, tied his white handkerchief to the branch of a tree, and preceded the Archbishop to the first barricade. The venerable man got up on the barricade, holding out the promise of mercy : there was a shot fired from a window, and, mortally wounded, he fell, exclaiming, "May mine be the last blood shed !" ("*Que mon sang soit le dernier versé!*")

dealing out so largely to her now. She has her saints who are praying for her and will save her. You are somewhat of these, if you will suffer me to say so, and I say it quite seriously. We have each and all our own power in God's Kingdom, and however feeble we may be individually, collectively we can do great things. And therefore it is that I have

(See Vie F. Ozanam, p. 447.) Dr. Neale's stirring poem on the subject is less known than it ought to be :—

.   .   .   .

Who come towards the barricade with steady steps and slow?
With prayers and tears, and blessings to aid them as they go?
Among the armed no armour the little cohort boasts,
Their leader is their Prelate, their trust the Lord of Hosts.
And the brave Archbishop tells them in voice most sweet and deep
How the Good Shepherd layeth down His life to save the sheep;
How some short years of grief and tears were no great price to give,
That peace might come from discord and bid these rebels live:
Rebels so precious in His Eyes, that He, Whose word is fate,
Alone could make, alone redeem, alone regenerate!

One moment's lull of firing, and near and nearer goes
That candidate for martyrdom to the midmost of his foes:
And on he went, with love unspent, toward the rifled line,
As calm in faith, in sight of death, as in his church's shrine:
And the war closed deadlier round him, and more savage rose the cheer,
And the bullets whistled past him, but still he knew no fear:
And calmer grew his visage, and brighter grew his eye,
He could not save his people, for his people he could die:
And following in the holy steps of Him that harrowed hell,
By death crushed death, by falling upraised the men that fell.
They bear him from his passion, for the prize of peace is won;
His warfare is accomplished, his Godlike errand run;
They kneel before his litter, in the midst of hottest strife;
They ask his prayers, the uttermost, who gave for them his life.
So, offering up his sacrifice to God with free accord,
The city's Martyr Bishop went home to see his Lord!

.   .   .   .

great confidence in the future, far greater than I had in the last reign.   Then one was forced to believe in the success of egoism and corruption ; now that dreary belief is swept away.   We are certain that France will not tolerate the rule of a materialistic government or caste, and this conviction is my greatest hope.   There is nothing in the world that I should not think preferable to the triumph of such times and doctrines as those of '30 to '48.   Better suffer than decay.   You see I am nowhere near converted !   I shall always be a poor solitary man, weather-beaten, struggling with the difficulties and delights of solitude. That is the enigma of my whole career ; I have never had any party on my side, because I have never belonged to any party.   I have been obliged to make my way through indifference and repulsion, with God alone, and some few friends He has given me, on my side. . . . Chalais is a blessing which fills my heart, nature and grace dispute which shall do the most for it.   I am writing on a delicious evening, with a clear calm sky, trees, corn-fields, woods, rocks, valleys, all lit up softly by the moon, all breathing peace divine. The thought of you touches me deeply, because I know how much sorrow I cause you by all the complications of my life.   Probably it will be my lot to the end."

Lacordaire's review and forecast of the political

situation, as expressed to Mme. Swetchine, September 15, 1848, is interesting : " You are right, *chère amie*, the horizon is darkening *à vue d'œil*, although the elements of strength and security are great in Paris since the June days, and there is a strong bent in men's minds towards the truth. But there are such divers elements around, such balance among passions and parties, so little that is fresh for use in the minds of our leaders, that one can hardly imagine how any fixed order is to come out of it all without a struggle which should definitely eliminate some of all these incompatible elements. Our society is composed of three ruins, a resurrection, and a chimera. The three ruins are the Empire, the Restoration, and the Revolution of '30 ; the resurrection is the Conventional Republic ; the chimera is Socialism. Throw into the bargain an almost universal religious ignorance, a heap of antichristian prejudices, an overwhelming terror of truth in what pertains to God, and you have the sum-total of our troubles. But, mind you, there are three things for us : the light produced by this desperate accumulation of ruin and disorder ; the holiness of a multitude of souls who have preserved an unequalled faith ; the state of the Church which claims some quite extraordinary help from God. So you may lay it down as an axiom that we shall be saved. . . . How, when, by whom ? It would be a very welcome prophecy to make, but these things are only known at the last moment. It is evident that we must pass through a mighty struggle to which June is a mere prelude. I say it is manifest, because in the moral as well as physical order of things, when irreconcilable materials meet and accumulate, explosion must follow. So it will surely come, though what will be the issue is God's secret. If the Republic fails, Henri V. is the inevitable presumptive heir. I do not say so that you may bespeak me in such case a Court chaplaincy! for the experience I have had of political life will last me a thousand years and a day! You cannot imagine how thankful I am to have escaped that danger, especially having done in all faith and conscience all that I could during the emergency. If I had entirely abstained, it would have been a prudence bordering on selfishness; as it is, by jumping into the fire I burned myself a little, but all the same, I acquired a right not to be quite reduced to ashes, and to drop some little oil upon my wounds. If it were not that God overruled the whole matter, I should think myself rather a deep kind of man! Look here, when the whole thing has tumbled to pieces—Assembly, Republic, and Constitution—people will say, '*Ma foi!* that Father was sharper than we were! he foresaw it!' Ah, *chère amie*, we cannot laugh in such serious times! But we can take comfort in the blessed certainties of our faith. Nothing in this world is greater than the Christian edifice ; God has made all else small, and we are like a great living cathedral in the midst of a waste solitude. If God takes pity on the remnant of our life, we shall see before we die the wonders of His Right Hand ; we shall have trusted Him alike in the sorrows of darkness and the joy of light. One of my troubles in Paris was lest death should come upon me away from my brethren, disguised as a journalist ! But under this age-worn, consecrated roof, at my post, among my own people, the storm, should it reach hither, whether it brings ruin, exile, or death, will be but the end of a fair pilgrimage."

IX.

PRIVATE LIFE—THE *COUP-D'ÉTAT*—FLAVIGNY—OULLINS—TOULOUSE—LAST CONFERENCES.

FROM this time Lacordaire's public life ceased, and for the remaining years which were given him he never suffered politics to engross his mind. His friend and biographer Montalembert explains, while regretting, the line of opinion he expressed upon the Italian question, concerning which the former says, " He did not perceive at once the dangers which were evident and inseparable from the line of the Italian patriots.   The sacred and most legitimate aim they set before them of freeing Italy from foreign rule cast a veil over the immorality of the means they employed in her emancipation."   He had ceased to read the newspapers, and his sympathies with a national cause were rather ideal than based on deliberate facts. Ten days before his death Lacordaire dictated a letter to M. Guizot (it was apparently the last he ever dictated) which is interesting as characteristic of both men :—

SORÈZE, *November* 2, 1861.

"MONSIEUR ET CHER CONFRÈRE,—I had just finished reading your work on the Church and Christian Society in 1861, when I received a second copy sent to me by yourself as well as your note of October 29th. These tokens of your kindness were all the more acceptable that I was still enjoying the pleasant impressions left on my mind by your book. It is a great light shed by a great authority. Naturally I cannot agree with you on the theological question of Protestantism, and I should also make a reservation on the Italian question up to the moment when Piedmont invaded the Neapolitan States, and that part of the States of the Church which had remained in full obedience to the Pope. This seems to me the limit where justification ceased to be possible, and where the Italian Revolution assumed a character of violence, conquest, and usurpation. As to the great outlines of your work, the errors and merits of our day, that which has been wanting to us in success and in defeat, the necessity of religious liberty honestly carried out for the good of the State and of all Christian communities; as to the difference between the liberal and the revolutionary mind; as to our fears and hopes for the future, I accept your thoughts as the only ones whereby the world and the Church are to be saved. You must have undergone many attacks in consequence, *monsieur et très honoré confrère*, but you have long been accustomed to this, and one can never hope to serve mankind without being exposed to their ingratitude. My health, to which you kindly allude, is very frail, and makes me envy your fine old age, which has suffered nothing from the long and arduous work you have undergone.

(Signed by himself.)

"FR. HENRI DOMINIQUE LACORDAIRE."

I have anticipated somewhat in quoting this letter in order not to return to political matters. Henceforward the interests of religion, as more especially connected with his Order, were to occupy and absorb Lacordaire's attention. In the autumn of that same 1848 he was at Dijon, in compliance with the Bishop's urgent request, preaching the Advent Station; and some of the clergy of the diocese, who possessed the old Benedictine Convent of Flavigny, about fifteen miles from Dijon, offered it to him for an establishment of Dominicans. The climate was less severe than that of Chalais, and Lacordaire was glad to remove his novices thither; but the beginning was humble. "At first we had but seven chairs in the house; everybody carried his own with him wherever he went—from his cell to the refectory, from the refectory to the *salle de récréation*, and so on. One person brought us a sack of potatoes, another of turnips ; flour, wine, oil ; all the population of Flavigny was friendly and helpful. But this did not last long. A committee of clergy and laity was formed at Dijon under the Bishop's presidency, which guaranteed us certain help for a time." How plainly Lacordaire anticipated the turn events were soon to take is evident from the same letter which describes the foundation of Flavigny to Mme. Swetchine, in which he says (December 14, 1848) : "Louis Napoleon has had an overwhelming majority here, and in the whole department, and I hear the same thing from the neighbouring departments. It seems to me quite certain that we shall have him as President, and as the Presidential position would destroy him in six months, it appears to me only probable that his party will speedily push him higher, all the rather that the rights of the National Assembly, now that it has accomplished the Constitution, are very questionable. So another Assembly will be called with the object of re-establishing the throne on behalf of the Napoleonic dynasty ; subject to the resistance of Republicans of all shades, and of such fortuitous events as are known only to God's Providence. I voted for General Cavaignac, so as to be clear of all the evils probably involved in such a combination."

The new Archbishop, Mgr. Sibour, wrote cordially to Lacordaire, speaking with gratitude of his work hitherto at Notre Dame, and desiring that it might continue ;' accordingly, in Lent 1849, the important series of Conferences on Man's Intercourse with God was given. The three first of these, on Man's Supernatural Intercourse with God, are very wonderful in their clearness and power ; the three next concern Prophecy, and the seventh and last is upon the Blessed Sacrament. Apparently Mgr. Sibour was well satisfied with the continuation of the work, for during that spring he privately proposed to Lacordaire that the former Carmelite convent in the Rue de Vaugirard should be made use of for a Dominican Community. While negotiations for this work were pending, the Archbishop, together with the well-known Abbé Gerbet—since Bishop of Perpignan—proposed the establishment of a religious newspaper, in which he asked Lacordaire's co-operation. But "I would promise no assistance, direct or indirect," he says. "After two attempts, and with plenty else to do, I feel justified, without selfishness, in keeping aloof." Accordingly, November 4, 1849, Mgr. Sibour formally installed the Dominicans in the proposed convent, and while a numerous gathering assisted at the ceremony, there was no opposition even from the hostile press. Churchmen fondly hoped in those days that religious liberty was a thing really and permanently

¹ "Ce digne archevêque a conquis en quelques semaines une popularité qui est encore un des phénomènes remarquables de ce temps" (À Mme. de la Tour du Pin, November 21, 1848).

established in France. When M. de Falloux was able to bring in a *projet de loi* for freedom of instruction, supported by such men as Montalembert, Cousin, Dupanloup, Thiers, Laurentie, Dubois, etc., Catholics and Universitarians (as they were called) united; so that March 15, 1850, saw free instruction become the law of the land. Alas for the present day, when under the insulted name of Liberty, religious instruction has more than ceased to be the law of France!

As soon as he was established in the Rue de Vaugirard, Lacordaire began a regular course of preaching of a simpler character than his Notre Dame Conferences, given every Sunday during Mass. This proved most useful, and was greatly valued. "Only fancy," he wrote, November 29, 1849, "I have turned into a Curé! Every Sunday after the Gospel I preach for half an hour on that same Gospel for the day. Our church is full, and people seem to think that this sort of thing will do as much good, perhaps more than the Notre Dame Conferences."

In July 1850 the Pope appointed Père Jandel, one of Lacordaire's earliest colleagues, to the important post of General of the Dominicans, a tribute to their work which was highly prized by their founder in France, without a moment's surprise that he himself had not been selected. "It is the most welcome reward for all my labours," he writes, July 19, 1850, to Mme. Swetchine. ". . . Père Jandel is myself, without any of the drawbacks to myself; and I have but one mind in the matter, hearty gratitude." That September Lacordaire went to Rome to promote the canonical erection of a French Dominican province, which was accordingly done, and on the 15th September 1850 the act was signed which confirmed that province in its rights and privileges, Lacordaire being the Provincial. Writing from Genoa on his journey, he alludes to his occupying the same hotel where in 1831 he had been with de la Mennais and Montalembert, adding plaintively, "Alas! the three pilgrims have been widely separated since then, and will never meet again save, as we may humbly hope, in the presence of God;" and in another letter of nearly the same date he says, "All those with whom I hoped to work harmoniously have taken paths so far apart from mine that I grow more and more what David calls a sparrow alone upon the housetop!"

Yet in spite of such passing melancholy, Lacordaire was active and happy in his work. In 1850 his Conferences in Notre Dame had been a continuation of the last subject—The Fall and Restoration of Man; and in 1851 he went on, treating the Providential Economy of Man's Restoration. "There was nothing visible to make him foresee that the pulpit he had so long and so honourably occupied would henceforward be closed to him," Montalembert says; "and yet, as though moved by some hidden presentiment which he shrank from even admitting, he involuntarily closed the Station by a solemn farewell, which is remarkable as containing a sort of *résumé* of his past life, and as being one of the rare occasions on which Lacordaire brought his own history upon the scene."

" Twenty-seven years ago," he said, in opening the Conference,[1] "when God restored to me the light which I had forfeited, He likewise inspired me with the wish to consecrate myself to Him in the sacred ministry, and henceforward my uppermost thought was the conviction that innumerable men were estranged from Christianity solely because they knew it not ; and that they knew it not because no one had taught them. I remembered my own boyish days, and how little was given me when once I left my home ; and I marvelled that in the heart of a Christian country souls should be left to grow up to manhood with no more religious teaching than some three months' catechising when they are mere children. I resolved if God gave me life, strength, and gifts, to do whatever in me lay towards repairing this pitiable defect of education among a civilised nation. Ten years from the time when I cherished this hope— perhaps overbold on my part—I was summoned to this pulpit by Mgr. de Quélen, the first, kindest, truest protector of my youth. Separated as he was

[1] Conferences, lxxiii.

R

from me by many opinions, surrounded by men who were unfriendly to me, he sheltered me with an affection at once generous and fatherly, and despite my faults and my foes, he never withdrew the kindly hand which he had laid upon my head at my ordination. Now that he is gone from among us, and that seventeen years have confirmed this work which he began, I cannot review the course we have travelled without a grateful memory of him, without offering the public tribute of a son to a father. I was thirty-three when the office of teaching you the Faith from this pulpit was committed to me; of teaching it after the way most adapted to your mental attitude, to the instincts of the century, and the importance of the place whence the instruction issued. Was I sufficiently prepared for the task or not? I cannot tell—God knows. When I recall the years which had preceded this Notre Dame period, my childhood's faith, my youthful denial thereof, the keen, unexpected restoration which cast me suddenly from out the aberrations of civil life into the calm of the priestly career; then after a long and studious interval the turn of events which brought me all at once face to face with public opinion; it seems to me that the Lord's Hand had led me, and that in appearing before you I was obeying His call." Towards the conclusion of the Conference Lacordaire takes up again this thread: " This is our hope and our faith; here I leave you, here where dogma ends, and truth demands of you in return for her light, holiness of life. It may be that God's Providence will suffer me to open this second issue ·before you ; I alike fear and wish it. I fear from mistrust of myself; I wish it because I love you. But even if a fresh career should be opened by God's Will to my interest in you, I cannot now refrain from speaking as though I were taking leave of you. Suffer me to do so, not as a presentiment, but as a consolation. A consolation, because I experience two opposite feelings—one of joy in having accomplished a work which has forwarded the salvation of some, and that in a century which has been called the century of abortions ; the other of sadness, as I realise that no man can accomplish any work without leaving the best part of himself behind him in it—the firstfruits of his strength and the flower of his days. Dante begins his great poem by saying—

> ' Nel mezzo del cammin di nostea vita
> Mi ritrovai per una selva oscura.' [1]

I too, *messieurs*, have reached that middle stage of life's journey in which a man lays aside the last thought of youth, and descends rapidly to the shores of helplessness and forgetfulness. I ask no better, for it is

---

[1] " In the midway of this our mortal life
 I found me in a gloomy wood, astray,
 Gone from the path direct."
>   CARY'S *Dante*, *Inferno*, i.

the lot which a merciful Providence provides ; but at least at this marked dividing-point, whence I can yet once more behold that which is wellnigh ended, you will not grudge me the delight of looking back, and of calling to mind with you, my companions, some of the memories which make both yourselves and this Cathedral so dear to me.　It was here, when my soul was brought back to God's Light, that my sins were forgiven and put away, and at that altar my lips, strengthened and cleansed, received for the second time the Lord Who had come to me before in my early youth.　It was here that by degrees I rose to the priesthood, and that after long wanderings seeking after my hidden calling, it was revealed to me in this pulpit, which for seventeen years you have sur rounded with silent respect.　It was here that after a voluntary exile I brought back the religious habit which for half a century bigotry had driven forth, and that before an assembly, formidable alike in number and quality, it won the triumph of unanimous reverence.　It was here that the day after a revolution, when the very pavement was yet strewed with *débris* of the throne and with warlike symbols, you gathered to hearken to that Word which alone can survive all ruin, from my mouth ; and that, carried away by an emotion which none could control, that Word was saluted by your applause.　Here, close beneath that altar, rest my two first Archbishops ; he who called me in my youth to teach you, and he who summoned me back to the charge, when mistrust of my own power had caused me to retire. Here, on this same archiepiscopal throne, I have found a third pontiff with the like kindly heart. In a word, it is here that every affection which has gladdened my life has arisen, and that I, a solitary man, unknown to the mighty, estranged from all parties, alone among the crowds which gather together, have found souls to love me. O ye walls of Notre Dame, sacred walls, which have borne my words to so many souls which were without God in the world; altars which have blessed me, I am not taking leave of you, I do but say what ye have been to me, and overflow within myself at the memory of your gifts, even as the children of Israel when in exile sang the song of Sion. And you, *messieurs*, already a numerous generation, in whom I may have planted truth and holiness, I shall abide one with you in the future as in the past; but if the day should come when my strength refuses the demand of my will, if you should cease to welcome the voice that once was dear to you, know that you will never be ungrateful, for nothing henceforth can ever hinder you from having been the glory of my life or the crown of my eternity."

Lacordaire's presentiment, for such it surely was, was a true one. He never preached again in Notre Dame. After the *Coup-d'État* of December 2, 1851, he was only once again heard in Paris on any occasion of public note, and that was February 10, 1853, when he preached on behalf of the Écoles Chrétiennes at Saint Roch, the same church where his first unsuccessful sermon had been preached. Though apparently without cause, there was great susceptibility in high quarters about this sermon, which was preached before the Archbishop of Paris and Cardinal Donnet. His concluding words—"Let us bring up Christians in our schools, but before all else, let us train up Christians within our own hearts. Children of Christ, be as great as your Father, be generous as the Cross on which He bore you. The world may not acknowledge you, but suffering souls will seek you; they will learn the beauty and power of Christianity from you, and whatsoever age or soil may be your lot, you will be of those who uphold reverence for God and for man, the two great sources which combine to save the world"—would seem to us absolutely true and harmless; but "from this day forth," Montalembert says,[1] "it be-

[1] Lacordaire wrote, January 3, 1852, "Our country is lost unless it restores religion. You, dear child, are called to work for this regeneration, and the thought must be your consolation, or at least it must give you strength to endure. For myself, I feel an indescribable joy in the witness of my heart, that for twenty-seven years, since the day of my consecration to God, I have never spoken a word or written a sentence which had not as its aim to give to France the spirit of life, and to give it in a form that would be acceptable; that is to say, mingled with meekness, temperance, and patriotism. You will some day do

came impossible for Lacordaire to preach in Paris," although it would appear that the Archbishop more than once invited him to do so.

In May 1851, Lacordaire's valued friend Mme. de la Tour du Pin died, and we find him writing to the friend who had been as her second self: " You know how I loved and esteemed her who for twenty years had been one of the powers of my life by the loftiness of her spirit, her deep sympathy, and her wonderful self-devotion. I know all that you have lost, since I myself have felt its worth. But however sore the separations of this world, we always have Him Who is its Author left to us, He Who gives and Who takes away, Who will never fail us, and in Whom we shall all one day be reunited by the faith and love which He has given us. He will not forsake you, nor leave you lonely here ; for He has balm for every wound, even for those which seem as a bottomless gulf. Cast yourself wholly upon Him, and so in loving hope find her again whom you have lost. . . . Adieu ! May God help us both, you and me, to end this life well ! "

Lacordaire left Paris soon after these events to visit

the like. Prepare yourself by a constant control over yourself and your passions. If there is no good day in store for our country, at least there is God's own day in store for our individual souls ; for your soul and mine, which God has knit together in spite of the difference of our age, because it is the privilege of Divine Love to know no measure by time."

the various Communities of Dominicans which were under his charge as Provincial. "There is nothing tragical about my departure from France or the interruption of my Conferences at Notre Dame," he wrote from Ghent, February 2, 1852. "At a moment when both tribune and press are silent, I, as well as many of my friends, have felt that any strongly liberal and Christian utterance might lead to serious mishaps, whether through friends or foes of the new powers that be ; and therefore I determined on being silent, as the safest and most honest course. . . . This resolution once made, I preferred leaving France, on the one hand not to be exposed to all manner of contradictory observations, and on the other to use the first scrap of leisure I have had for long in visiting our houses in Belgium, Holland, England, and Ireland."

Lacordaire's visit to England was too brief to give him much acquaintance with our country. He writes to a young friend from

"HINCKLEY, *March* 7, 1852.

"This is a little town in Leicestershire, where we have a convent and a few fathers. I got here last night, after two days in London, during which I saw no one, in order to give myself up to seeing the town, which is large, and has some very fine parts, but which strikes me as inferior to Paris in several respects. Its very size neutralises its beauty; it becomes merely an interminable pile of houses, without harmony, without any connection; and when these houses are all in cold straight lines, as in most parts of London, their vastness is a wearisome weight, which gives no pleasure to mind or body. The finest part of London is happily enclosed in a quarter which is spacious without being overwhelming, and where parks, palaces, spacious streets, Westminster Abbey, the Houses of Parliament, and the Thames combine admirably. I shall enjoy seeing it all again as I return."

From Oxford he writes :—

" March 16, 1852.

"After ten days (among the Dominican houses) I came here alone to rest, and write quietly to those I love. What a beautiful charming place this Oxford is! Imagine a plain surrounded by hills and watered by two rivers, in which you find a whole heap of Gothic and Greek monuments; churches, colleges, courts, porches, scattered profusely, but gracefully, in quiet streets, ending in trees and meadows. All these buildings devoted to literature and science are open; the stranger enters them as a home, and they are truly the home of beauty for all who can appreciate it. You cross silent quadrangles, meeting no one save here and there a young fellow in cap and gown;

there is no crowd, no noise; the air seems solemn, like the age-stained walls around, and it seems as if they never made any repairs for fear of sinning against antiquity. Nevertheless there is an exquisite cleanliness everywhere supreme. I never saw so much apparent ruin with so much preservation. In Italy the buildings seem young; here time leaves its stamp, but without dilapidation, and after a majestic fashion. This town is small, and yet it is grand; the number of public buildings takes the place of mere size, and makes it imposing. How I longed for you as I went about solitary, amid all these men of your age! Not one who knew me or cared about me; I was for all of them absolutely nothing at all, and often the tears came into my eyes, thinking how many friendly faces I should have met elsewhere. London has some splendid quarters, but as a whole its uniformity is depressing; and it has an immense insignificance, which deprives it of the gracefulness of a well-turned-out thing! The population, though lively, scarcely conceals great poverty; nothing can be greater than this people in its institutions, nothing meaner than its appearance in the streets."

To Mme. Swetchine he wrote :—

"OXFORD, *March* 16, 1852.

"I got here yesterday alone, and feeling quite lost, but with a childish delight at finding a quiet town

that is not smoky, but all full of literary interests;
Gothic and modern buildings, with an inconceivable
number of quadrangles and cloisters, where here and
there one meets young students in a very quaint little
cap and gown. I am delighted to pace these quiet
streets, these beautiful river-lapped avenues, and I
never remember seeing anything that made so pleasant
an impression on me. I can quite conceive that the
young fellows brought up here can never forget it, and
must retain an ever-increasing affection for the place.
We have nothing like it in France; the University
means to us nothing but a College—that is to say, four
walls, with five or six professors and as many tutors.
Here the University is a world in itself, and a very
charming world. All these colleges are open freely
to strangers, who can enter as into a home belonging
to any who love literature and art. The colleges are
large and not crowded, so that solitude adds to their
grandeur. . . . One seldom hears a word of impiety
in England; there is such a thing, but it is powerless,
vague, despised. This people possesses more liberty
and more religion than any other, yet withal an
amount of poverty which forces itself upon one in all
large towns. The population of London, which is
so lively and vigorous as a whole, is in detail most
terribly piteous to behold. I never saw such rags or
more degraded physiognomies. The Englishman, who
is so brilliant, so almost femininely beautiful in the

upper classes, is horrible to behold in the poorer throng. Christianity has evidently suffered, and does suffer, greatly here. Another feature of London is that you see much more of the statues and monuments of its great citizens than of its princes. Westminster Abbey, S. Paul's, and all public buildings are full of monuments raised to the memory of all manner of celebrated Englishmen, whereas we have few save in commemoration of our kings—great and small."

By the end of March Lacordaire returned to Flavigny, crossing Paris hastily to avoid seeing people; but to his great satisfaction he met M. de Montalembert in the station, and they were able to travel together for some hours, which recalled to both friends the time (1832) when they had travelled from Munich to Paris together. They discussed now, as then, a host of weighty matters. " Alas, what a mere journey this world is ! " Lacordaire writes, " and how great a blessing it will be to arrive at the end, where all will be clear and certain ! " From Flavigny Lacordaire wrote at length, explaining the motives of his withdrawal from Paris, to Mme. Swetchine. The letter is so entirely the man himself, in all his strength both of feeling and of will, and in the resolution of a powerful nature, never swerving before right, that it must be given at length.

" May 6, 1852.

" The most serious matter I have had on my hands since my return is the loosening my connection with Mgr. Sibour. Living so close to him, and receiving so much kindness from him, I have by slow degrees lost some of the independence I have hitherto always kept, and which is more than ever necessary in the position where God has placed me. As early as 1836 I felt the need of isolation, when I left Paris and went to Rome for retirement ; then the Order of S. Dominic opened the way for me to be for fourteen years absent from Paris, save the short time required for my Conferences. At the end of 1849 the foundation of our house at the Carmes inevitably recalled me to the place I had so perseveringly avoided ; but after two years' trial, I once more am convinced that the position is a false and dangerous one, that it links me with men and things whose solidarity is to my mind doubtful, and, moreover, that it involves too many calls and occupations to be consistent with the leisure I require. The Revolution of December 2, 1851, supplied a suitable opportunity for loosening these ties ; everything was changed, and the fact of Monseigneur pledging himself to a policy which I could not but disapprove, opened a wide door of separation. I could not go on working with a man who changed so quickly from one pole to the other, and in spite of my gratitude towards him, it was impossible for me consistently to remain in the personal contact with him of heretofore. Above all things I am sensitive to straightforwardness; the more I see men fail in it with respect to their religion, the more I desire, with the grace of Him Who holds all hearts in His Hand, to keep clear of whatever can possibly compromise or weaken a high Christian honour in myself. Were there but one soul which hung on mine, I should owe something to that soul; but whereas by God's Providence I have been made the link between many souls, the point to which they look for strength and consolation, I am bound to do everything in my power to spare them from falling back or from the bitterness of doubt. In a week's time I shall be fifty; for the last twenty years I have gone through numberless trials, in which I seemed likely to fail a hundred times, but this upholding hitherto of Heaven's protecting Hand does not dispense me from striving on my part to co-operate with God's goodness towards me. I can no longer continue the struggle with the inexhaustible passions of men, and I have acquired the right to use the shield of retirement. I am perfectly convinced that no party will ever support me, because nothing will ever make me pledge myself to any earthly party; I am also perfectly certain, that if I continue in a public position, I shall always invite the assault of my enemies by the *naïveté* of my feelings and the boldness of my words.   The very nature of my audience, made up as it is chiefly of youthful hearts, carries me away; I grow young when in contact with their youth, and as all deliberate preparation is an impossibility to me, I can never undertake to subject myself to these prudential rules which would absolutely fetter me.   'To be or not to be?' that is the question.   I have done a great deal in the way of public speaking, why should I be denied the ineffable comfort of a peaceful life spent in writing for God's service during the rest of my life?   Writing is never stormy, and I have had no troubles in connection with what I have written.   Not a line of my writings has ever raised any discussion, although I have dealt with the most delicate and controverted points of theology. But then in writing the mind has absolute self-control, nothing springs up between it and God in the shape of urgent expression.   By-and-by, if men read my writings, they will not understand why my career has been one of such excitement; indeed I hardly understand it myself.   I know myself to be naturally gentle, averse to extremes, given to simple and moderate opinions, and when I see all that has come forth from such a peaceful source, I am thoroughly amazed. My only explanation lies in one word—I never belonged to any party.   Why should I not henceforth reap the fruits of this solitude?   If it were a case of breaking all the chords of the lyre, I could understand that I should have no right to do so ; but if one is severed, the rest remain.   Certainly I have at times thought that in some quiet parish I might still teach souls of a less inflammable character than those with which hitherto I have dealt ; but is not all Christian morality put forth freely and with sincerity a source of provocation ?   I gave homilies in our Church des Carmes ; did they give satisfaction ?   I may grow as old as you please, but my speech will retain its natural, inartificial *fougue ;* and even if hereafter I could return to this work, I must leave it for a time. Were I to return to Paris next winter, I should be overwhelmed with pressure to preach in Notre Dame, and I should never have the courage to resist it ! From every point of view the spell must be broken, and if I am intended to take my place hereafter in humbler pulpits, people must have grown used to the idea that the work of my youthful days is ended.

" These, *chère amie,* are the motives which have determined me.   I almost feel as if God had always warned me of definite duties at the very hour they were due. In 1832 I was the first to sever myself from poor de la Mennais ; in 1836 I left the pulpit of Notre Dame at the right moment, to resume it hereafter with more authority ; in 1848 I bade farewell to my seat in the Legislature the day after that outbreak which shattered and dishonoured the Republic, and although every one was not prompt to see that it was slain, I was fortunate enough to foresee the fact ; now I withdraw before other breakers ahead, not out of cowardice or selfishness, or heedlessness of God and man, but in order to serve both more heartily in such measure as may yet be permitted me. It is in this manner that hitherto I have triumphed over the difficulties of my nature and my situation ; other men might have done better, I do according to what I feel and what I am. Forgive this long explanation. I greatly desire you to be satisfied, for however firm I am in my own convictions, the concurrence of your mind is always so much additional strength and a great consolation. Good-bye. I am going out to look at some lilac-trees which I have planted in a thicket below our convent, and which are very slow to flower."

About the same time, writing in a similar strain to Henri Perreyve, Lacordaire says (June 3, 1852) : " At no time, I can assure you, would it have been more acceptable to me to be in Paris. My spiritual family and my dearest friends are there. To pass there the rest of my life, after so much movement and so many troubles, would have been a great blessing to me, but my Dear Master will not have it so. Doubtless He saw that I loved too much, and was too much loved; and He has called me forth from the scenes amid which He has never suffered me to linger long. Many very serious and urgent calls are settling my movements at present, and although I seem free to go where I will, in truth I am simply obeying what seem to me imperative duties. When I left the Assembly in 1848, no one understood me, but now who is there that regrets that I did so? What use could I be in that collection of powerless passions, and how thankful may I not well be to God for warning me in time that my place was not there? Neither did my friends understand it, when in 1836 I gave up Notre Dame to go to Rome; and yet I returned reinforced, authorised, more fitted to perfect the work, and, moreover, in the interval, I have established a religious Order in France. Was this time lost? To-day other things call me away, and sorry as I am to leave you especially, I make the sacrifice conscientiously. That which is good does not fade away, as you say; but all pleasant things are mixed with what is bitter, and we must learn to bear the vicissitudes of enjoyment and separation. For many a long day God has moulded me to solitude, absence, loss and gain of all things; and though no stoic at heart, I am better adapted than many a man for such a storm-tossed destiny. Don't be angry with me. You are ever close to my heart as my cherished child. We shall meet from time to time; we will take the opportunities God gives us, and live upon their memories. I shall come to you, and you to me, as we may, until such time as eternity unites us to each other for ever in God's Presence. It will soon come! I am glad you are moving near our house. Is your new room larger than the last? I thought you had not air enough for your delicate chest. . . . I abhor tyranny, but if ever I am king, my first decree shall be fixing the square cubic feet necessary for a Frenchman to live in. The greed of builders will soon bring all our lodgings to the level of those famous cages in which Louis XI. used to shut up people he didn't like! People cry out at that, not seeing that in his time it was an exception, and now it is a general thing! Tell me all about your cage; whether you can stand upright, stretch yourself out at full length, and receive a friend in it—three things which in this world are very precious. I could go on about no-thing for ever, but I must say good-bye on behalf of *messieurs* the Hindoos, concerning whom, as a Catholic monk, I am reading somewhat at present."

"July 6, 1852.

"All that you say about my absence from Paris touches me deeply, save one sentence in which I cannot agree with you. You are afraid that I shall be forgotten. Alas! *cher ami*, the best thing in the world is to be forgotten by all men, save only those who love us and whom we love. All else, as they buzz around, give us more trouble than joy; and when one has finished one's task, ploughed one's furrow, be it great or small, and sowed what good seed one might therein, the happiest thing that can happen to one is to leave oneself in God's Hands and disappear. So I am no ways moved at the thought of being forgotten; I rather rejoice, and the only thing which is a cause of sorrow to me, except the separation from my friends, is the thought that perhaps I might have been useful to some youthful hearts like your own. But no man can do everything at once; what he gains at one end he loses at another, and God Alone knows how in the arms of His Mercy to embrace all times and all places."

Now that he had thus forcibly set himself free from his more public engagements, Lacordaire turned his vigorous mind to the subject which had from the first been prominent among his interests—education. He never forget how he himself had lost all Christian faith as a boy in the Lycée of Dijon, and he knew well that his own history was that of the greater part of the lads of his country. The *Universitaire* education was excellent as a technical thing, but as a matter of faith and morality he knew it to be worse than useless. Freedom of instruction had been his watchword long before he became the member of a teaching Order, and now that that freedom had been confirmed as a political fact by the law of March 15, 1850, his energies were bent on returning to the short-lived avocation of past years, and he would fain be once more a schoolmaster. But Lacordaire was too practical not to see that his rule was too ascetic for men whose life was to be spent in so exhausting an occupation as teaching; besides which their choir duties were incompatible with it, and he decided at once on founding a new branch with the more elastic rule of the Third Order. The College of Oullins gave a favourable opening for this work; it had been founded in 1833 by secular clergy, among whom was the Abbé Dauphin, a Canon of Saint Denis; and these, who entirely agreed in Lacordaire's opinions as to education, now invited his co-operation, so that the affiliation was soon accomplished. Four professors of Oullins took the Dominican habit, and on S. Thomas Aquinas' Day, July 25, 1852, the transfer was effected in the presence of a large gathering of friends and relations of the pupils.[1] He wrote the day before to Mme. Swetchine: "How I wish you could see this fine house, on a hill overlooking the Rhone, and whence you can see Lyons, the hills of Bugey, the Alps, and the plains of Dauphiny. God spoils us with giving us such beautiful sites; each one is more wondrous than the last, and sometimes it quite frightens me, I feel so unworthy of it all! God does really treat me *in*

---

[1] "Here I am," he wrote, "at fifty, with an entirely new work in hand! Ask God that it may be blessed like the rest, and give me as much comfort."

fanciullo, as a mere child.   One finds everything in Him, even tenderness, which amazes one, because it seems so undeserved !"   He had just visited Toulouse for the first time, and had taken great delight in a pilgrimage to all the places connected with the history of his founder—Montpellier; Prouille, where S. Dominic's first monastery was established, and where the church remained as in his time, and where the *Seignadon* or *Signe Dieu* is still so called, the spot indicated for building the monastery by the saint, with the sign of the Cross; Muret, where Lacordaire said Mass in the chapel where S. Dominic was praying during the battle known by its name, where the King of Aragon and the Count of Toulouse were defeated by Simon de Montfort.

That autumn Lacordaire took four novices with him to Flavigny, who were to be the foundation of the Third Order, and a religious ceremony of some importance marked its initiation. The procession wound about the woods and hills, singing, and finally a stone cross was raised on a prominent rock, in front of which Lacordaire addressed the surrounding band. "This foundation is a great burden at the close of my career," he writes (October 9, 1852), "but it offered itself so naturally, and under such favourable circumstances, that I should have felt myself resisting God's Will if I had refused to undertake it. Five young professors from Oullins join me. . . . Of course the future is uncertain, but what should we ever do here if we refuse to act without the certainty of stability for a century? The whole world is built of dust upon a volcano; but God underlies it, and gives stability where He sees fit, even amid all our upheavals and ruins. . . . God is the moving Power; He sometimes chooses to found upon a quicksand in order to prove to men that it is He Who works, not them. Besides, I am always resigned beforehand to fail in anything, and my consolation is that even in failure I may be at rest because I have done my duty, and striven for that which is right." In this spirit Lacordaire set to work at training his Third Order, becoming their Novice Master, and devoting himself to them. Three times daily he held a conference with the novices, and all day long he was accessible to them, ready to discuss, explain, and teach, as they might require. In August 1853 they returned to Oullins, where a great desire was felt to keep Lacordaire among them, but this was incompatible with his duties as Provincial. During that summer he was thoroughly carrying out his retirement from public life—expeditions with the boys from Oullins, when he piqued himself on finding the way amid the mountains and woods of Chalais and the Grande Chartreuse; some occasional preaching, such as a ' panegyric " of Fourier, the saintly priest of Mattain-court in Lorraine (the great apostle of education who in the seventeenth century founded the congregation of Notre Dame, of which he writes, " It is the first time I ever preached a panegyric. As one grows old one finds oneself doing impossible things !"), a sermon at Sens on the translation of S. Colomba's relics, and the like.

On the 8th September this year his dearly-loved friend Frédéric Ozanam died at Marseilles on his way back from Italy, where his family had vainly hoped to see his health restored. Lacordaire's notice[1] of him will strike most readers as infinitely more valuable and impressive than the lengthy, somewhat cumbrous Life published by his brother.

This autumn too was marked by the foundation of a Dominican house at Toulouse. Lacordaire writes to Mme. Swetchine, October 24, 1853 : " I go to-morrow to Toulouse, and I feel as if I were going there to my last resting-place, and should there find my grave. God could give me no nobler or more welcome one, and so it is not likely that it will be so, but I like to go there with the pleasant hope. No other foundation—and this is the sixth, includ-ing Oullins—has given me such vivid and pure pleasure. I feel as if I were going home, and as if S. Dominic and S. Thomas Aquinas were receiv-ing me in their arms. I should have liked long

---

[1] Published in the *Correspondant*, November 1853.

before this to see you, but I was afraid. The older I grow in the art of government, the more I see how necessary it is for superiors to set the example of welldoing, and never to do themselves what they would not suffer others to do. . . . The consequences of my every act follow upon me so quickly that the thought thereof makes me exceedingly cautious. And that is why you have not seen me at Fontainebleau, where I have a brother and a cousin; too many things attracted me for me to be able to go there. . . . I hear that you are suffering and sad; alas! the Cross comes sooner or later to each of us, and so far from its being averted by a holy life, that is an invitation to God to touch us with the mysterious sceptre of His Dear Son. But how much courage we need to accept it! and surely faith itself is quite as much a torch to light up our own deficiencies as to clear our way. I hardly dare say that I am continually with you in thought, for what is man as a support and comfort? Even God can sometimes hardly comfort us, such sorry creatures are we! But after all, so far as the affection, gratitude, and devotion of one creature can help another, I am present with you, and share your troubles. Remember sometimes that you have helped me, and perhaps through me many others who do not know you now, but who will know you some day."

The week before the Archbishop of Toulouse

solemnly opened the new house Lacordaire writes, December 27, 1853 : " Though for ten years I have been accustomed to receive such blessings from God, this one touches my heart more deeply than any other has done. It seems like the crown of all His graces through my life, and that there is no-thing beyond, save not for me not to prove myself too unworthy, during the remainder of my days, for all that I have received. Every time I walk in or about Toulouse I fancy how S. Dominic walked there, and comparing his life and my own, I marvel that God should have chosen one so far distant from the founder as the instrument of re-storation in France. Every Wednesday I celebrate at Saint Sernin, at the tomb of S. Thomas Aquinas, with intention for our Order and the French province in particular."

In this same letter Lacordaire alludes to the series of Conferences he had undertaken to give at Saint Sernin, and which he intended to supply what had been left imperfect in those of Notre Dame. He says that his general scheme has been made out, and that the series will occupy six years at the least, seven at longest; and he adds that he himself is satisfied with the plan, and thinks it will complete the work happily. But this was not to be. Let Montalembert's suggestive words be given : " Invited by the Archbishop of Toulouse to resume his

Conferences on behalf of the young men of that intellectual southern metropolis, Lacordaire gave early in 1854 six Conferences, the last, and I think I may safely say the most eloquent and perfect of all. He treated of Life in all its stages ; life in general, the life of the passions, moral life, supernatural life, and the influence of this last upon private and public life. At the end of the sixth Conference he announced his intention of taking as the subject of his further discourses God's established means of communicating the supernatural life to us, namely, the Sacraments ; but this last discourse had contained certain explosions of truth, grief, and pride concerning the moral degradation of the private life of nations as were not at this time seasonable. It behoved Lacordaire to give up public speaking henceforward."

The passage which gave special offence, striking as it did at the Second Empire, is as follows :—

" Let us consider what that other life, which we call *public*, is. In private life a man confronts himself; in public life he confronts a people. There it is his duties and his personal rights, his own perfection and his own happiness which demand his solicitude ; here it is the duties and rights, the perfection and the happiness of a people which preoccupy his thoughts. And inasmuch as evidently a people is more than a man, so evidently public life is superior to private life. Private life alone verges on egoism ; its very virtues, unless they aim at a higher region, are easily corrupted beneath the empire of a restricted fascination. Do you ask for proof? turn to history. It sets forth but two manner of peoples : the one moulded to public life; the other frustrated on all sides in the management of their own affairs, and kept in tutelage beneath a master who leaves them barely liberty to live without complaint beneath the shelter of the laws he gives them. Now see the consequences to these peoples of their condemnation to private life.

" All public activity being an impossibility to them, there remains no mode of raising themselves save riches, and no serious pursuit save that of wealth. The spirit of gain takes possession of souls. A man's country, the scene for great doings, becomes a mere commercial sphere. Its citizens are stockbrokers, its tribune the counter, its Capitol the Bank or the Exchange. Such a people despises literature because it does not lead to fortune ; and if nature, fertile in the very spite of men, brings forth some gifted minds, they will soon be seen, faithless to their gifts, renegades of genius, prostituting their muse, and betraying modesty and truth for the love of gold. Her poets aim rather to be financiers, and the bruit of glory is less real to them than the jingle of coin. Every post is measured by its stipend, every honour by its profit. The greatest names, if so be great names there are in such society, are appended to industrial undertakings ; and such undertakings, useful enough in their own secondary places, push adroitly to the front, whence they are not dismissed. Even those who administer the general funds do not disdain to enrich themselves like ordinary individuals. No one knows how to be poor, not even the rich. Luxury grows with cupidity; and this overflow of wants divides the people into two classes, which have nothing in common—those who enjoy everything, and those who enjoy nothing. And whereas in the country where real public life prevails, the honour of sharing in public affairs kindles a generous ambition, and puts before all men a glorious make-weight against the grovelling tendencies of human nature; here, in the people steeped in private life, nothing checks the downward course. Cupidity begins, luxury carries on, corrupt morals finish the tale. For one consequence of riches in those nations which are held, if not in servitude, yet in tutelage, is idleness, and idleness is the inevitable parent of depravity. What is a man to do with himself when there is no need to earn either fortune or bread ; when amid an abundance which averts all trouble he sees no call of responsibility which sets him to work ? Where public life is the order of the day, every rich man is, or may become, a patrician. The moment he ceases to be occupied with his personal interests, the general interests of the community present them-

selves and demand his powers and heart. He reads
in the history of his fathers of those who did honour
to a great inheritance by a great self-devotion, and if
the elevation of his own nature in any way corresponds
to the independence he has acquired or received, the
thought of serving his country opens a perspective of
sacrifice and toil. He must needs speak, write, rule
with his gifts, and sustain those gifts, however grand
in themselves, by that other power which never suffers
itself to be eclipsed with impunity, goodness. From
his earliest years the young patrician, that is, the son
of the public man, contemplates ardently the future
which awaits him before his contemporaries. He
does not despise literature, for he knows that therein
lies mental supremacy. It is combined with eloquence
and taste, the history of the world, the knowledge of
despotisms and liberties, the light shed by time, the
shadow of all great men shedding their glory upon
the soul which aims at their similitude, and bringing
together with their glorious memories courage to
follow in their steps. Literature is the palladium of
all true-hearted nations; and when Athens arose, she
had Pallas as her divinity. None save those peoples
which are on the road to extinction refuse to recognise
the value of literature, and that because, esteeming
matter beyond spirit, they cease to perceive that which
gives light, or to feel that which moves. But among living nations the culture of letters is next to religion the

greatest of public treasures, the aroma of youth, and the sword of manhood. The young patrician takes delight in and gives himself up to literature; he delights in it like Demosthenes, and gives himself to it like Cicero; and all this portraiture of what is great, while fitting him for the duties of his citizenship, also arm him against the all too precocious errors of the senses. From letters he goes on to law. Law is the second initiation into public life. If among enslaved nations it leads merely to the defence of common interests, among free nations law is the entrance-gate of creative and protective institutions. Thus amid lofty thoughts and worthy habits the national *élite* of a country is formed. If riches still produce some voluptuaries, they also make citizens. If they enervate some souls, they strengthen others. But there where the country is an empty temple, demanding nought of a man save that he pass through it silently, will arise on all sides, through a formidable idleness, energetic debauch. Whatever strength there may be left in souls will be expended on self-destruction. Empty heads bear the weight of great heritages, and worn-out hearts drag wearily after dignities no less worn out. The corruption of subjects and rulers is mutually exchanged. These last, who have neither anything to do, because all things are lawful to them, take the lead in the degradation of morals, and the whole machine treads on with a uniform step towards those regions which Providence has provided for nations unworthy to live.

"One last word. In those lands where the public, not private, life is considered, a citizen's rights are inviolable; that is to say, his property, his honour, his liberty, and his person are sheltered from all arbitrary assault, and protected alike by the sovereign legislature and invincible opinion; he is amenable solely to the law, and that no effete law, but one that resides in a magistracy itself independent of everything save duty. This absolute security, which nought save crime can ruffle, lifts up men's characters. Every one feels in himself that he is the subject of lawful government in all honourable obedience, but he also feels all-powerful against the frailties of any power whatsoever. A noble respect for public welfare, a sincere devotion to the authority which can do no wrong, spring from this self-confidence. The whole country breathes at ease upon the soil which God has given it; such misfortunes or injustice as may yet befall are no more than the inevitable accidents of human events, like to the clouds which pass across the sky sometimes in the most favoured climate.

But how far otherwise it is in those countries where private life is foremost! There the law itself bows before the caprice of a will which cannot be anticipated; the magistracy, movable and dependent, obeys other commands than those of justice; and every one, conscious that his fate lies in the hands of a single man, draws back in fear which rules and paralyses his acts, his words, even his thoughts. The people's soul becomes possessed by the lowest of passions—fear. Hypocrisy slips in behind fear to diminish it, adulation to disguise it. Between these three vices, which mutually sustain and justify each other, men's hearts grow mean, their characters degraded; nothing is left standing save slavery, nothing certain save contempt."[1]

These words were not unnaturally looked upon as having a marked reference to the *Coup-d'État* and the Second Empire, and though Montalembert says that he is not aware of any formal prohibition having been laid upon Lacordaire, there was a general feeling, in which he pre-eminently shared, that the time had come when his bold, vigorous eloquence, which had unhesitatingly spoken forth under such various *régimes* without hindrance, was no longer likely to be tolerated. The present were days of luxury and idleness, and much that Lacordaire was ever foremost to condemn; his strong, unyielding pose, "*en Libéral impénitent,*" was well known; in a great measure, too, he felt that he had done his work; the seed would surely spring up, whether men would or whether they would not, and the Chrysostom of France was henceforth silent. "I became dumb, and opened not my mouth, but it was Thy doing."

[1] Sixième Conférence de Toulouse.

T

Several years later Lacordaire said, "I left the pulpit from a spontaneous fear lest my liberty should be shackled amid a world which had lost its own;" and on his deathbed he said, "I felt that in my thought and expression, in my past, and what little remained to me of the future, I was myself at liberty, and that the time had come for me to disappear like the rest."

Lacordaire was still only fifty, and in the prime of his intellectual vigour and strength, and probably the words he had spoken over the grave of his friend Mgr. de Janson in 1844 fully expressed his own heart's feeling: "He was forty-five; the ripe age, when whatever throughout a man's life he has sown is bearing its fruit-laden branches; and this was precisely the age at which Mgr. de Janson was to lose all his past, and to see his life cast down like a tree cut at the roots. It is difficult for those who have never sounded the depths of sorrow of such a position to realise them, or the courage a man needs not to break down under it. He did not break down. He was not indifferent or without regrets, but his own heart was strong to sustain him in God's Sight, to uphold his honour before men, and to enable him to go on working for his brethren."

Lacordaire was never molested, he underwent no persecution, and those who knew him best unite in saying that he never displayed the slightest token of bitterness or animosity towards the ruling powers. He only seemed to intrench himself in a stiff neutrality, slightly tinged with the disdain which he more or less instinctively felt for all powers. But there is no doubt that he was sorely wounded to see his country, of which he had hoped such great things in every shape of liberty, turning round after what he felt to be so fawning a fashion, and "not merely accepting, but craving a master." His regrets over France, and his admiration for England in her greater consistency and stability, are strongly expressed in the last thing he ever wrote, which indeed was but the beginning of a series of Letters upon Christian Life,[1] addressed to a former pupil. The only three ever finished make one earnestly desire that the work might have been accomplished; they are as powerful and picturesque as anything he ever wrote. "One may have intellect, science, even genius, and yet be deficient in character," he writes. "That is the case with France in our times. She abounds in men who have accepted everything at Fortune's hands, all the time without having betrayed any trust, because in order to betray you must have held to something at least! But to these men all events are as mere passing clouds, a spectacle, or a shelter—no more. They submit to them without resistance, after having paved the way for them involuntarily; mere toys of a past over

[1] Lettres à un Jeune Homme sur la Vie Chrétienne.

which they had no power, and of a future which does not deign to unveil itself to them. . . . Nothing can stand against thirty millions of men who do not know how to keep steady on any foundation, and who have lost all political feeling as to religion and their own rights." [1]　And again almost the last words of the third Letter are as follows :—

" Men will tell you that love for the Church is incompatible with love of your country ; that sooner or later you will have to choose between them, and that you can only remain a faithful member of the one by becoming an undutiful son to the other.　I greatly desire to clear away this error, inasmuch as love of our country and love of the Church are, taken together, the most sacred feelings of the human heart, and were it possible for the one to be the enemy of the other, it would in my apprehension be the most terrible crisis that God has ever suffered to try His people here below ; but it is nothing of the sort.　A man's country is his Church in Time, as the Church is his country in Eternity; and if the orbit of one is more vast than that of the other, they have alike but one centre, and that is God ; but one interest, which is justice ; but one home, which is conscience ; the same citizens, the souls and bodies of their children.　It is true that the Church may be at variance with the Government of a country, but

[1] Lettre i.

the Government is not the nation, much less the country.[1] Who among us ever imagined that his country is in the head or the heart of the men who govern it ?   Our country is the soil on which we were born, the blood and the hearth of our fathers, the love of our parents, the memories of our childhood, our traditions, our laws, our customs, our liberties, our history, and our religion.   It is all that we believe, and all that we love, protected by those who were born at the same period of time and the same given place with ourselves, in heaven and earth.   The Government is for us merely a means of preservation for these possessions in their right place and full security; and if, so far from fulfilling this mission, it betrays or dishonours it, we take refuge in the love of country for succour, hope, and consolation.   When Nero governed the world, Rome existed in those who loved her, and her deserted Forum was the country of such as still possessed a country.   If, then, the Government of any nation persecutes the Church, either that nation is Catholic or it is not.   If it is Catholic, it is not the Church which attacks the country, but the country which is itself oppressed in one of its dearest, most holy rights—its religious Faith; and the Church, when defending itself by the words or the blood of its sons, is simultaneously defending an

[1] "Country" fails wholly to reproduce the meaning of *patrie*, as Lacordaire uses it.

outraged, insulted country. If, on the contrary, the nation is not Catholic, it is true that the Church is not one of the component parts which make it what it is ; but even then it is included in the natural right of all men to truth, grace, and eternal salvation ; and the Church enduring persecution forwards two benefits to the country—one in the future, its conversion ; the other present, namely, liberty of conscience." [1]

Lacordaire felt keenly that those men who had clamoured so lustily for liberty really were bent but on their own, and that liberty of conscience too often among them only meant freedom to disbelieve and neglect everything, however sacred. He put a powerful check, however, on his utterances, for he was no demagogue, and merely to stir up passions by strong words was not the course in any way acceptable to his mind. Two hundred young students in Toulouse presented a petition eagerly calling upon Lacordaire to resume his Conferences, but in vain. He answered them in warm, pathetic words, alluding to similar petitions of an earlier date, which had touched him less ; " since now, growing old as I am, I advance more speedily towards the time when I shall be forgotten, and the need of souls never yet found me passionless and without the craving to minister to them. But God calls me to fulfil more hidden duties ; I must give myself up to these, and

<hr>

[1] Lettre iii.

forget the past." [1]   His own phrase, "the poignant grief of the men and things of to-day," was a picture always before his eyes; and Montalembert does not scruple to say that this grief shortened his days, although disappointment never degenerated into discouragement, and his sorrow was never without hope.

But all the same, while withdrawing from the more public sphere in which he had cut his footprints so deeply, Lacordaire was very far from lapsing into inaction or spiritless indolence. Probably such would have been an impossibility to him. Henceforward he gave himself up with all the vigour of a young man to the working of education under his Third Order.

It was just at this time that the venerable College of Sorèze came into his hands, and the remainder of his life was spent there.

[1] March 31, 1855, letter in the *Écho de l'Ande.*

X.

SORÈZE—THE ACADÉMIE FRANÇAISE—DEATH.

THE original foundation of Sorèze dates back to Pepin le Bref, 757. It remained in the hands of the Benedictines until 1840, when it was bought by a body of Churchmen who wished to see the institution kept for its original purpose, and in 1854 it passed into Lacordaire's hands, to be, as he said, his earthly rest, and at last his grave. (" *Viventi sepulcrum, morienti hospitium, utrique beneficium.*")

He set to work with vigour to make the College all his imagination realised as the possible perfection of an educational house, and " you can have no idea of what such an administration is, above all in the first beginnings, when everything has to be created. Besides, I am a very systematic person, never hurrying myself, doing each day's work as it comes, and consequently there is no end to it."

Writing to Mme. Swetchine, November 4, 1854, of the various changes he is making at Sorèze, all of which seem to have been accepted and even appreciated by the pupils, who, Lacordaire says, seem to wish to co-operate heartily in the restoration of tone to the school, he goes on to look back upon the past touchingly :—

" All our best men have died prematurely. It is as though they had traced out our path, and their tomb is but the symbol of our own. I feel deeply how little that is good I have thrown into a work which required so much. I have a strong faith, patience, and flexibility, but all that falls very far short of the Saints! And what great work has ever been founded on earth without holiness? On the other hand, our success has been so marked by providential gifts, by such marvellously *à propos* succour, by men sent us so precisely at the right moment, that sometimes I think I have merely been the feeble forerunner of better times than ours. God makes use of whom He thinks fit. He lifts up and casts down, and though the instrument was nothing worth, the work has not the less been blessed and prospered. It will all be as God sees fit. I have often offered it all up in my heart, and this is easier to me than it might be to many, because I am naturally very moderate in all things, and am easily satisfied. I think I wish now for nothing more than to die at peace with God."

Comparatively speaking, it was now a very quiet, uneventful life. When, early in 1855, Montalembert urged him to write upon the public difficulties of the times, he entirely refused, though not without laying his heart open to his friend as to the reasons for such a refusal. "I think," he said, "that I can do more for the Church and the convictions of a lifetime now by building up in education, than by entering into the lists with men whose doctrines I have already withstood in everything I have said or written." He threw himself heartily into the interests of Sorèze, even to the minutest details of repairs and beautifying. "I am in all respects a *père de famille,*" he said of himself. "At my age one begins not to live any longer for oneself. When I was young, I sought stir and fame, but now the repose of a useful obscurity is the only thing which attracts me." His system of education was not built up on theories; his object was to make the boys under his care into large-hearted, true Christians, and his own conception of what that was could scarcely be surpassed. He believed that in forming character and confirming faith, constraint and fear were feeble as compared with persuasion and love. Accordingly from the first he left the fulfilment of all religious duties absolutely free, and no boy was *obliged* to perform any. The consequence was that the irreligious tone which had of late years prevailed, quickly disappeared, and the boys almost needed to be kept back rather than pushed on in their religious ardour. It must have been a touching sight to see them hanging about him, whenever he was to be found in play-times, some-times shyly taking hold of his white robe as if some virtue came from out it. He preached constantly and regularly in the chapel, dividing the work with the chaplain, but never taking less than one sermon a week in Lent, or in a fortnight at other times; and he took just as much pains, it is said, with these sermons to his boys as he had ever taken with his Conferences in Notre Dame. On one occasion Lacordaire told a young preacher who made his gift of improvisation too much an excuse for idleness, that he always took a week to prepare his school sermons, and it would seem that their effect upon the young hearers was striking. The boys always looked forward eagerly to Lacordaire's sermons, and often left the chapel moved to their heart's core, lifted out of themselves. In many respects his influence over them reminds one much of that Dr. Arnold exercised over a similar congregation. He worked upon a regular plan, treating of Christian life and its foundations—prayer, penitence, etc. The general sketch of his courses has been found, but merely as a sketch, in no way filled up. Besides this he gave himself freely to all who liked to seek him as a confessor; his door was always open to his boys, and no occupation, however pressing, but was gladly laid aside to listen to their difficulties and troubles. On one occasion Monta-lembert tells how (I think it was in connection with his election to the Academy, though his friend does not say so) he pressed Lacordaire to remain in Paris for business of some importance, but he entirely refused, saying that by so doing probably some of his dear boys at Sorèze would miss the confession for which they were preparing, " and no one can pretend to calculate the loss of one Communion in a Christian's life," he added.   He was constantly impressing on his boys that true religion avoids equally all hypocrisy and all human respect.   A good Christian must be stedfast in what are called natural virtues—in uprightness, straightforwardness, honour ; he must have " the courage of his opinions " (a phrase we have thoroughly adopted in English).   "While you are looking out for the supernatural," he used to say, "take care you don't lose the natural !"   His great gifts of conversation were freely used on these lads' behalf. Every evening he used to join the upper classes in the large schoolroom and talk with them for an hour or more, trying to draw out their ideas and thoughts on all possible subjects, one only excepted—politics. This he scrupulously avoided, and could never be induced to touch upon.   Sometimes he read or recited to them, and his gifts in this line being so great, it is easy to imagine what delight he gave. The military form was kept up, and there were sergeant-majors, captains, etc. ; but the literary Academy within the College, which was called *l'Athénée*, and which was only entered by those who achieved certain school attainments ; and the *Institut*, a select body of twelve, always chosen from the former,—these were the most highly-coveted honours of the place, only exceeded by the title of *Étudiant d'honneur*, which the best and most respected scholar received on leaving Sorèze yearly, and which entitled him to keeping up a close connection with the place, spending a fortnight there yearly, and other like privileges. At Easter, Lacordaire delighted to go off on long expeditions with his boys, on some picnic in wood or meadow, and pouring out the endless stores of his fascinations for their amusement. The number of scholars rapidly doubled itself, and in spite of sundry attempts to depreoiate the work, there was no doubt of its thorough hearty success. On one occasion Henri Perreyve was present at some little festivity at Sorèze ; the boys had crowned Ozanam's bust with flowers (chiefly because Lacordaire had been writing his Memoir lately), and Perreyve made a speech in which he spoke affectionately of the two friends. As he sat down he whispered something to Lacordaire, which caused the latter to rise smiling. " Gentlemen," he said, " there is a report in Toulouse that the students at Sorèze have hung their Director in effigy !" Instantly one of the head boys, " Sergeant-major " Serres, jumped up and answered, " *Mon Père*, they know a great deal at Toulouse, but there is one thing they don't know which we should like to teach them, and that is that every single one of us would very willingly be hung for you!"   But his popularity was not sustained by any over-indulgence or weakness, it need scarcely be said.   Like Dr. Arnold again, Lacordaire was resolute in expelling boys whom he felt to be really vicious, and therein absolutely dangerous to those with whom they associated.   It cost him grievous pain, and the boys knew it; perhaps one of the most touching tributes paid to him as Director of Sorèze was the fact that at his burial four young men whom he had expelled as boys were in the funeral procession, and as heartfelt mourners as any present.

In respect of education, it was said by competent judges to be equal to any school in France, and unquestionably the tone of everything seems to have been raised, as might be expected from the impression Lacordaire's individuality was continually renewing upon masters and pupils alike.   The standard of literary taste, both classical and modern, was raised, and what was really good and beautiful was rather aimed at under his influence, than the more meretricious beauty which the actual French world sought after.   Against all luxury he set his face steadily. Even the silk and woollen sashes worn by some of the boys were set aside, because, as he said, " a real sword can only hang on to a leathern belt;" and when some of the boys sported *duvets* on their beds, he reproached them publicly. " Leave such things as those to women and sick people !" he exclaimed. " When I was cold at my school at Dijon, I used to put my portmanteau on the bed !"

June 8, 1855, Lacordaire writes to Mme. Swetchine : "I grow fonder and fonder of Sorèze. I have been here nearly a year, and the next two months will be fuller of work than before. I must prepare a *discours* for the Prize Day; it is the first, for last year I merely spoke without premeditation, and I felt it was not quite the thing. It requires a certain turn of thought not suited to improvisation, and everything calm and quiet requires more reflection than inspiration. Then the Examinations are coming on, and a thousand details which take up all my time."

September 19, 1855.—" I have finished my sketch of Ozanam. . . . Every day I hear of changed opinions and altered attitudes among men that I have known, till it makes me feel giddy ! How thankful I am to be out of it all ! In giving me this solitude, God has repaid me a hundredfold for all my life's toil, and all I ask of Him is that I may end my days in it. Adieu, *chère amie;* you are one of the few souls who have remained faithful to their post. It is a great thing, and I thank God for it daily."

In a letter of about this date (October 5th) Lacordaire first mentions Henri Perreyve, whose name has since become so well known, to Mme. Swetchine, as "one of the few men in whose opinions I have found consistency and faithfulness, things so strangely rare that I make a careful note of them for the credit of human nature and my own special consolation." The last letters in this most valuable correspondence go on still expressing Lacordaire's thankfulness for being removed from the scene of political passion and excitement. "I am growing old, and the tears sometimes fill my eyes at the thought that I shall go hence pure from all that sort of thing. How good God has been to me! What a happy retirement He has given me, just at the moment when I had no course left but to stand aside and be silent! and among the general apostasy I have kept some faithful friends who cleave to our common Faith!" And when his old friend had gone to Fleury, he writes: "When I was at Issy, we used often to go there, and I have a very pleasant memory of it. If my letter finds you there, I thank God for sending you to rest beneath the same shades which I enjoyed in youth. How young I was then! What a slave still to imagination! seeking fame for myself by means of God, and yet sincere in my wish to serve Him. Now I am like an old lion who has crossed the deserts, and who lies with his great paws stretched out, looking somewhat mournfully at the sea and its waves. How much has happened between those Issy days and now!"

The interest of the next letter is chiefly that mysterious one which nevertheless exists for most of us ; it was the last Lacordaire ever wrote to the trusted mother-like friend, who had been so much to him through his animated career :—

"SORÈZE, *August* 24, 1857.

" At last, *chère amie*, our *fêtes* are over, and I have time to say how sorry I am to have been so long silent. Providence has been very good to us in the way of unforeseen incidents, striking meetings, splendid weather, and everything which could give us perfect success. Only Montalembert was wanting, but he was represented by M. Werner de Mérode and the Duc de Mirepoix, whom he had promised to meet here, and who kept their engagement better than he did. We had Marshal Pélissier, whom we did not expect, and the former Abbot of la Trappe, de Staonéli. . . . Several unforeseen incidents turned out most happily. Among our guests there was an American, the *Chargé d'Affaires* of the Republic of La Plata, whom nobody knew, but who spoke admirably. . . . The Marshal spoke amid great applause. In short, it was the best festival I have had, and will pro bably be the last. God has been very good to me, as sometimes one sees in things which happen once and never again. Several people have brought me tidings of you, M. Cartier among others. Do you

U

remember him, Besson's friend? a man as modest as he is remarkable, a race you don't find nowadays! The complete edition of my writings is just coming out, the first time they have been regularly collected. I still from time to time receive tokens of their continuing to do some good. This is now my greatest reward, and God has been very good to me in this way. This third year at Sorèze has been good and happy. The ground has grown from beneath our feet, and I quite believe the school is saved. I have seen many young fellows improve markedly during these three years, and there can be no gladder sight to a Christian soul. I hope to see you again here below. Let me hear of you, and believe that no one is nearer to you in spirit or values your affection more than I do. Pray for me, as I pray daily for you. We shall find one another again for ever in God."

Mme. Swetchine was then lying on her deathbed, and M. de Falloux, who took the place of a son beside it, says that when he arrived in Paris he found her greatly preoccupied about Lacordaire, not having heard anything about these same doings at Sorèze. M. de Falloux found a newspaper which gave an enthusiastic report of the whole proceedings, which gave her great satisfaction. She specially rejoiced in Marshal Pélissier's presence. "It is enough, and not too much," she said, "to satisfy everybody." Shortly after this, hearing of her serious illness, Lacordaire hastened to Paris to her, and spent six days in constant attendance upon her. "Not the smallest detail was forgotten in her questions," M. de Falloux says, "and never was Lacordaire more attractive in his geniality and filial piety. Both seemed aware that they were drawing to a close of the earthly intimacy God had granted them, and they expressed it continually, though without words. Mme. Swetchine's weakness increased rapidly. But nothing interfered with her meditation, frequently of some hours, in her chapel, nor daily Mass and frequent Communion. Père Lacordaire had the comfort of celebrating several times for her. . . . On September 1st she seemed really better. I left her at six o'clock, and returning a little later, I found her talking earnestly with Lacordaire and M. Fresneau, and she asked to have an article on Sœur Rosalie, written for the *Correspondant*, read to her." All this inspired Lacordaire with a confidence he had not as yet felt, and having left Sorèze hastily, with much business weighing on his mind, he thought he might safely go back now, fully intending to return almost immediately to his dear old friend. Accordingly, on September 2nd he said a very early Mass in her private chapel, had a long confidential conversation with Mme. Swetchine, and left by the nine A.M. train. She said not one word to detain him, though it seems probable that she foresaw it was their last earthly meeting; but one striking characteristic all through her illness was the way in which she accepted every blessing and comfort God gave her without ever asking anything for herself. Very soon the dropsical symptoms from which she was suffering increased rapidly. Extreme Unction was given her, and during that evening Mme. Swetchine sent her special blessing to Lacordaire and his work through Père Chocarne, then Superior of the Dominicans in Paris. How constantly he was in her mind was shown by her conversations respecting him with M. de Falloux. She reverted again and again to his correspondence with her, saying, "He will never be really known except by his letters." One day she sent M. de Falloux to a little *étagère*, and made him bring her a book bound and carefully kept in a case; it was the MSS. of the "Vie de Saint Dominique." She looked at it with evident pleasure, and then asked de Falloux to read the letter it contained [1] aloud to her;

[1] "I send you, *chère amie*, the manuscript of the 'Life of Saint Dominic.' I have not effaced the corrections you made, in order that they may remind you, and whoever may see them, what you have been to me in friendship and counsel. They are a manner of hieroglyphics of which I hereby give you the key. I do not know if God will ever permit me to write any longer work. I have many things in my heart; it seems as though my thoughts expanded and grew stronger daily; but how many trees wither in full leaf, without supplying much fruit to the planter! If public speaking leaves me no time to write, or if death snatches the pen from my fingers, this 'Life of Saint Dominic' will remain a sort

and then sending for the whole collected series of letters, she gave them over with the MSS. to him. Early in the morning of September 10th she passed to her rest at the ripe age of seventy-five, happy in the surrounding of many that she loved, though perhaps he who was missing, Lacordaire, was almost the dearest of all her dearly-loved friends. On the 6th he wrote to M. de Falloux: "I have just received your telegram telling me that Mme. Swetchine is *in extremis*. I have no hope ever again to see this dear friend, who has been a second mother to me during the most trying periods of my life. I have to thank you for having seen her so lately once more, and for the opportunity of taking counsel once more with that fine mind, kindled by such a soul as I have never really seen the like. I was able once more to give her the Body and Blood of Him Whom she loved above all else, and Who is doubtless now her sure reward. Her last glance at me was one of benediction, and if

of isolated obelisk which from that very fact will obtain a certain value. If, on the other hand, I am to do a man's work, and leave a more finished record of labour behind me, the following pages will possess for you, loving me as you do, the attraction of a youthful period which you have known and cherished. I should like that some day when your nephews come upon these MSS. among your papers, they should know how they had an ancestress who was worthy to share Saint Jerome's friendship with Paula and Marcella, and to whom the only thing lacking was an illustrious and saintly pen to record what she was indeed." Paris, February 22, 1841.

I must grieve not to be by to close her eyes, at least I have stood with her at the edge of the grave, and the memory thereof will abide with me to my own last hour."

October 26, 1857, he wrote to a lady: "I have a great loss to bear. Mme. Swetchine, who has been a second mother to me for five-and-twenty years, is taken from me. I went to Paris to be with her at the last, and stayed six days there, but unfortunately duty recalled me to Sorèze, and I could not close her eyes as I should have earnestly desired. Hers was a first-rate intellect, and her heart was full of kindness, faith, devotion, and love. I shall always think of her as one of those souls whom God has placed in my path as a light and a guide. Although latterly her help had been less needful to me, and distance lessened our intercourse, her loss is very great to me. It renews my sorrow for that of our mutual friend, Mme. de la Tour du Pin, who was also so remarkable a woman, so good, so self-devoted! It is a curious thing that I have found all my best friends among our aristocracy. Mme. de la Tour du Pin, Mme. Swetchine, Mme. de Mesnard, Montalembert, etc., although I have so little to do with the world and its *salons.* . . . Sorèze is now my Versailles; it is as solitary as Louis XIV.'s great palace, and it also has its own measure of celebrity, which we revived by a great *fête* last August. . . . I am above all happy in the steady progress of our pupils in discipline, work, religion, and good general habits. I assure you I was never happier. I am weary of the world, and hope to end my days here. But all that will be just as it may please God."

Some of Lacordaire's most interesting letters to Henri Perreyve and other young men among his friends were written about this time, when the pressure of public affairs no longer hindered his free expression of the large loving heart which was always ready to pour itself out upon those he loved. Thus he writes, March 6, 1854 :—

" MON CHER AMI,—You were wrong to check your impulse of writing because I had not answered your last letter. Don't let it happen again. Write as often as your heart moves you, as often and at as great length as you will, only don't be hurt if I am not so quick about answering as I should like. If you really love me you will hear my answer through all space, you will know that I rejoiced to read your letter again and again, and you will forgive the delay in my written utterances.

" These lovely days remind me, too, of our walks together, in like weather, in the Bellevue and Meudon woods. Shall we ever enjoy such again, here or else-where ? God knows; but one thing is sure, that we shall resume them under more lovely conditions, in an unfading spring. We must keep our real *rendezvous* for that.   All else is but a preparation, a prelude, a doorway; it is the weakness of men without faith to look for all the joys they can expect in friendship, here on earth.   Perhaps we may meet but seldom here, but the day will come when we shall be always together.   You will be full of beauty then, and I shall regain my youth like yours.   But before that I must grow old, and so will you; but this old age is merely a dream which hides the approach to renewal and immortality. Between times we must have some sad days—everywhere it is so.   Melancholy is the powerful ruler of all sensitive souls; it comes upon them without their knowing how or why—suddenly, secretly.   The ray of light which gladdens others is a cloud to them, the festival which brings delight and gladness to some is as a spear to their heart.   It is only God and Our Lord Who can avert idle, weary clouds from the hearts of those who truly love Him.; the less real the cause of our suffering, the harder it often is to relieve.   You ask my opinion about the Eastern War.   I think it is a just war.   The union of France and England against the arrogance of schism and despotism is a grand thing. . . . Nevertheless I do not think that the Turks can remain much longer in Europe.   God seems to me to be carrying out two ends—the expulsion of the Turks and the restriction of Russia.   .   .   .

"I agree with you about the mountains, the sea, and the forests; they are the three great works of nature, and very full of analogies, especially the two last. I love them as you do; but as one grows gradually old, nature becomes less and souls more to one. One learns the beauty of that saying of Vauvenagues, 'Sooner or later one cares for nothing but souls.'[1] And so one can always love and be loved. Old age, which withers the body, renews the soul if it be not selfish and corrupt; and the hour of death is the spring-time of the spirit."

Henri Perreyve's health was failing rapidly, and Lacordaire writes to him :—

"I have a world of reproaches for you, dear friend. First of all, your signature is a very hieroglyphic! unpardonable save to business men, who are afraid of forgery if they write their name legibly? And then your article has a false name, which is horrible! People ought to write nothing to which they cannot put their name, and above all I hate a *nom de plume.* If one dare not sign one's name boldly, it is a sure sign that the thing in question ought not to have been written or published. . . . How are you? Have you courage to do nothing but go out, and sleep well? If you only knew how useful it is in life sometimes to know how to lose time well! Look at Ozanam. What a difference, if instead of forcing his life as he did, he

[1] "Tôt ou tard on ne jouit que des âmes."

had slept eight hours out of the twenty-four, and only worked six ! He would be alive now, and have thirty years of life before him ; that is to say, six hours of work multiplied by three hundred and sixty-five days, themselves multiplied by thirty! I don't know whether it is indolence or the spirit of worldly calculation, but except the rare occasions when something must be finished at any cost, I have a horror of hurry and interference with the ordinary natural course of things. Each day brings its own work and rest in a welcome succession, one makes up for the other, and the soul, always active, ripens amid an unfailing youth. Sometimes I fancy that is mere Sybaritism, and yet only look at the results of the opposite course! Are you quite sure when you give way to your feverish eagerness that it is for God's Sake you are so urgent, and are not influenced by the disguised ambition of production ? Pride is very crafty, and so, I must confess, is the charm of a quiet life. God knows all that, and He sets thorns before us on all sides, so that when we strive to avoid them on one side we fall into them on the other.

"You are very simple, and *naïf,* and innocent, and everything else, to talk to me about writing books ! It is very clear that *you* are not at the mercy of two hundred boys who have a right to run in and out of your room from morning to night about every manner of trifle ; or to come down upon you, just when you least expect it, with some very serious matter which puzzles you terribly as to whether you ought to be firm or yielding, severe or indulgent. Be so good as to know, *monsieur le malade*, that I never could do two things at a time, and that is why I am so well now, although I am not losing my time. If I were to do what you want, I should write a very poor book, and have a College even worse than the book on my hands. It is all very well to say that years pass by, and I am growing grey! It is quite true, and were I here by my own seeking I should take it greatly to heart. But being certain that it is God's Will which placed me here, I give myself up to His gracious dealing, leaving my years to Him for what they are worth, and my intentions the same! Undoubtedly if I were master of my own life, I should be inclined to shut myself up and write, taking part thus in the political and religious affairs of the day, but God has ordered things otherwise. Since 1830, just a quarter of a century, my life has been one continual worry, without leisure, without any certain future, without ties, almost without a country! I have been carried along like a leaf before the wind; and I am so entirely used to this, that even Sorèze, where I fain would die, only seems to me the tent of a temporary sojourn. God will most likely uproot me from this as from elsewhere, and it is not likely that He will leave me to write at leisure in a home of my own choosing. So don't urge me to write any more than to love you; the first is impossible, the second is done!"

To Henri Perreyve :—

"*October* 11, 1859.

"I know not if you feel as I do, but I cannot love any one without the soul slipping in as well as the heart, and so making our Dear Lord the medium betwixt us. An intercourse which fails to become supernatural ceases to be intimate, for what true intimacy can there be without sounding the depths of those thoughts and affections which fill the soul with God? I see friends who do not make their confessions to one another, do not help one another in the paths of penitence, and keep their spiritual life closely shut away even from those they love best. But is this real friendship? Is not friendship a full gift of oneself? and when our Lord has become one with us, can we really give ourselves without giving Him Who is thus part of ourselves? And how can we exclude conscience from this self-devotion, if it be entire? And how can you make that gift without a full confession of whatever is in you, of good and evil? It is so sweet to humble oneself before those one loves! And if pride restrains one, if one would fain be an actor even to one's friend, does one really love him? Confidence is undoubtedly the first element of friendship; one might in fact call it the entrance, inasmuch as sacrifice is the sanctuary; and can there be confidence without confession, or is confession anything but a supernatural confidence? . . . I am preparing for death, and it seems to me that nothing is more helpful in the hour of death than the services of a priest who has been one's friend. Friendship furthers openness, humility, unreserve, so wonderfully! What a blessing to die in the arms of a man whose faith is one's own, who knows one's inner heart, and who loves one!"

In September 1858, Lacordaire was re-elected Provincial of the Order, greatly to the joy of the Dominicans in France, who for the last four years had missed his kindly presence among them. But he did not feel that he could resign either the headship of Sorèze or the post of Superior to the Third Order; and while accepting the additional work of the Provincialate, he looked forward to accomplishing some of the work he still craved after when the quieter days should come.

"When my four years as Provincial are over," he wrote, September 23, 1858, "I shall be sixty; that is a solemn stage of life, if one attains to it. My great regret is that I cannot go on with my 'Letters on the Christian Life,' of which three have been published, and seem to be useful. But God orders it otherwise. If I should attain the age of sixty, I hope I may be able to retire and devote my remaining days to this work for God's glory."[1]

The privacy of his latter days was to meet with one more, and that a most honourable, interruption. In bygone days the Literary Societies of Lyons,[2] Toulouse,[3] and Marseilles had all been proud to enter Lacordaire's name on their books, and now the Academy sought to confer upon him the highest honour France can offer her literary men, by making him an Academician.

It was no mere vanity that made this tribute acceptable to him. As on the occasion of his election to the National Assembly, the point on which he rested with satisfaction was that such honours were in his person a "symbol of liberty accepted and strengthened by religion," as he said in his *discours de réception.*

He wrote, November 16, 1859, on this subject: "You may be sure that I appreciate the honour of being received into the Académie Française, and that I feel the spontaneous kindness which has been shown

---

[1] It was during this second Provincialate that he was able to recover for the Dominican Order the old church and convent of the Preaching Friars at Saint Maximin in Provence, whence they had been driven during the great Revolution. In the summer of 1859 he had the great satisfaction of installing a number of student novices, who overflowed the convent at Chalais, in their own rightful abode at Saint Maximin.

[2] 1845.   [3] 1854.

by some of the most illustrious Academicians on my behalf. This kindness which has found me out in my retirement, wholly unsought on my part, is perhaps the only public honour I have received during my life. I say *perhaps*, out of respect to the choice of me made by the town of Marseilles as their deputy to the last Constituent Assembly. But except that election, there has been nothing in the course of my life such as is commonly called an honour conferred. This honour is quite compatible with my position as a Religious. There have been bishops members of the Academy, and other ecclesiastics from among the regular clergy have been elected; no one is surprised, because literary fame is the thing of all others the most free from all mere rank or position. The Roman Academies are full of Religious, and I know one Dominican, who fills a high post at the Pontifical Court, who is a member of the Academia dell' Arcadia, and is known within it as Titiro or Melibeo. So he might well be a member of the French Academy. All so far is plain. Now perhaps you will say, Then why not come to Paris? why not come forward as a candidate, since you value the position of Academician, and think it compatible with your habit? Bossuet was not so fastidious. True, my dear friend; but first of all, Bossuet was at the Court; he was not living in a school some two hundred miles from Paris. That makes some difference: he was free, and you who have been at Sorèze, know how far otherwise it is with me. There is another difference. Bossuet, as you mention him, lived in religious days; his name and his cross were safe to meet no opposition in the Academy, he could come forward in all his talent. But could I do the like, without his talent or his period? Could I knock at the Academy door with absolute certainty of not exposing my name or my cross to obloquy? Can I do this? What certainty is there as to the majority or minority which might come forth? If it were only a question of myself, I might do it, but I carry the gods of Rome with me, *Dii indigetes*, and that in times which have but a very doubtful liking for them as yet. Is it not worth keeping my honest and respected obscurity out of the way of such risks?

"Moreover, even as to literary honours, does it altogether become a Religious to seek them? or if it is not out of place in Rome, is it not somewhat a risk in Paris? I appeal to your tact and your friendship. And what is wanted? That the Academy be sure of my grateful acceptance. This they are already. I gave my word as to this when the first suggestion was made. Whatever may be the result, *cher ami*, I feel the honour of being thought of by so many men who are eminent in the literature of our age and country. If their vote should not confer upon me the title of colleague, I shall at least remember gratefully that they did not count me unworthy to bear it."

To another friend he wrote, December 7, 1859: "You seem to fancy that I want to be an Academician. You are mistaken. I never gave it a thought. The proposal was made to me, not only by my friends, such as Montalembert and de Falloux, but by others, such as MM. Cousin, Villemain, and Guizot. Then the question became whether I was to refuse or to let the thing go on. Mme. Swetchine, when dying, thought it would be a mistake to refuse, because in such a spontaneous movement among eminent men on behalf of a Religious, there seems to be a certain homage paid to religion. And would it be right to reject homage offered to God in the person of one of His ministers who has done nothing to seek it, and who can honestly say that he had never even wished for it? I took Mme. Swetchine's view of the matter, although there is a bondage as well as an honour in the matter, and I am unwilling to forego any link of my entire independence."

The election took place, and Lacordaire was chosen by twenty-one votes as against fourteen. The day before he wrote, "It seems certain, but one should never sell the bear's skin until the bear is on the ground, even when for 'bear' read 'Academy'!" He went to Paris for his reception, making the usual oration, January 24, 1861, in the presence of a more than ordinarily large and illustrious gathering, which, according to custom, turned mainly on de Tocqueville, whose successor he was. His concluding words carried the motive which made him rejoice in his new position: "When your votes suddenly called me among you, I seemed to hear, not merely the voice of a literary body, but that of my country itself summoning me to take my place among those who are, so to say, the Senate of her thought and the prophetic *représentants* of her future. I have watched the prejudices which twenty years ago would have separated us, and these prejudices, which your choice of me has conquered, set forth the progress won in sixty years of an experience full of dangers, of successes, of deceived wisdom, and of helpless though noble courage. M. de Tocqueville was among you the symbol of liberty nobly interpreted by a great mind; I shall be, if I may say so, the symbol of liberty accepted and strengthened by religion. I could receive no nobler reward on earth than to succeed such a man for the advancement of such a cause." [1]

[1] Surely a liberty-loving nation might be satisfied with such opinions as Lacordaire expressed in speaking of de Tocqueville : "Certainement M. de Tocqueville, comme tout vrai chrétien, aimait le peuple ; il respectait en lui la présence de l'homme, et dans l'homme la présence de Dieu. Nul ne fut plus cher à ce qui l'entourait, serviteurs, colons, ouvriers, paysans, pauvres ou malheureux de tout nom. À le voir sur ses terres, au sortir de ce cabinet laborieux où il gagnait le pain quotidien de sa gloire, on

He was not to retain the post of earthly honour long. He never sat there again. Already the words, "Friend, come up higher," had been spoken; and returning to Sorèze immediately after the ceremony with a heavy cold and very much exhausted, Lacor-

l'eût pris pour un patriarche des temps de la Bible, alors que l'idée de la première et unique famille était vivante encore, et que les distinctions de la société n'étaient d'autres que celles de la nature, toutes se reduisant à la beauté de l'âge et de la paternité. M. de Tocqueville pratiquait à la lettre, dans ses domaines, la parole de l'Évangile : *Que celui de vous qui veut être le premier soit le serviteur de tous.* Il servait par l'affable et généreuse communication de lui-même à tout ce qui était au-dessous de lui, par la simplicité de ses mœurs qui n'offensait la mediocrité de personne, par le charme vrai d'un caractère qui ne manquait pas de fierté, mais qui savait descendre sans qu'il le remarquât lui-même, tant il lui était naturel d'être homme envers les hommes." In America de Tocqueville saw " pour la première fois un peuple florissant, pacifique, industrieux, riche, puissant, respecté au dehors . . . et cependant n'ayant d'autre maître que lui, ne subissant aucune distinction de naissance, élisant ses magistrats à tous les degrés de la hiérarchie civile et politique, libre comme l'Indien, civilisé comme l'homme d'Europe, religieux sans donner à aucun culte ni l'exclusion ni la pré-ponderance, et présentant enfin au monde étonné le drame vivant de la liberté la plus absolue dans l'égalité la plus entière. M. de Tocqueville avait bien entendu dans sa patrie ces deux mots, liberté, égalité ; il avait vu des révolutions accomplies pour en établir le règne ; mais ce règne sincère, ce règne assis, ce règne qui vit de soi-même sans le secours de personne, parce que c'est la chose de tous, il ne l'avait encore rencontré nulle part. . . . Il n'admira point l'Amérique sans restriction ; il ne crut pas toutes ses lois applicables à tous les peuples . . . . enfin il ramena sur l'Europe un regard mûri, mais ému, qui le remplit,

daire insisted nevertheless on preaching as usual through Lent in his school chapel, which was more than he had physical strength to do, so that when Holy Week came he was quite ill, and obliged to stay in bed.   His weakness was so great that the friends

selon sa propre expression, *a'une sorte de terreur religieuse.* Il crut voir que l'Europe, et la France en particulier, s'avançait à grands pas vers l'égalité absolue des conditions, et que l'Amérique était la prophétie et comme l'avant-garde de l'état futur des nations chrétiennes.   Je dis des nations chré-tiennes, car il rattachait à l'Évangile ce mouvement progressif du genre humain vers l'égalité ; il pensait que l'égalité devant Dieu, proclamée par l'Évangile, était le principe d'où était descendue l'égalité devant la loi, et que l'une et l'autre, l'égalité divine et l'égalité civile, avaient ouvert devant les âmes l'horizon indéfini où disparaissent toutes les distinctions arbitraires, pour ne laisser debout, au milieu des hommes, que la gloire laborieuse du mérite personnel.   Mais malgré cette origine sacrée qu'il attribuait à l'égalité, . . . malgré sa conviction que c'était là un fait universel, irrésistible, et voulu de Dieu, il n'envisageait qu'avec une sainte épouvante l'avenir que préparait au monde un si grand changement dans les rapports sociaux.   Il avait vu chez les Américains l'égalité agir naturellement comme une vertu héréditaire ; il la rétrouvait trop souvent en Europe sous la forme d'une passion, passion envieuse, ennemie de la supé-riorité en autrui, mais la convoitant pour soi, mélange d'orgueil et d'hypocrisie, capable de se donner à tout prix le spectacle de l'abaissement universel, et de se faire de l'humiliation même un Capitole et un Panthéon . . . il la rétrouvait en Europe in-quiète, menaçante, impie, s'attaquant à Dieu même, et sa vic-toire inévitable pourtant, lui causait tout ensemble le vertige de la crainte et le calme de la certitude," etc. (Discours de Réception.)

nearest him were seriously alarmed, and though he rallied for the time, he was never the same man he had been before. He had been engaged to preach at S. Maximin in May, on the occasion of the translation of some relics of Saint Mary Magdalene, and he had looked forward to the occasion, for the foundation of the College of S. Maximin was one of his most cherished works. Eight Bishops were to assist, and numbers of old friends and admirers from Paris, and indeed all the country, were counting on this—now rare—opportunity of once more hearing the voice which had thrilled from one end to the other of France. His doctor endeavoured to dissuade Lacordaire from the attempt, as beyond his strength, but he would not give in, and started; but when at Montpellier, he found himself so completely unequal to the exertion that he turned back with that calm acquiescence in God's Will which had become a part of his very self. He spoke of the matter in the school chapel, saying, " It is a great mercy when God warns a man of the uncertain tenure of his life by sickness. He has mercifully dealt thus with me, and I would have you join me in thanking Him for it."

Yet the discipline was sharp, as may be judged by an expression in a letter of May 28th: " This is the first time that my body has refused to obey my orders." In everything from this time forward it was plain that he was, in Jeremy Taylor's quaint but expressive

language, " undressing for the grave."   The very day
after his return to Sorèze Lacordaire wrote to the
Priors of his Order explaining his physical incapacity
for all his work, and saying that as he felt that work
would be seriously injured were he to forsake either
the school at Sorèze or the still new Third Order, he
asked permission to employ a secretary for his correspondence, and to appoint a visitor who would relieve
him of his duties as Provincial, duties which were
only compatible with his school-work by being performed during the brief periods which ought to be
spent in real rest.

That summer Lacordaire was sent to Rennes-les-
Bains with Henri Perreyve, but not even the com-
panionship of one he loved so well could make the
sort of life tolerable to him ; he could not endure the
manner of life which all frequenters of " *les Eaux* "
know to be imperative and—intolerable !   At the end
of three weeks he returned joyfully to Sorèze, and for
a little while seemed really better.   On August 12th
he wrote, " The machine is fairly good yet, only it
won't bear so much jolting as of old."

That September he presided at a meeting of Priors
at Flavigny, in order to choose a Provincial *Vicaire ;*
but, as one of his Community observes, it was not in
his nature, so intensely subject to all claims of duty,
to make much use of such help, and practically
Lacordaire continued to govern his Province as

before. His last Lenten course, preached to his dear boys, was on that, to him, most congenial subject, Duty—duty, the greatest and noblest of claims, the source of all that is high, holy, and happy. Once more he visited S. Maximin, where every evening he gave an instruction to the company of white-robed novices, now sixty in number; but every effort became more and more laborious, and in the spring he was reluctantly obliged to leave Sorèze, and suffer himself to be nursed a while by some kind friends at Becquigny (Somme). There was some slight amendment in appetite and vigour, but as he passed through Paris on his return, and consulted two celebrated doctors, Rayer and Jousset, they thought ill of his case. Internal inflammation and anæmia, or impoverishment of the blood, were two dangerous enemies for a man of his age. His return to Sorèze was a sort of triumph. Not the College only, but all the inhabitants of the place greeted him eagerly; floral arches, inscriptions, flags, everything that the scene-loving French nature could invent was provided to testify the public delight at seeing him again. A few days later he received tidings of the death of one of his first companions, the Dominican artist Besson, who died in the midst of an Eastern mission. He had loved Réquédat, Piel, Hernsheim, and de Saint Beaussant all tenderly; perhaps it was only because Besson was the survivor of that little company that he seemed to love him best.   One of the last days of his life, Père Chocarne, kneeling beside him, spoke of his speedy departure, adding that whereas the loss was all to those left, it would surely be an accession to the joy of those gone before to be reunited to him.   "All those you have loved, father!"   "Yes," he answered softly, "they are many."   Père Chocarne mentioned several by name, and Lacordaire himself added, "And Père Besson!" with a kindling eye and a tone of voice not easily to be forgotten, says the still living friend.

As the summer of 1861 advanced, Lacordaire grew visibly worse, and so feeble was he that syncope not unfrequently came on.   He still was able sometimes to go out driving, and feast his eyes with the rich fertile country that he loved.   August 27th, he resigned his office of Provincial.   September 12th, he wrote, "I had very good news from Rome yesterday ; Père Jandel had an audience of the Holy Father, and told him of my condition.   He expressed great interest, and desired the Rev. General to convey to me his apostolic blessing."   Many friends from all quarters flocked in to take leave of one who could not fail to leave his mark wherever he had been known.   Henri Perreyve, himself so soon to follow his elder friend, came twice.   Montalembert arrived, September 25th. Lacordaire dragged himself with effort to meet him on his arrival on the *perron* of the College.   He was very feeble, and the pallor of his fine though wasted countenance invested it with wonderful dignity. Montalembert spoke of it with tears. " I never was so transfixed," he said; " I never saw such over-whelming beauty." October 10th, M. Foisset, one of Lacordaire's earliest friends, who had read law with him at Dijon, and had been faithful to him through everything, came; and he was followed by M. Cartier, who, as he said, was something more than a friend. He liked to have him at the Mass said by his bedside, and they had a drive together, a rare thing now for the sick man. Lacordaire talked much to M. Cartier about Père Besson, and urged his writing the Life which appeared not long after.

Mass was said in his room daily, and he liked every day to have some part of Bossuet's "Préparation à la Mort" or the "Acte d'Abandon à Dieu" read to him. But it scarcely needs to say that the thought of death had long been familiar to him. In his extremest weakness he said, pointing to his Crucifix, "I cannot pray, but I can look at Him." Every day too he had some part of the Bible read to him, selecting specially the Acts of the Apostles, the Gospel of S. John, and some of S. Paul's Epistles.

On Sunday, October 10th, the Provincial Chapter which was to elect his successor was held. Before it the Fathers went to Sorèze to visit the sick man. " He received us with his wonted kindliness," Père

Chocarne says, " gave us his blessing, spoke of the affairs of the Order, and also of himself. 'I did not expect to leave you so soon,' he said, 'God calls me to Himself. It is well that I should go. If I remained longer, it might be thought that the work depended on one man. I shall be more useful to you *there.* Pray for me.'"

October 30th, he had a severe *crise* during the night, and the combination of rheumatic symptoms gave him acute pain. That afternoon, at two P.M., Dr. Houlès thought him so feeble that he proposed administering the last Sacraments. His confessor spoke to Lacordaire. "Not yet," he answered; "I will tell you when it is time." Some better days followed, and for the third time the Pope sent him his blessing, together with a plenary indulgence for the hour of death. During the night of November 5-6 another *crise* occurred, with great increase of pain, and in the morning he asked for Extreme Unction and the Viaticum. All the available Community, and the pupils forming the *Institut,* took part in this ceremony, and after it was ended Lacordaire took leave of each individually, giving them his blessing, and saying to the lads some little word of encouragement. His own nephew, Frédéric Lacordaire, had been at Sorèze for some days, and of him too Lacordaire took leave, specially commending to him Louis, the faithful attendant who had nursed him, and whom he loved with all the warmth of his loving, grateful heart. And indeed Louis deserved it, for his devotion had been great ; for twenty days and nights he had not been in bed, and the tender care with which he watched the sick man could only come of true, heartfelt affection. Sometimes when excessive pain caused Lacordaire to cry out, he would look up at Louis in touching apology, and throwing one arm round his neck, draw him close to himself, speaking gently of his own impatience.

After having received the last Sacraments, Lacordaire remained absorbed in recollection, but always ready to speak kindly to those who came to see him. Among these were the Fathers from Oullins, who had been summoned by telegram. He was specially pleased to see Père Captier [1] and Mermet, who had been the first members of the Third Order, and talked in detail with the former about the House at Oullins, of which Père Captier was Prior, going with interest into the question of buildings, plantations, etc. On Sunday, November 10th, he was so much better

---

[1] He was one of the victims of the Commune, May 25, 1871, being then Prior of the House at Arcueil known as the École Albert le Grand. The Dominicans were seized on the 19th and carried off to Bicêtre. The most touching account of these terrible days, as given by one who, while actually under the *fusillade*, escaped as by miracle, will be found in "Paris Brulé," by Louis Énault (pp. 2,34). He speaks of Père Captier as "une des plus belles et des plus nobles intelligences de son temps ; il était massacré."

that hope revived in all around.   " If it might be ?"
one who loved him whispered trembling.   But he
made an expressive sign indicative of his own conviction, and indeed his strength failed him daily.

Through these long anxious days his own calmness
and recollection were most striking, and nothing was
suffered to break in upon it.   Those who loved him
best went quietly in and out of his room, often only
kneeling for a few moments at the little altar there,
and going away silently, after receiving a look of affection from the dying man.   One of these was specially
near his heart, M. Barral, the " Emanuel" of his
" Letters to a Young Man."   So it went on, each hour
as it passed wearily by doubtless accomplishing its own
appointed work : he scarcely took any food, rarely
spoke, and then scarcely to be understood; no one
could do anything to relieve him ; and all his former
eloquence was now reduced to the grateful expression
of his languid eyes, which still strove to thank those
who sought, however vainly, to minister to him.   A
final *crise* came on the evening of Wednesday,
November 20th—the most trying of all—and in spite
of his weakness, he started up convulsively, stretching
out his wasted arms as though seeking something,
looking eagerly into every face and towards Heaven,
until at last with a great cry he exclaimed, " *Mon
Dieu, mon Dieu! ouvrez-moi! ouvrez-moi!*"—" Lord,
open Thy way to me!"   They were his last words.

The Father Provincial's voice rose up in broken accents with the last commendatory prayers, and 'at the sound Lacordaire fell back upon his pillow and seemed to recover self-control. There was no further expression of suffering; he seemed to be rapt in the prayers, absorbed in God. The Crucifix being offered him, he tried to put it to his lips, but his feeble hands could no longer guide themselves; a friendly hand fulfilled the office, and then the Cross remained lying on his breast. The Father Provincial paused as he came to the solemn words, than which none can be more full of deep longing and weight—" *Proficiscere, anima Christiana, de hoc mundo*"—almost as though he could not bid one so loved to leave them ; but after a moment Père Chocarne signed to him to go on, and as he proceeded—" *Mitis atque festivus Christi Jesu Tibi aspectus appareat*"—a sob, half of sorrow, half of triumph, rose from all around. He remained calm, peaceful, neither sleeping nor as yet departed—the stillness of God's Own Presence. So the whole of the 21st November was passed, until about nine o'clock in the evening, failing to hear him breathe, the faithful Louis fetched a light, and found that the happy soul had indeed fled beyond the troubles and griefs of this world.

"The perfection of life lies in self-abdication." They were Lacordaire's own words, and he had fulfilled them. He died a humble Religious, and the only worldly honours which surrounded his deathbed were the fervent love and veneration of all who had come in contact with him.

The body was placed in the chapel, the College flag, veiled in crape, beside it, and every one connected in any way with the work came to look once more upon that noble face, and count over what they had lost. "If my sword is rusted, *messieurs*," he said not long before to the boys of Sorèze, "it has been in your service."

"Rusted it was not," one who loved him answers, "but now it is broken indeed!"

For three days crowds came from all quarters to look upon the "remains of a sublime intellect, the head which had enlightened so many others, and which, though for a time separated from the living intelligence which had kindled it, would yet one day possess it anew," as he had himself said before the remains of S. Thomas Aquinas.[1] The simple country-folk were no less eager in surrounding him with tokens of their reverence and affection than those whose intellectual level was nearer his own. On Thursday, November 28th, he was laid in his grave,

[1] "Cette tête sublime dont vous avez là l'enveloppe extérieure, cette tête qui en a illuminé tant d'autres, et qui, quoique separée de l'intelligence qui l'animait, cependant ne cessa pas d'en avoir été l'organe, et même le redeviendra un jour, et nous présente ainsi tout ensemble l'immortalité de sa poussière avec l'immortalité de sa pensée" (Discours, Saint Sérnin, Juillet 18, 1852).

Mgr. Desprey, Archbishop of Toulouse, saying the Requiem Mass, while Mgr. de la Bouillerie spoke the funeral oration which custom demanded, and which in this case was called for by the strong feeling of all present.

No fitter summing up of the Christian warrior's life can be found than the words of his own dearest friend, Montalembert, who, after speaking of that deathbed— *"propter quod non deficimus, sed licet is, qui foris est, noster homo corrumpatus; tamen is, qui intus est, renovatur de die in diem "*—says : " I am not writing a funeral oration, I am only speaking as an eye-witness. . . . As Lacordaire himself said of Mme. Swetchine, ' During life, modesty and friendship itself lay a constraint upon our words; but there is this to rejoice over in death, that it sets free alike our memory and our judgment.' . . . And now, what will remain of him in this world ? I believe that his fame will reach to distant generations. But meanwhile, who can say ? No doubt it will be with him as with all those who have been beyond their times, and have left their impression behind in their words or writings. It will be with Lacordaire as with greater than he—Dante, Shakespeare, Corneille—succeeding centuries will not wholly accept his utterances. Some points of his genius will be questioned anew; some forms of his eloquence will grow antiquated. The ideas, the passions, the struggles which kindled him will seem insignificant or superannuated. Those immortal truths of religion which he defended, assaulted by new foes, and compromised by new follies, will require fresh champions, and fresh testimony. His foundations, already threatened by covetous greed, will very likely be overthrown by cowardly persecution. But neither time, nor man's injustice, nor the 'treacheries of glory' can ever deprive him of the true greatness of his character, of the dignity of having been the most stedfast, the most powerful, the most hero-like man of his day; of having grasped and proved, as no one else had done, that alliance of faith and liberty which alone can redeem modern society; of having combined with such wondrous power and brilliancy that intrinsic tenderness and gentle pathos which win and touch men's hearts even more than genius. To all time his memory, like his living presence, will be yet more loved than admired. When I seek for a greater, more eloquent Frenchman than he was, I can find none save Bossuet, and it is in Bossuet's words that I find what seems to me the summary of my friend's life—I behold him shining with 'that Divine fire which is in us, and which displays, as in a world of light, the everlasting union of honour and goodness.'"

Printed by T. and A. CONSTABLE, Printers to His Majesty
at the Edinburgh University Press

www.ingramcontent.com/pod-product-compliance
Lightning Source LLC
Chambersburg PA
CBHW031134120726
47905CB00006B/1697